The Janitor Brigade

Robert Bush

PRESS

Dedicated to:

T his book is dedicated to those who will soon be facing their final hour. Although we think we may know who these people are, the fact of the matter is that this time frame cannot be predetermined by any of us. Every single one of us will be faced with this ultimate hurdle, even though none of us want to think about it as we tackle the personal challenges we face on a daily basis. All of us will someday be faced with this moment of truth, as our momentary stop in this world will undoubtedly come to an end. The challenge we all face rests upon the purpose we have while we are here on earth; how each of us can truly make a difference in the lives of those around us. Since our stop here is temporary, we must work diligently to determine where our final resting place will be. We must never believe that it is too late for any of us (or those we love) to be saved; therefore, we must not rest on our laurels and wait because we do not know what tomorrow may bring.

The Janitor Brigade is designed to make all of us think about our current faith walk and honestly determine if we are truly where we need to be. Pay close attention to the characters in this book, as their journey may in fact reflect yours as well. As the battle for our soul continues to rage on, the world around us does not take notice and continues to move at record pace. However, this perpetual, mindless trap will eventually slow down and someday, just like everything else; it will come to an abrupt end. I hope and pray that all who read this book begin to search from within because this is where the answer lies. God is only concerned with what resides in our hearts because only He knows the truth. *The Janitor Brigade* is going to make you think about your life in ways that have created nothing but fear and trepidation in the past. I hope and pray that from this point forward, the fear that may be consuming you today is replaced by the peace of our Lord. This is the one book that will make all of us truly assess our personal actions, ultimately converting the unthinkable over to the tangible.

I dedicate this book to my ***loving wife and daughters***, who by God's grace epitomize His love in all that they do. Without their undying faith in me, I would be nothing…merely an invisible vapor in this daunting world. As I stare into their eyes, I see the Lord's reflection looking back at me, and I know we will all be together when we leave this world. I know that they are the reason for my own personal salvation because each of them is a constant reminder of just how blessed I am. Their continual support for me regarding this message has made me stronger in my own personal walk, and for that, I am forever grateful. Thank you for showing me the eyes of Jesus, and for giving me the strength and perseverance to fight the most important fight of all. I love you with all my heart and soul…you are my true heroes in a life where there are none anymore. Once again, thank you for believing in me and supporting me in this journey. Without your constant encouragement and trust in me, none of this would be possible.

I would also like to dedicate the importance of this message to ***my parents***, as they have literally been taking care of their parents for nearly 50 years. Since my first book, ***Shortcut to Heaven***, was published, we lost my grandmother. She was 102 years old when she went to be with the Lord, and she was the final parent left from either my mom or dad's side of the family. What my parents have taught me throughout their lives is that our ability to care for our loved ones as they grow older is something that all of us must do. They have never complained about how their lives were changed due to this responsibility, but instead, they tackled the task at hand with a love that can only be described as unconditional. I am sure God has looked down at them as only a proud parent can do. At the same time, I have looked up to them as only a proud son can do as well. Thanks, Mom and Dad, for showing me what it means to truly love and treasure our parents…through your actions, you have done wonderful things for those around you for many years. The strength I have seen in you has provided me with the desire to continually push harder, to somehow follow your footprints regarding my own personal journey. Thank you for providing me with the intestinal fortitude to keep my head held high in all that I do…and no matter how difficult the race may be, to never give up.

Contents

Chapter 1

"Foundation for the Future"

The man lay motionless; however, he could feel the wires and tubes attached to him move with his every thought. After everything he had been through, how in the world did he end up here in this kind of condition? One minute, he felt like any other normal guy his age, and the next, he was here surrounded by strangers. He was grateful for one thing...his mind was still as sharp as ever. This was important to him because it allowed him to look back on the life he had been given. He felt privileged to have known so many wonderful people, so many supporters who clearly loved him in every way possible. But where would he be going now? The thought of his next stop made him start to shake on the inside, and he didn't like this feeling one bit. This would be a path he would be crossing very soon because he certainly wasn't going to be getting out of this place. He was in no condition to get up and walk out, and after the most recent feedback from his oncologist; his prognosis did not look good. The man was living on borrowed time, and he knew it. As much as he hated to admit it, he knew deep down inside that this would, in fact, be his last stop here on earth before he moved on. The man was sound asleep and ready to revisit his life once again. Waking up would be very important to him, as his final destiny was being aggressively pursued by the enemy. Escape may be futile at this juncture; however, it was still a possibility as long as he was alive. Death was knocking on the man's door but he wasn't answering...not yet anyway. Soon, the option would not be his, and he would be gone from this world forever. However, until that happened, his mind would go back to what seemed like a world far, far away...one last time.

At the age of 12, nothing was more important to Jonathan Gunn than his personal batting average. After all, hitting .300 was a prerequisite for him if he expected to start on his father's Little League team. His dad expected a lot from all of his players, but even more from his only son, Jonathan. He was always held to a higher standard than the rest of the team in all phases of his game, as the bar had been raised to the highest level. Jonathan's father made it all the way to the major leagues; therefore, the inherent pressure he felt early on in life was nearly unbearable at times. He often wondered how his friends were able to take everything in stride, yet here he was playing every game like it was his last. Jonathan wanted so much to be just like them, but his desire to please his father far outweighed his feeble attempt at just being a kid. He was a strong leader and did everything he possibly could to set a good example on the field. On that faithful day in late July, Jonathan's leadership would be put to its greatest test. Little did he know it at the time, but this would be the day that would define his character. The day started out like so many others that summer; however, this was all about to change…

The Valley View All-Stars had breezed their way through both the district and regional tournaments with no problem; just one more win and they would be making the trip out west. Every kid on the team dreamed about playing in the state championship, and now this dream was about to become a reality. Never before had any team from rural Wyoming ever won the Little League All-Star State Championship; however, this team was unlike any the area had ever seen before. The community had fallen on hard economic times recently, and discouragement had taken up residency with no signs of leaving anytime soon. The only positive common thread among the area's residents was that of a special team of 12-year-olds. Despite insurmountable odds against them, this was a team that absolutely refused to listen to the voices of negativity that tried desperately to engulf their every move. The state championship would be played on hometown soil because the entire state had long ago recognized just how important a game like this could be for the local economy. Never in their wildest dreams did they actually think that Valley View would be a participant; the scheduling had much more to do with personal survival than anything else. Although Valley View would be playing on their own stomping grounds, they would not be afforded home team status due to their lower seed in the championship game. After all, they would be playing the mighty Lolo Springs All-Stars. Since the first game of the season, it was a given that Lolo would be one of the teams that would eventually make it to the championship game. Their talent was unmatched by anyone else in the state, and everyone on the team knew it. Valley View could care less about the final seeding, as they had finally made it to the elusive championship game they coveted so dearly. If the team could somehow find a way to bring home a win, it just may provide the spark the entire community needed. This was more than just a game; it was an opportunity to change the negative mindset that had gripped nearly everyone in recent years. People were down and out, and lives were being ripped apart. The pressure on the entire team nearly suffocated every player that day; however, all eyes were focused on the coach's son. He was the one who would be expected to save the city, to somehow make life worth living once again…

The day was absolutely perfect for a baseball game, as the sun quickly rose above the rugged terrain that surrounded the small community. There was a feeling of optimism and hope that hadn't been experienced by anyone in the area for a very long time. Jonathan Gunn was about to tackle one of the most important days of his young life; however, even he had no idea what this truly meant. After all, he was just a 12-year-old who loved the game of baseball. Little did he know that this day would reflect much more than just a game between kids. How could anyone, including Jonathan, be prepared for the events that were about to unfold? This would be one of those special days that would begin the maturation process for him, one that neither he nor the rest of the town would ever forget. He would be pitching the championship game for the Valley View All-Stars, which was something he had dreamed about since he first started playing catch with his father years ago. The team would be forced to depend on his dominance; however, this was something he had grown accustomed to since the beginning of this magical season. Jonathan had an intimidating presence that was felt by nearly every player on the opposing team. Standing in the batter's box against him was something that nobody looked forward to doing, and his fastball was already being noticed by local scouts in the area. Although he was by far and away the best player on the field, he always exerted a tremendous amount of pressure on himself to perform at a very high level. This kind of inherent pressure ran deep in his veins, as his father's mindset was identical during his playing days. His stomach was in knots as the game edged closer, but this was just normal for him. Jonathan's father had convinced his son long ago that butterflies were, in fact, good for the soul. "Son, if you find yourself all wrapped up in knots before a big game, that isn't necessarily a bad thing," William would say. "That feeling in the pit of your stomach shows you care. Just make sure those butterflies fly away after the game starts because you need to play with confidence. You need to go out there and expect to win. In your mind, watch yourself win…and then go out and do it." His father knew exactly what these words meant because he had lived them firsthand during his playing days. William Gunn was regarded as the greatest pitcher the area had ever seen, and he helped create a belief among other young men in the area that dreams absolutely can come true. The pressure that was exerted on Jonathan came from within because the performance bar in the Gunn household had been set very high. Would this be the day that he finally lived up to his father's expectations? Up until now, no matter how hard he tried, he always seemed to fall a little bit short. Hopefully, this day would be different…

Nobody in the little town of Rocker ever argued baseball with William Gunn, better known as the pitcher with the golden arm. He was still idolized in the small Wyoming town because he had taken his baseball career all the way to the major leagues. Things like this just didn't happen to folks in Wyoming, and everyone in the area took ownership of his accomplishments. William was drafted by the New York Yankees, and this made it even more special. Jonathan wanted so badly to follow in his father's footsteps; however, the chance of this happening was very slim. Maybe this would be the day that finally convinced everyone in the area that he was just as good as his father, that he was something special too.

Although Jonathan was not as gifted as his dad, he was a fierce competitor who hated to lose. It was very important for Jonathan to find a way to make his dad proud because this was something that had eluded him up until now. Quite possibly, this could be the day that he would finally set the record straight. Jonathan had a lot riding on this day, far more than just a state championship. Gaining his father's approval was his ultimate goal, as this had never come easy to him. William never told Jonathan that he was a believer in his talents because it just wasn't his style to hand out accolades on a routine basis. Jonathan had a chip on his shoulder at a very early age that just wouldn't go away. Controlling this edge was difficult; however, it was also his distinct competitive advantage against his opponents. Preventing this aggressiveness from spilling over into an uncontrollable rage was one of his dad's greatest challenges as a coach. However, even he wasn't prepared for what was yet to come…

Both teams battled through the first five innings and traded runs, and the score was knotted at three heading into the final inning. Jonathan started out slowly, but he was picking up steam and was nearly unhittable over the last nine batters he faced. The 6th and final inning would prove to be the ultimate challenge for Jonathan, in more ways than one. How would he respond to the events that were about to unfold around him? And how would the others on his team respond as well? Pressure was beginning to intensify, and everyone knew the game was heading for a wild finish. Soon, heroes would be crowned, while others would wallow in defeat. Nobody on the field of play would ever leave this particular game unchanged, as young men would soon be forced into premature adulthood. This game would ultimately define the true backbone of the players involved, and many would fail the test. Life's foundation for those involved was about to be laid, and some would never change.

Jonathan was getting stronger by the pitch, and everyone in the stands was beginning to believe that this miracle finish would, in fact, take place. There was a feeling of confidence that was starting to build, and the entire team's mindset was gaining valuable momentum as they made their way into the final stretch. Lolo Springs was favored to win; however, Coach Ramsey could sense that his team was beginning to let this one get away. Inner confidence was starting to build for Valley View, and the crowd was becoming more and more energized by the minute. There was an incredible amount of electricity in the air, as the sound of the ball cracking into the catcher's glove got louder and louder after every pitch Jonathan threw! Ramsey knew he had to resort to the game plan he had thought about for quite some time; one that he promised to use *only* if he absolutely had no other choice. In his mind, he had reached that point. Ramsey was the kind of guy who did his homework on every opposing player his team faced. He looked at every single way he could beat an opponent, and then he went for that specific weakness, regardless of the damage it caused. It made no difference what that particular deficiency was, as he could stoop to just about anything when it came to capturing a competitive advantage. More often than not, the tactic he employed became personal, and this particular game would be no different.

Jonathan was getting stronger and stronger over the course of the last three innings, and Ramsey knew the time was right for his plan to go into effect. Lolo was simply overmatched with Jonathan on the hill; therefore, it was important for Ramsey to move quickly before the game got out of reach. He was the kind of coach who epitomized everything that could possibly go wrong with youth sports. Ramsey had been nothing more than a third string first baseman in his playing days, and his only option now was to live his life vicariously through his own son's accomplishments. His life revolved around winning at all costs, and he had no care whatsoever regarding who he took out in the process. The Valley View All-Stars stood in the way of the championship he had dreamt about all year long, and he wasn't about to let this team of hicks take away his ultimate prize. Ramsey had done his homework on Jonathan, and he believed he had uncovered his "Achilles' heel". He was getting ready to squeeze as hard as possible, with hopes that the kid would break…and the game would be his at last.

Jessica Gunn attended all of her son's games, as his tender heart continually reminded her of a younger William from years gone by. That side of William hadn't been seen in a very long time, and Jonathan did everything possible to continually fill this void. Nobody matched Jessica's athletic prowess when she was younger; however, this was all a distant memory today. She did everything she possibly could not to go back to the day that changed her life forever, but this was an impossible task. Like so many others, the life she cherished was taken away in an instant by a selfish drunk driver. Jessica did everything in her power to remain strong and not let the bitterness eat away at her soul, but it wasn't easy. Somehow, her faith had gotten her through some very difficult times in the past, but nothing could prepare her for what was yet to come. Never in her wildest dreams did she ever think it would be tested in this fashion, 19 years later at her son's Little League baseball game. There was no way she could have ever prepared herself, or her family, for what was about to happen…for the real curveball that was about to be thrown their way.

Coach Ramsey had his plan in place, and the timing was perfect. The first batter up in the 6th inning for the Lolo Springs All-Stars struck out on three consecutive pitches. Ramsey knew it was time for his plan to go into effect, as his window of opportunity had finally arrived. The setting for his dubious plan was just how he had pictured it to be, and he began to mentally play out the sequence of events. Even Ramsey felt bad about what was ready to unfold, but nothing would stop him now. His team had no other chance to win the state championship, and he knew it. He gathered his team together in the dugout, and he began to communicate the plan. Even the kids were uncomfortable with his directive, but after all, he was their coach. Ramsey looked up at the stands to make sure everything was in place and there she was; the scenario he had been waiting for was absolutely perfect. Jessica was seated in her regular spot, just adjacent to the Valley View dugout. Ramsey knew his scouting report was accurate because his attention was immediately drawn to the wheelchair Jessica was seated in. His opportunity had arrived, and he wasn't about to let it slip away. After all, the Gunns were no friends of his…why should he care about what was about to happen?

Jessica Daly was a beautiful girl with an incredible jump shot. She and her dad began practicing together at a very early age, and all of her hard work had evolved into the most accurate shot the school had ever seen. Upon graduation from Little Cedar Springs High School, she was offered a full-ride scholarship to go to school in North Carolina, and her positive impact on the team was immediate. As a true freshman, she scored an average of 12 points per game, which was the third highest on the team. Since she had been blessed with a 5'11" frame, she soon became a formidable rebounder, averaging six boards per game as well. The only thing she loved more than basketball was her high school sweetheart, William Gunn. Her heart skipped a beat every time he was near because he was the only one she had ever truly loved. He always made her feel so important, no matter what they were doing. Over the years, something had disappeared and she rarely saw this level of engagement in William. His zest for life had deteriorated and had almost come to an abrupt stop. Thank God for Jonathan, as he was the one who filled this gap today. He had become her best friend; the one that she turned to for almost everything. No matter how hard she tried to resist, her mind continually took her back to the day that changed her life forever, the day that she somehow wanted to forget.

Jessica's sophomore year was about to start, and she was thrilled to get reacquainted with her friends who made it home for the summer. All of them came back to the Rocker area with stories to tell about their first year away in college. What an incredible time it was for everyone involved, as the summer provided the perfect forum for comparing notes. Unfortunately, the time off that summer went by way too fast, and before Jessica knew it, she was getting ready to head back to school for her sophomore year. Just as he did the previous year, William reluctantly drove Jessica back to the university. He hated the fact that she would be away, but oh, how he loved this girl so. Her long, dark hair and big, brown eyes were something he dreamed about every night as he turned out the lights. Without any doubt whatsoever, William knew that Jessica was the girl he wanted to be with for the rest of his life. They both agreed they would not give in to the pressures that surrounded them, no matter how difficult that may be. William kept telling himself that he was stronger for it, even though his love for her was unlike anything he had ever experienced before. He knew from the very first time he laid eyes on her that she would, in fact, become his wife. Jessica had stolen William's heart on day one, and he had no desire to take it back.

What started out as one of the best nights in their young lives would soon take a sharp detour and prove to be one of their worst as well. This would be the night that would change their lives forever; the night that would undoubtedly put their love for one another to the ultimate test. Little did either of them know that this night would change everything in a matter of seconds... and ultimately threaten their reason for existence. If only they could take a mulligan, they would erase this night and simply throw it away, somehow pretend it never existed. Why did this have to happen, and what in the world did they ever do to deserve the outcome? Unfortunately, these would be the questions that would never be answered, the ones that would haunt the two of them forever. The night started out like others before; however, this was all about to change. Soon, it would unravel and come apart, with pieces scattered everywhere.

William and Jessica left the party at about 10:00 p.m. because Jessica wanted to get a good night's sleep in preparation for her intrasquad game the following day. William would also be leaving after the game to get back to Virginia Beach, where his Triple A team was preparing for their playoff run. The five days off had allowed William to rest his throwing arm, as his inflamed rotator cuff had been acting up for quite some time. After all, a pitcher with a bad arm is like a sprinter with a bad wheel...not much use to anyone! William wanted to spend some quality one-on-one time with his Jess; therefore, he was thrilled to be leaving the party. They giggled and laughed, finally making their way out the back door. Who cared if anyone noticed, they thought, as they held each other tight. Finally, they were together, and that was all that mattered to both of them. Triple A baseball didn't pay too well, and William had the truck to prove it! He just loved that old Chevy, even though it became the laughing stock of the entire team. William and Jessica decided to take the shorter route, Highway 42, back to the school because she needed to be in her dorm by 10:30. Within minutes, they were well on their way and alone at last. The rain was really starting to come down hard, as William did all he could to focus on the sharp turns that quickly confronted them. The corners were getting more and more difficult, and the rain pelted the windshield with a pounding action that seemed to hypnotize the two of them. William was starting to have a very difficult time seeing the road ahead, as the visibility was worsening by the second. If only he would have replaced those old wiper blades…maybe, just maybe, their trip back to the dorms would have been a whole lot different.

As the old Chevy came around the corner, William barely caught a glimpse of the bright lights that came upon them in a flash. The massive piece of steel immediately cut through them like a knife, as they could hear the metal eat through their layer of protection before they knew what hit them. Without notice, the force of the crash was so intense; it spun the truck around like a top. Finally, the old truck came to an abrupt stop, and stillness grabbed the air. William did all he could to gather his senses; however, he felt an incredible pain on his left side. Fortunately, it wasn't his throwing arm or shoulder, he thought, as he frantically began to search for his Jesse. She was nowhere to be found. He jumped out of the truck and ran around the mangled grill to the passenger's side. The door had been jammed open, but still no sign of Jesse. His heart felt like it was going to pound out of his chest, and panic began to suffocate him. He gasped for air and screamed her name. He begged for a return answer but all he could hear were the echoes of his own voice in the distance. The louder he yelled, the louder the echoes came back at him. It was as if they were laughing in his face, knowing the outcome would not be good. Tears streamed down William's red cheeks, and his heart felt like it was being dismantled piece by piece.

William made his way to the top of the hill and could feel his knees begin to buckle. There she was, thrown to the ground like a rag doll, his precious Jesse. Her body lay motionless at the bottom of the ravine. "Jesse, I'm coming to get you," William screamed, as he tried to somehow gather his composure. He scaled his way down the rocks and finally made his way to where she was lying. She didn't move, but she was somehow still alive. William expected to be greeted by a massive pool of blood and a disfigured Jesse, considering how far she had fallen from the truck. However, this was not the case at all. Despite the impact of the crash and the fall she had taken, her scrapes and bruises were miraculously minor on the outside. However, the fall had severely taken its toll on her internal organs and structural frame. William fell to his knees and began to scream, "No, please, don't let this happen to my Jesse. Please, let it be me instead of her." Jessica looked up at William and whispered, "It's going to be ok, William. God will find a way to take care of me, just like He always does." All William could do was shake his head and scream even louder than before. How could he have allowed this to happen? Why didn't he protect his beautiful girl, the one who meant everything to him?

William looked down at Jesse and he knew right away that she was in trouble. Her beautiful life, as they knew it, had been taken away in a matter of seconds. William's nightmare was about to become a reality because the results would confirm his greatest fear. Jessica's spinal cord had been severed due to the fall, and she would never walk again. Life, as both of them knew it, would be changed forever. William Gunn and Jesse Daly would never be the same, but this would not take away his love for her. He would go on to love Jesse with all his heart, but a significant part of his life was taken away on that tragic evening as well. Despite the fact that these events would haunt William until the day he died, he would never turn his back on his one true love. No matter how difficult it was for him, he made a promise to himself that evening that he would never, ever leave her side…no matter what the cost may be.

Coach Ramsey gave his players the sign, and his plan was immediately set into motion. The only way his team could win would be by targeting their malicious taunts directly toward Jonathan Gunn. They needed to do everything in their power to go right after his heart and truly shake up this kid. Ramsey had to find a way to penetrate Jonathan's psyche; he needed to see just how much Jonathan could really take. Ramsey had a feeling the collateral damage would undoubtedly be extensive, but it was well worth the risk. The second batter for Lolo Springs in the 6th inning stood in the batter's box, and the ill-advised chant began to resonate throughout the stadium. "Hey, lady, stand up and cheer for your son!" the team shouted. Jonathan looked over at the opposing players and immediately knew their words were directed at both him and his mother. He could feel his blood begin to boil, as his attention was now directed toward the opponent's dugout instead of the batter who stood in their way of the championship. Oh, how he wanted to throw his pitch in their direction rather than toward the batter he faced! They were talking about his best friend; the one who meant more to him than anyone. He proceeded to throw eight straight balls, and the chants pulsated in his head. He could not shake the voices, as they seemed to get louder and louder by the second. Runners on first and second base; the noise was ringing in his head, and no matter how hard he tried, it just wouldn't go away! William Gunn called time out and went to the mound. "Settle down, son, let's get through this inning, and we'll put this one away when we come to bat," he said, as he choked back the tears and the incredible anger that gripped him like a vice. He knew his son would lose all composure if he, in fact, lost his cool as well. "They're talking about Mom right now! I can't let this happen to her," Jonathan said, as his eyes filled up with tears. William patted Jonathan on the backside, and he slowly made his way back to the dugout. His eyes pierced through Ramsey like a knife, but Ramsey could care less. He had now exposed Jonathan's weak spot, which was exactly what he had hoped to achieve. Finally, Ramsey knew he had Jonathan right where he wanted him...

Ramsey's plan was working to perfection. The bases were loaded, and Jonathan continued to struggle with every pitch. Ramsey had a bad reputation before the game, but this had taken his lack of character to its lowest level yet. Jonathan needed one more strike to get out of the inning, as the count was full at three balls and two strikes. The stands grew silent because everyone knew the next pitch would either determine their survival or immediate demise. He felt as if his entire body was moving in slow motion. "Stand up, stand up, stand up!"...the noise was deafening. Jonathan looked for his mom in her regular place. There she was...his hero, right by his side just like every time before. They made eye contact, and she mouthed the words, "I am so sorry, sweetheart. I am so very sorry." Jonathan just shook his head and said, "It's okay. I love you, Mom." And with that, he delivered the final pitch of his Little League career. Ball four. Game over. Lolo Springs All-Stars 4, Valley View All-Stars 3. The crowd went numb, and every heart in the city slowly began to crack wide open. Their hope for a better tomorrow seemed to evaporate along with Jonathan's last pitch. Regrettably, it was back to life as they knew it. The dream was officially over...

Jonathan slowly began his long walk back toward the losing dugout, but his only concern right now was outside the field of play. He jumped the fence and pushed his way through the crowd. He had to find his mom; she was his only concern right now. Finally, he pushed his way through the mayhem, and there she was. Tears streamed down Jesse's face, as she put her arms around Jonathan and held him as tight as she could. "I've humiliated you, Jonathan. I'm so sorry I came to the game today. I'm ashamed at what has happened. This was all my fault. Please, forgive me," Jesse said, as she continued to cry even harder. However, Jonathan would have none of that. He reached down, held her hands, and looked her straight in the eyes. "Mom, I have never been more proud of you than I am today. I'm so lucky to be your son. Now, let's go home. No matter what happens, you'll always be my hero." Jonathan began to push his way through the crowd. With his head held high, he patiently waited for the bleachers to clear. This was Jonathan's finest hour; when the chips were down, he stood up for what he believed in. He had become a man in a few short hours...and someday, everyone would take notice.

Chapter 2

"A Wolf in Sheep's Clothing"

The high school years were like a dream for Jonathan, as he had become one of the most popular kids in the school. He was an exceptional athlete; lettering in football, basketball, and baseball all three years. While he was able to set a number of records at Rocker High School, Jonathan's true passion was his love for helping troubled kids. Beginning with his freshman year and running all the way through graduation, he spent two nights a week at the Timber Lake Juvenile Detention Center counseling kids who were struggling with personal issues. More often than not, the kids at the center grew up in abusive relationships at home and, in many cases, many of them would need years of counseling before going out on their own. Jonathan had become attached to many of the young men and often wondered who would fill the void when he was gone. Most of the attendees had very few visitors, if any; it was almost like a nursing home for kids. Jonathan's care group consisted of himself and four other close friends from school who had the same passion for kids. Their desire to make a difference in the lives of these young men was incredible, and they spent nearly all of their free time at the center. All five would soon be heading off to school, and each of them knew things would never be the same once they were gone. Not for them, and certainly not for the kids. Jonathan's greatest worry was for one boy in particular; Jimmy Hidalgo…what in the world would happen to him after Jonathan was gone?

Jimmy was one of those special cases that ripped Jonathan's heart out from the first time he met him. He was unlike the typical resident at the Timber Lake Juvenile Detention Center because he was extremely gifted in many aspects of his life. Jimmy had an above average IQ, and his intuition was far greater than any of the other kids at the center. He had numerous gifts that would soon be going to waste unless they were nurtured and encouraged to grow. He was one of those special kids who just wasn't supposed to be there, and Jonathan knew it. Although he was surrounded by other residents who had no intention whatsoever to get back on track, Jimmy was different. Deep down inside, he wanted to do better than the other kids who surrounded him. Jimmy still felt like there was a chance he would someday be going home; therefore, his dream of having a normal life remained alive. He wanted to believe that he was loved by his family, even though he had never been given any signs since he arrived that this was the case. Jonathan vividly remembered the day that Jimmy was brought to the center and, without any warning whatsoever, became one of them. The scene would be forever etched in Jonathan's mind, and he could still see the events play out as if they happened just yesterday. Many lives would be changed on that day because visible sadness would leave an imprint on everyone involved. However, none would be more impacted than Jonathan's…it was a day he would never, ever forget.

The silver Lincoln pulled up in front of the building and slowly came to a stop. Ironically, Jonathan just happened to be looking out the window of the second floor, as the brake lights faded from red to black. He instantly became focused on the 12-year-old boy, who was seated on the passenger's side. He was sobbing uncontrollably and pleaded with his father. "I'm sorry, Daddy. Please, I don't want to go. No, no, no," cried Jimmy. His father calmly got out of the car and proceeded to walk around to the passenger's side where Jimmy was sitting. Immediately, Jonathan got a very bad feeling about this guy. The tension that followed him around the car was suffocating, as a darkness took hold of the man that seemed to come from somewhere else. Although he was well-dressed and conveyed a perceived impression of success, Jonathan's intuition told him it was all a facade. He was not a good man, and Jonathan was already afraid for the young boy's safety. As his father made his way to where Jimmy was sitting, he looked around to see if anyone was watching. He opened the door, and by the young boy's reaction, Jonathan knew his words were powerful. He leaned over to his son, grabbed him by the scruff of the neck, and yanked his head into the side of his face. Jonathan could see the man whisper into his boy's left ear. The father's words ripped straight to the heart, and Jonathan could tell from Jimmy's reaction that they were cruel and cutting. He had sent a strong message to the boy that he meant business. Jimmy Hidalgo wiped away his tears and got out of the car. He held his father's hand and walked slowly to the front door of the center. Although Jonathan had only been on the job for three months when this happened, he felt a strong desire to get involved. He couldn't help with the way he was feeling; it was just his way.

Jonathan quickly ran to the top of the banister and began to move quietly until he reached the ground floor. By the time he got to the bottom of the staircase, he could hear the conversation that was taking place in the other room. "My wife and I have decided that my son is in desperate need of a place like this," the man said. "My name is Anthony Hidalgo, and this is my son, Jimmy."

"Hello, Mr. Hidalgo, it's nice to meet you," said the woman from behind the desk. "Is your wife here as well?" "No, unfortunately, she's not feeling well and couldn't make the trip," responded Jimmy's dad. "She desperately wanted to be here, but she was far too tired to be with us. She feels terrible about our need to bring Jimmy to the center, but she's in full agreement that this is the right decision for our family." Jonathan was careful to make sure he wasn't heard, and he continued to listen to the conversation from the other room. After seeing the interaction that took place just moments before, he knew something was wrong with this picture. His intuition kicked into overdrive, and he plotted his next move. He had to find a way to help this kid. Something about him was different, and Jonathan knew it.

Finally, with all the paperwork filled out, Jimmy was handed over to the center like some kind of unwanted pet. Robert Fisher, the Director of Operations at Timber Lake, personally met all new residents and was immediately available for the Hidalgos. The Hidalgos represented increased revenue for the center; therefore, Mr. Fisher was more than happy to oblige. Trivial conversation took place between the two men; however, it soon transitioned over to the inevitable. Jimmy was being left behind, and Anthony reached out and shook his hand. He told Jimmy he loved him and then quickly turned his back on his only son. Jonathan was still standing motionless at the bottom of the stairs, as Anthony made his way across the room. Jonathan stood still and did all he could to go unnoticed. He knew this man would not take kindly to his eavesdropping. Anthony began to reach for the door, but he could feel the presence of someone else in the room. He could sense that he was not alone. He calmly turned around and saw Jonathan standing approximately 20 feet behind him. Their eyes met, and Jonathan could feel his knees begin to buckle. He was only 15 years old, and he realized he was no match for this man. Anthony could sense this kid was on to him, and that Jonathan somehow knew there was another side to his well-scripted charade. As his eyes peered deeply into Jonathan's inner being, the look he gave Jonathan told him everything he needed to know. He felt as if this man had exposed his soul and that he would do everything he possibly could to take it for his own. He was afraid of this man, but why? It was only a matter of time before he would find out...

Jimmy's first days at Timber Lake were spent sobbing behind closed doors. His heart was broken, and his purpose for living was clearly undefined. Oh, how he longed for the family he once knew, even though he realized it would never be the same. He and his father were never very close, but oh, how Jimmy loved his mother. She was the one who always said the right thing to him, the one who provided a glimmer of hope in a world filled with darkness. It was Jimmy's mother who did all she could to offset the environment that had been created by Jimmy's father. He was a violent man, as his unpredictable temper erupted within the Hidalgo home on a regular basis. The final episode that played out before Jimmy's arrival at the center would sever any ties between them forever. As Jimmy reflected on the chain of events that played out nearly one week earlier, his heart became heavy with sadness. His lasting image of his father would haunt him for many years to come. No matter how hard he tried, he just couldn't shake the events that changed everything. This would be the night that robbed Jimmy of the innocence and the life he once knew. He closed his eyes and began to go back in time, even though this was the last place he ever wanted to visit again.

Anthony Hidalgo was one of the most feared and hated businessmen in the entire mining industry. Although he called Rocker his home, the actual number of days he spent with his family over the course of the year numbered less than 50. He was a ruthless individual, one who had accumulated his wealth by walking on anybody who dared to get in his path. Unfortunately for Jimmy and his mother, Maria, business deals that went south typically spilled over into their home as well. Over the last six months, Anthony's business relationships were starting to unravel. He had burned far too many bridges in his lifetime, and now the rivals he had grown to hate were finding a way to get even. The tension within the Hidalgo home was unbearable, and something was about to give. The images Jimmy could still see were very real…something he would never forget, no matter how hard he tried. No matter how hard he closed his eyes, he just couldn't make them go away. Jimmy's mother meant everything to him, but this would be the night that her smile would be taken away from him forever, just when he needed it the most.

Jimmy and his mother were having dinner alone that evening, just like they did almost every night. Although Jimmy was now 12 years old, he still had a lot of little kid in him. He loved his nights alone with Mom because those spent with his father typically ended with somebody getting hurt. When his dad was in town, he made it a habit of his to always stop by the local watering hole for a few drinks after work. As the drinks increased in number, the more dangerous the Hidalgo household would become. Jimmy could tolerate his father's outbursts; however, he knew his mother's physical condition was deteriorating due to the punishment she was taking. Jimmy had gotten to the point where he just couldn't allow this to happen anymore. His mother was all he had; she was the only one in his life who truly cared about his well-being. On this particular evening, Anthony's stop at the local drinking establishment extended much longer than usual, which was never a good sign. Jimmy went to bed early, praying that he would somehow find a way to go right to sleep before his dad got home. Just as he was about to doze off, he heard the door to the garage slam shut. His worst nightmare was about to come true. Jimmy and his mom were no longer alone, and they both lay still hoping that the temporary silence would somehow take them into the morning. Unfortunately for both of them, this would not be the case. Jimmy could hear the heavy footsteps work their way from the main floor on up toward the staircase that led to the two bedrooms upstairs. Closer and closer they came, as they were about to come to rest on the second floor. Take a right, and the steps would be directed to Jimmy's room... take a left, and they would be in Mom's. The steps slowly began to veer off to the left, and Jimmy felt his stomach begin to churn. He knew exactly where they were heading. Dad was officially home...

Within minutes, Jimmy could hear the confrontation immediately intensify from behind the wooden doors to his mother's room. Maria pleaded with Anthony to stop, but the old man was just getting started. The alcohol had taken over his entire thought process, and his rage was beginning to kick into high gear. Jimmy could tell by the sounds coming from her room that she was in real trouble. He could almost feel the pain she was going through, and he knew he had to do something before it was too late. As Maria pleaded for Anthony to stop, Jimmy's adrenaline began to rush at record speed throughout his entire body. It was as if he could feel every single blow firsthand, and he knew right then and there that he had to move quickly. Never before had Jimmy experienced such an absolute disdain for his father; what little respect he had for him before the evening started was evaporating like the morning dew as it awaits a hot summer day. This would be the night that Jimmy had finally heard enough, as the time had come for him to take action. He simply had no other choice.

Jimmy got out of bed and made his way straight to the closet. He searched for the closest weapon he could find, and there it was...his aluminum bat. Since Jimmy didn't own a gun, this 33-inch piece of rounded metal would have to do. Jimmy knew he could inflict a considerable amount of damage with his newfound friend, but would it be enough to stop his father? He picked it up from behind the hamper and made his way down the hallway. When Jimmy arrived at the door that led to his parent's room, he felt his hands start to tremble as he slowly reached for the knob. He had no idea what waited for him on the other side of the door, but he could tell from the unwanted noises that it wasn't going to be good. He was immediately drawn to his mother's bloodshot eyes, as her body lay motionless on the bed. She looked up at Jimmy, with tears streaming down her swollen cheeks. Jimmy's heart seemed to skip a beat, as he contemplated his next option. He would need to make sure he moved with precision and laser-like focus...the man he was taking on was now his enemy.

Anthony had his back to the door, and he began to laugh out loud at the damage he had done. Jimmy's mom, defenseless and unable to do anything, could only sob in disbelief. Jimmy had seen enough. He hated his father for what he was doing to the one he loved, the one who was always there for him. Jimmy's blood began to pump faster and faster, and he made his way into the room. He needed to make sure he hit his dad with everything he had because he knew the retaliation would be severe. Jimmy swung the bat as hard as he could, and the result was a direct hit. The bat cracked the back of Anthony's knees with incredible force, as his father went down and cried out in agony. Jimmy took another shot and solidly connected with his father's rib cage. Anthony went down once again in pain, and Jimmy went over and held his mother just as tight as he could. Oh, how he wished he could freeze this moment, that he could somehow hold on to her and never let go. Jimmy needed to get some help quickly before his father came to, but just as he began to dial 9-1-1, he saw his father's image move out of the corner of his eye. Anthony was a very strong man and somehow was able to garner up enough strength to yank the phone cord out of the wall. He staggered over to his dresser and pulled out a walnut-colored humidor box that had been hidden under his clothes. Unfortunately, this box didn't contain his personal stash of cigars, as he had other intentions for Jimmy right now. Out came the pistol, and he slowly walked back over to the bed, where Jimmy held his mother tight.

Anthony cocked the trigger and gestured Jimmy's way. The words pierced through Jimmy's body like a dagger, as he said, "If you ever turn on me again, boy, your mother is going to pay. Now, if you truly love her like you say you do, then you'll go back to your room and pretend like this night never happened." Jimmy's eyes met his mother's, and she slowly nodded in agreement. With that, Jimmy pulled himself off the bed and gave his mother one last kiss. He told her he loved her and made his way back to the door. As he turned around, he stared back at his father with a look that said it all. Anthony had no doubt in his mind that from this point forward, his son would never look at him the same way he did before the night unfolded. This was undoubtedly the night he had lost his boy forever. He knew his only choice now was to get rid of him, to take him far away with no intentions of ever bringing him back. Jimmy's walk back down the hallway to his room felt like the longest walk of his life. He would never be the same after the sequence of events that just ripped his family apart. Every emotion imaginable ran through him like firewater. Anger, fear, fatigue, and disbelief; but most of all…sadness. Tears streamed down his cheeks, as he lay on his bed. His body and mind were in a state of shock, and all he could do was think about his mother's sad eyes. On the worst night of Jimmy's life, he was immediately thrown into adulthood. Oh, how he wanted to be a little boy once again.

Jimmy's life would soon take on a dramatic change, and Timber Lake would become his home. Somehow, Jimmy had found a way to persevere through the difficulties he had faced. No parents and not a lot of friends, except for Jonathan, was all Jimmy had right now. He loved being with Jonathan because he was the one person who seemed to understand him the most. Jonathan was an incredible listener and showed a genuine interest in Jimmy's daily activities. He was the brother Jimmy never had, the one who somehow filled a void that should have been embraced by his father. What would he ever do if he didn't have Jonathan? How in the world would he ever make it if the only one he cared about went away? Unfortunately, there would be a day that he would be forced to find out...

Jonathan spent his last summer at home with mixed emotions. On one hand, he was extremely anxious about heading off to school in Central Washington. He had been targeting their university for quite some time and the thought of finally stepping foot on campus was exciting. On the other hand, he felt completely empty inside regarding the idea of leaving his parents behind, especially his mom. She had always been his strongest advocate growing up and seemed to routinely say the right thing when he needed it most. Jesse's paralysis was beginning to take a major toll on her entire nervous system, and her mobility had been severely impacted over the past couple of years. Jonathan knew it would only be a matter of time before she would need additional assistance regarding just about everything she had grown accustomed to doing. However, no matter how bad she felt, her beautiful eyes continued to light up each and every day. Nobody had any idea just how much pain she was in because she continually refused to let her guard down. Jonathan could sense that her special spark would soon be going out, and the thought of it happening when he was gone to school was almost too much to bear. Saying good-bye to his mom would have a different meaning now because of the uncertainty that was in front of him. His best friend in the whole wide world was beginning to fade away, and Jonathan's heart was slowly breaking right along with it.

William was never the same man after the car accident took Jesse's legs. The blame game had consumed him long ago, and no matter how hard he tried to move on, it seemed to always bring him back to the many "what ifs" that consumed his every thought. He was able to find some solace through coaching Jonathan; however, he never seemed to truly connect with his only son. Jonathan absolutely idolized his father, but he always felt like he had let him down. William was an incredible athlete, and here was Jonathan, turning his back on sports so he could run off to school. Although he felt confident about his decision to head out to Washington, he didn't see any passion in his father's eyes when he shared his plans with him. Instead of passion, Jonathan saw disappointment, and that feeling of despair left an emptiness in Jonathan's heart that would be tough to fill. Jonathan knew he would miss his dad far more than his dad would miss him, and that was hard for him to understand. For an 18-year-old kid, this was a difficult pill to swallow. What did he do wrong? If only he knew...

The last shift before his departure to school was going to be extremely difficult for both Jonathan and Jimmy. The two of them were very close, as Jimmy had become highly dependent on Jonathan for just about everything. Nearly four years had passed since Jimmy first arrived at Timber Lake, and nobody at the center had made more progress than him. Ever since the day he was dropped off at the front door, Jimmy had done everything possible to become a better person in all facets of his life. The bitterness he felt toward his father had started to subside, and as a result, he was able to embrace nearly everything around him. Jonathan had become his biggest fan and his greatest supporter. As the two of them became the best of friends, Jimmy eventually opened up to Jonathan and told him everything about his difficult upbringing. He told him all about the way he loved his mother and how much he had missed her beautiful smile. Jonathan was the only person Jimmy talked to, and this wasn't until after he had been at Timber Lake for nearly a year. Jimmy trusted Jonathan with everything he had, and this had never happened to him before. Fear had been his greatest enemy, but now due to the friendship he had built with Jonathan, that fear had been replaced with peace. Unfortunately, this mindset was about to be put to the ultimate test...

Jonathan decided that the best way to let Jimmy know about his departure for college would be over dinner, when the two of them were alone. His final shift before departing for school would be the following Monday; therefore, time was running out. No matter how hard Jonathan attempted to avoid the inevitable, he knew the discussion he was about to have was something he needed to do. He had to find a way to somehow communicate the inexplicable to Jimmy. How would Jimmy react to the news that could eventually take him back to his old world, the one that he had shaken off through many sleepless, frightening nights? Jimmy was about to be left alone just like when he was a young boy, which was a dangerous thought to say the least. Isolation would soon be knocking at his door and with it, like in so many other instances, this silence would undoubtedly bring the enemy as well. Jonathan meant everything to Jimmy, but their friendship would soon be put to the ultimate test. The conversation that Jonathan had dreaded for months now was about ready to take place...and Jimmy had no idea what was coming his way.

Dinner at Timber Lake was the best meal of the day, but on this particular night, Jonathan's appetite was nowhere to be found. Jonathan made it a priority of his to have dinner at least one night a week with Jimmy, as this had become their special time together. Over the years, this was when Jimmy opened up to Jonathan about everything. This was, in fact, the time when Jimmy did all he could to put those unwanted demons from the past to rest. Hopefully, these uninvited guests would not be coming back to life in light of the conversation that was about to take place. Jimmy was in extremely good spirits on this particular evening because he had been waiting all day long to share something very special with Jonathan. The news he was about to communicate was something he had set his sights on for quite some time. Finally, he would be able to enjoy the accomplishment with the one who meant everything to him. The test scores were in, and Jimmy had reason to celebrate. Never before had he ever attained marks so high, never before had he ever felt so special...

Anthony Hidalgo continued to pay for his son's care at Timber Lake, but this was only to keep him away from the life he once knew. Neither Anthony nor Maria had ever visited Jimmy since his arrival on that first day nearly four years ago, but somehow Jimmy had made it through the fire. There were times when he didn't want to go on; however, he was able to close his eyes and continually find a way to see a new day. Over time, those days turned into weeks, months, and years...and here he was today on the other side. How could he have ever made it without Jonathan by his side? The one constant in his life had always been there for him, but the news of Jonathan's imminent departure was about to come his way. There was no way he could have ever prepared for what was about to happen. Hopefully, he would find a way to somehow make it through the silence once again.

"Jimmy, I need to talk with you about something," Jonathan said, as he pulled his chair closer to where Jimmy was sitting. Jimmy sat back and took a deep breath because he could sense something was up. "First of all, I want you to know that you've been one of the most important people in my life since you arrived here at Timber Lake. I really don't know if I would have lasted here this long had it not been for you. However, I'll soon be leaving the center, as I have decided to go to college out in Washington. I'm going to be heading out there on Monday, and I'm not sure when I'll be back. I will be giving up my position here at Timber Lake in order to start the semester this fall, which means I'll need to get out there and get things ready." Jimmy sat motionless, unable to speak. His eyes filled with tears, and he rocked slowly back and forth in his seat. "Whenever I get back home, this will be the first place I visit, I promise. I'll be here to make sure everything is ok. Please, don't change anything you're doing, Jimmy. You're doing a terrific job. I'm so proud of the young man you've become. We will always be best friends, I promise," said Jonathan, as he could see Jimmy fading off into the distance right in front of his eyes. Jimmy slowly got out of his chair and began to walk down the hallway toward his room. Jonathan called out his name, but Jimmy never turned back. He eventually made it to his room and shut the door behind him. The empty feeling that consumed Jonathan, while he stood alone in the cafeteria, was overwhelming. He felt like he had ripped Jimmy's heart out with the words that Jimmy feared most. As he got back to his room, Jimmy buried his head in his pillow and screamed at the top of his lungs. Just like when he was younger back at home, nobody was listening, and his cries were drowned out by silence. Jimmy glanced over at the report card he had saved for Jonathan. These were his best grades ever, but now he had nobody to share them with. They would simply go unnoticed, just like everything else in his life as of now. Jimmy's life, as he knew it, was over.

Jonathan's shift came to a close, and it was time for him to go home. However, there was one last thing he needed to do. He walked back down to Jimmy's room and knocked on the door. There was no answer. Jonathan attempted to turn the doorknob; however, the door was locked. Jimmy was in his room, but he was too devastated to respond in any way. Jonathan reached into his coat pocket and took out a sealed envelope. On the outside of the envelope were the words "To My Best Friend…Jimmy". Underneath the inscription, Jonathan had written the words "I will always love you…Jonathan". Jonathan closed his eyes, kissed the envelope, and slipped it under the door. With tears in his eyes, he turned and walked away. The good times they had experienced together were still fresh in Jonathan's mind, as he reached the end of the corridor. Jonathan felt empty inside because he knew he had let Jimmy down. He slowly made his way down the stairs and out to the parking lot. As he pulled out of his regular parking space, he took one last look at Jimmy's second floor room. Oh, how he hoped Jimmy would peek out and at least wave his way. Jonathan kept looking at the window, but there was no movement. It was as if death had entered the building and taken up residence in Jimmy's room. His lifeless expression, with very little hope, had moved back in.

Jonathan would never forget that final look in Jimmy's eyes the evening he broke the news to him about leaving for school. The passion was gone, and the sadness was back. As Jonathan drove home that night, he had to stop three times to wipe the tears away and gather his senses. His summer was officially over. He would be leaving for school on Monday, and life would soon change. Coming home would never be the same for all involved, but nobody would be impacted more than Jimmy. Jonathan should have been excited about leaving for school, but his excitement had converted over to sadness in a flash. His heart was with Jimmy, no matter how hard he tried to break free. The young boy, who came to the center with no hope and a world of pain, would be vulnerable once again.

Chapter 3

"Don't Ever Look Back"

Jonathan's freshman year at Central Valley State University got off to a strong start, as he was able to make the transition over to his new lifestyle with relative ease. Although he missed his parents more than he ever thought possible, the opportunity to get out on his own was something he embraced... except for the cooking and cleaning part! Jonathan did a very good job of separating himself from past accomplishments and instead focused his energy on how he could truly make a difference on the future. Unlike many of his high school classmates who continually reflected back on their personal accolades, Jonathan was bound and determined to make a difference moving forward. Even though he was excited about all of the things that were in front of him, there were nights that he couldn't help but reflect back on the wonderful life he had been given up to this point. Leaving home on that crisp, cool, autumn day was one of the most difficult things he had ever done. Jonathan knew deep down inside that coming home from this point forward would have a much different meaning for everyone involved. As much as he tried not to think about the day he left home, it was nearly impossible for him to separate himself from the images that would be forever etched in the back of his mind. Just like every kid who makes the move from high school to college, the reality of this transition out of the house was something he would never forget. And as much as Jonathan tried to stay away from thinking back on the life that once was, there were times when this was nearly impossible. Jonathan's mind seemed to always go back in time when he closed his eyes for the evening, and this night would be no different. Tonight, his mind would be taking him back to a world that seemed so far, far away...to a time in his life that was now just a faded memory.

Buck was Jonathan's best friend and had been his constant companion for what seemed like an eternity. Life without him just didn't seem possible because he had become the trademark of the Gunn family since the day he arrived. His wagging tail had greeted each of them for the past twelve years, as he and Jonathan had practically grown up together. Jonathan was only six years old when William and Jesse surprised their only son with the little yellow lab of his dreams, and he would never forget one of the happiest days of his young life. The bumpy ride out to the old McCormick Ranch seemed like it would never come to an end, but that didn't make any difference to Jonathan. His new best friend would soon be in his arms, and that was all that mattered. Buck's whole life quickly revolved around Jonathan, as he became the official protector of his newfound friend. No matter where Jonathan went, there was Buck right by his side. Heading off to college would impact everyone, but nobody would feel the change more than Buck. Jonathan found himself going back to the day he left; he would never forget the look on Buck's face as he pulled out of the driveway. Their connection was real, and Jonathan knew that their lives together would be forever changed on the day he left for school. Their lives would undoubtedly never be the same again...

William and Jesse tossed and turned all night long, knowing that this would be the last time Jonathan slept at home before his big day. In the morning, the family would be leaving for Central Valley State, and they knew that silence would soon be replacing their only son. How in the world would they ever be ready for the change that was about to come? Their only consolation was that they knew they had prepared their son well for his new life, but had they prepared themselves? Jonathan had matured into a young man who always put others first, and both William and Jesse knew deep down inside that this gift would take him far. However, it was still very difficult to let him go because he was the focal point of their lives since the day he was born. Their only son was about to leave home, and they knew the void left behind would be impossible to fill. Jesse would be the one who would feel his absence the most because Jonathan was always there to take away the pain and somehow find a way to brighten her day. The morning they had dreaded crept upon them like a thief in the night, and the inevitable was drawing near. Soon, silence would be the enemy that moved into their home for good, as noises from the past would be nothing but distant memories. Like so many others in the same position, William and Jesse were about to embark upon their new journey as empty-nesters. More than anything else, it was the quiet time they feared the most. All of their wonderful memories seemed to rest dormant, waiting patiently for the sun to peek over the hills to the east. Oh, if they could somehow find a way to freeze time and stop this day from coming, they would do so in a heartbeat. The life they had loved seemed to evaporate without any warning, and now it was time to move on...whether they wanted to or not.

Buck was waiting for Jonathan at the foot of the bed when he woke up that morning, just like he did every day for the past 12 years. Buck had no idea why it felt different today, but it was almost as if he could sense that something in his life was about to change. Jonathan didn't get much sleep at all during the night because he just couldn't shake the thought of leaving in the morning. He slowly made his way down the staircase, with Buck following right behind. William and Jesse were already waiting at the table for Jonathan when he arrived, as they had prepared his favorite breakfast. As Jonathan sat down, he reached over and gently began to rub his mother's forearm. "Please don't cry, Mom. I'm going to be coming home as often as possible, ok? If you or Dad need anything at all, I'll get here just as fast as I can," said Jonathan, as he methodically started to pick at his food. With his stomach tied in knots, Jonathan did everything he possibly could to somehow force a smile. Jesse nodded her head and responded, "Jonathan, I'm so proud of you. You're going to do an amazing job at school, and I know in my heart that you're going to change lives. Don't you worry about your father and me; we're going to be just fine. I want you to go out there to school, have fun, and continue to do your best. We are so very happy for you." Her best friend was leaving, and no matter how bad her heart was breaking, Jesse never let it show. Just like she had done her entire life, she put her family ahead of herself. Jesse knew that Jonathan needed to go out to Washington with a clear state of mind. The last thing he needed from her right now was a guilt trip. On the other hand, Buck was just downright sad, and there was nothing anyone could do about it. Words would not take the pain away, and he continued to stay as close as possible to the only owner he had ever known. Buck lay his head down at Jonathan's feet and let out a sigh that seemed to say it all for everyone involved. His tail lay straight, with no wags to the left or to the right. It was hard to tell if that big, beautiful tail would ever move again. Only time would tell...

The last suitcase piled into the trunk of the car, and as the door slammed shut, everything seemed to move in slow motion. This would be the first time Jonathan ever left Buck alone, and he had no idea how his best friend would respond to his departure. Jonathan reached down and buried his head into the soft, yellow fur that outlined Buck's face, as tears began to slowly soak the collar that didn't want to let go. He whispered into his ear one last time before he got in the car, "Thank you for being my best friend. I'll always love you, Buck. I couldn't ask for a better friend than you. I'm really going to miss you, but I'll be back. I promise I'll be back." Jonathan looked over at his mother, desperately searching for her positive reinforcement once again. "Mom, do you think Buck is going to be ok? I'm afraid that he'll just give up on life after I leave. Could you please make sure that doesn't happen, Mom? Leaving him right now is turning out to be a lot harder than I ever thought it would be. I just need to know that he's going to make it after I'm gone." "Jonathan, don't you worry about Buck," said Jesse, as she continued to encourage her son just like she had since he was a child. "I've asked the Wilsons to watch him while we're gone. Jan's grandson is here visiting, and I'm sure he'll be over here playing with Buck the entire time. Buck is going to be just fine." Deep down inside, Jesse felt an uneasiness with the words she had just spoken because she knew this would be a huge change for Buck. Unlike the rest of the family, Buck had no time to prepare for what was yet to come. The most important person in his life would soon be leaving, and he would be faced with a loneliness that had never been part of his life before. Animals have an uncanny ability to sense change before it happens, and Buck was no exception. His eyes said it all, as he watched the car slowly begin to back down the driveway. As the Sedan started to pick up speed, Jonathan watched Buck do his best to keep up with the car. For the past 12 years, the two of them were inseparable. Buck was always there to console Jonathan after a tough game, a poor test score, or a scolding from Mom or Dad. He had been the one true constant in Jonathan's life, and no matter how bad Jonathan felt, his wagging tail would always turn out to be the best medicine possible. Finally, Buck stopped at the end of the dirt road, while the old, blue car made its way on to the main thoroughfare. College was on the other side of the world as far as Buck was concerned and, more than likely, Jonathan may never make his way back. Buck watched until the car slowly disappeared in the distance, and then his best friend in the whole world was gone. Buck stood there all alone for the first time ever, as he hoped to see the car's headlights coming back his way. He waited for what seemed like hours before he came to the realization that the old, blue car wasn't going to be back. Unfortunately for Buck, all that greeted him was the cool, autumn breeze and the reminder that winter would soon be on its way. He slowly walked back to the Gunn property line and made his way out to his favorite spot in the shade. Buck lay his head down, hoping this was all just a bad dream. How in the world was he ever going to make it alone? His best friend was officially gone and who knew when, or if, he was ever coming back.

As Jonathan tried to collect himself in the back seat of the car, he had a sick feeling in his stomach that he may have seen Buck for the very last time. He gazed out the rearview window and felt incredibly empty without his best friend. Buck was more than just a dog to Jonathan; he had become the most dependable friend he had ever known. Regardless of the situation, Buck was always there with a wag of the tail and a rambunctious spirit that had the ability to cheer him up, no matter what the circumstance. Jonathan and Buck had developed a relationship that was built on absolute trust. In light of the way he had departed, Jonathan somehow felt like he had been the one who had let his best friend down. He could still see Buck's eyes watching him make his way down the driveway, almost as if they were asking him why this had to happen. Tears rolled down Jonathan's cheeks, while he made his way further and further from home. This was supposed to be a happy day for him, but it wasn't. In fact, it had turned out to be one of his worst days ever. Nobody ever said growing up was going to be easy, but he sure didn't think it would hurt this bad. Maybe he should have just gone to the local college, he thought, because this would have kept him at home with friends, family, and Buck. Why didn't anyone warn him that leaving home was going to hurt this bad? He just wasn't ready for this empty feeling in his stomach, and he wished it would simply go away. Jonathan was experiencing a major life-changing event, and he wasn't sure how he would handle any more surprises that may be in store for him. Life was so easy when he was back in high school! Somehow, he would have to find a way to get through the move. And somehow, Buck would have to find a way to get through it as well. From this day forward, both of them would be on their own. They had to find a way to persevere and not give up, which was definitely not going to be easy.

Leaving Jonathan at college was something Jesse just wasn't ready to do… how in the world could she adjust to this sudden change in her life? Her best friend in the whole world was moving on with his life, while hers seemed to be stuck in neutral. Although Jesse was extremely proud of their only son as they pulled away from the dorms to start back home, she was scared of what life had in store for her. Now, she would be forced to find some common ground with William, to somehow find a way to fall in love with him all over again. Jonathan's void would need to be filled by William, and this was what scared Jesse the most. Jonathan was a terrific listener and always seemed to empathize with Jesse's position regarding any discussion the two of them would have; he just always knew what to say to make her feel better. William just wasn't this way at all, and Jesse knew deep down inside that this would be one of their greatest challenges. As William and Jesse arrived back in Rocker after Jonathan's orientation weekend, it was as if they had been alone forever. As the car came to a stop, the fear of having their arrival go unnoticed had now become a reality. In fact, Buck didn't even make his way around to the front of the house to check things out. This had never happened before because he was always the first one to greet them when they came home. "Old Reliable" was nowhere to be seen, and Jesse had a sick feeling in her stomach that something must be wrong. "William, please, go out back and see where Buck is," said Jesse, as her heart began to race. "Please, check on him and make sure he's ok." William made his way around back and there Buck was, lying in his favorite spot. William ran over to Buck and wrapped his arms around his big, fluffy collar. "Wake up, Buck. Please, wake up," shouted William, as he searched frantically for a pulse. William ran his hands up and down the side of Buck's neck; however, he was greeted with nothing in return. "Don't leave us now. We need you, please, don't go!" Jesse finally made her way out back, only to find William holding on to Buck and sobbing gently into his golden fur. She made her way over to his lifeless body and rested her head next to William's. She inhaled and could still smell the fragrance of her only son, which made the pain cut even deeper. They wrapped Buck up in a soft, blue blanket and put him in the back seat of their car. The vet's diagnosis of a broken heart came back as no surprise. How in the world were they ever going to tell Jonathan that his best friend was gone? Jonathan's life was moving at record speed, and now he would have to deal with this as well. The phone call that evening to Jonathan wouldn't be an easy one, but William and Jesse would find a way to do it. Somehow, they would garner up enough strength to say the right words once again, just like they did when Jonathan was younger. He took the news as well as could be expected, but the thought of never seeing Buck again was hard to accept. As Jonathan hung up the phone, he realized that Buck's death made his transition from high school over to college official. If he had any doubt before the news, the phone call confirmed what he had feared all along. He was definitely on his own now, and his life would never be the same.

The first three years of college went by like a blur for Jonathan. He became very involved with a number of school activities, with the majority of his free time being spent at the campus counseling center. While Jonathan continued to work with numerous kids and young adults at the center, he often looked back at his earlier days in Rocker at the Timber Lake Detention Center. He thought about Jimmy Hidalgo often and couldn't help but remember the look on Jimmy's face when he drove away on his last day. According to Jesse, she had heard that Jimmy walked out the front door of the detention center the day he turned 18, and that was it. Jonathan was hoping to see Jimmy one last time before he left town, but Jimmy was gone before anyone could have a word with him. Although Jonathan had stopped by numerous times to see Jimmy when he was home visiting his folks, Jimmy refused to see him time and time again. The counselors at Timber Lake indicated to Jonathan that Jimmy went right back into his shell as soon as Jonathan left for school. The confidence and trust that had started to build in him seemed to disappear. What would happen to Jimmy now that he was on his own? Jonathan could only hope the outcome would be good...

Jonathan's senior year at Central Valley State University was off and running, and just like the rest of his colleagues in class, he couldn't believe that his college career would soon be coming to an end. His life away from home had been difficult, but in the end, he had matured into a bright, young man with an incredible future. As Jonathan reviewed the classes that were standing between him and his degree, there was one class that rose above the rest. Every student was required to take the advanced marketing course, and for numerous business students, it would be the one hurdle that many would not overcome.

The infamous J.R. Tillman was the only professor who taught the class, and this was exactly the way he wanted it to be. Tillman had grown into the most talked about professor on campus because nobody ever left his class the same as before the semester began. Tillman was brought into Central Valley State to elevate the expectations of the business department, and the school's dependency on him made him even more arrogant than before he arrived. Tillman and their president, Dr. D. Wayne Evans, were close friends from way back, as they had worked together years ago. Tillman had promised Dr. Evans that he would consider teaching at Central Valley State only if his schedule would permit; however, Tillman made it very clear that certain expectations would need to be met in order for him to make the move. This was just the way Tillman liked it, as his desire to be in full control of everything he did was a given. Tillman had the ability to bring a lot of money into the school, and he knew his three-year agreement would undoubtedly provide the university with a huge increase in contributions. Well-recognized faculty members like Tillman could help the school attract new students and, more importantly, new boosters with big bucks as well. Tillman had negotiated a very lucrative deal with the school because he firmly believed that no other professor was his equal when it came to teaching students about the real business world. He made sure he was the highest paid faculty member at Central Valley State, as this was his primary condition for employment. No matter how close a friend Dr. Evans was, Tillman made it very clear that under no circumstance whatsoever would he ever do anything for free. His arrogance was only outweighed by his love of money. Both seemed to work hand-in-hand regarding his position at Central Valley State, which for everyone involved, was a dangerous combination.

Jonathan was the first student to arrive in class on that very first day because he couldn't wait to finally meet the man he had read so much about. Jonathan positioned himself in the front of the auditorium, while the room began to fill up with fellow students. The bell rang, and within 10 seconds, the door that led to the back of the room was slammed shut. Waiting in the back of the room was the man of the hour, the infamous, Professor J.R. Tillman. He methodically began to make his way down the stairway of the auditorium, and absolute silence immediately took hold of every single body in the room. Slowly, Tillman made his way to the podium. It was clear to everyone involved that he was about to establish his rules, and dissention from anyone would not be tolerated. Tillman immediately made a personal connection with all 147 students in class that day, as his presence seemed to hypnotize those on the receiving end of his immediate stare. Without saying a word, Tillman had captured the attention of everyone, and it was crystal clear from the start that he was in full control. Stillness seemed to engulf the entire auditorium, and nobody dared to move a muscle. This couldn't be Tillman; it had to be an imposter. This man standing in front of the class looked more like a middle linebacker in the NFL than he did a professor. Although he was pressing 50, he was definitely not somebody you wanted to mess with...J.R. Tillman's class was about to begin.

"Good morning. My name is J.R. Tillman. I'm sure every single one of you has heard of me, but please, don't believe everything you hear. Having said that, most of the stuff you've heard is probably true. However, I'd encourage you to have an open mind starting today and formulate your own opinion of me. Each of you can be rest assured that I'll be doing the same when it comes to my opinion of you. Today, your education is about to begin. Some of you presume you will be graduating from this university at the end of this spring semester. However, your papers will not be signed if you can't get past me. I am between you and the real world out there, and some of you will need to wait another year before you pass my class and get out. You see, I teach this course every spring, and I have no problem flunking you if you aren't up to the task. Simply put, if you flunk this class, you do not graduate. I hope I've made myself clear," said the looming figure from behind the wooden podium. As his small rectangular-shaped glasses rested on the bridge of his nose, he seemed to revel in the discomfort his words had caused. Hearts began to palpitate, and nobody said anything. It was obvious to all 147 students that nobody in this class was going to be the same after this semester. And nobody in this particular class was safe...

Just as the newly christened students began to catch their breath, the door in the back of the class slowly opened, and everyone turned to see who was there. Are you kidding me? Does this young girl have any idea what she's doing right now? Every student in the room turned around and there she was, certainly not what anyone would have ever expected. Jonathan immediately became enamored with the short petite figure as well. Tillman stood in absolute disbelief, as the young woman proceeded to find the only open seat available in the class, which just happened to be right next to Jonathan! Not one student in class would have switched places with Jonathan on that day because the last thing anyone wanted was Tillman's ire to get that close. She confidently walked in front of Tillman and sat down right next to Jonathan. He couldn't believe what he had just witnessed with his own two eyes...the great J.R. Tillman interrupted on the first day of class! Instead of embarrassment, Jonathan immediately found himself infatuated with this young woman. She was now getting settled in right next to him, and she was the most beautiful thing he had ever seen. His lips immediately became dry, and he felt like he needed some water. Their eyes met, as she brushed her hair aside. "Hi, I'm Erika Lewis, nice to meet you." Jonathan smiled and put his head down in disbelief. He wanted to laugh out loud, but he knew this would be a dangerous mistake. Tillman's face began to take on a darker shade of red. His gauntlet was about to be laid down...

J.R. Tillman was not the kind of man who was going to allow a distraction like this to take place in his class. Although Tillman touted himself as the professor with all the answers, his experience in the real world of business was shaky at best. On the outside, his bruised ego was never revealed to his peers or to his class. However, on the inside, his insecurity gnawed at him constantly without reprieve. The fact of the matter was that he failed miserably in the real world and decided to take his ego to the university setting instead. Never did Tillman ever think this would happen to him. After all, he was the heir apparent to a business that had thrived for many years. Losing it was not only his own worst nightmare; it also represented his family's greatest fear as well. All the blood, sweat, and tears had gone to waste, and nobody but Tillman was to blame. This was a part of his life that he wanted to forget, but the pain continually surfaced along with his temper, which meant it was almost always there.

The business he had owned nearly two decades earlier neglected to change with the market, and he still carried the evidence of this failure on his face every day. The pain masked itself as anger, but his was the worst kind of all. Unlike a temper that was easy to detect, his insecurity ran like a deep well with still waters. Rumor had it that Tillman's great grandfather started the company around the turn of the century, and it was eventually handed down to Tillman himself upon his father's death. His ability to assess the market strategically was not the company's downfall; his problems were internal. His great grandfather had been able to grow the business by importing numerous consumable products from the Far East. Much of his business came from Japan because his grandfather realized early on that the Japanese placed a high value on the relationship built behind the business. In fact, it became evident from the onset that deals would only be finalized if the relationship was in tact. However, J.R. Tillman's ego once again got the best of him, and this time the end result was disastrous for the organization. Tillman refused to invest the necessary time in these relationships and the Japanese culture, and it cost his company dearly. The key importers from Japan were so turned off by Tillman's refusal to treat them fairly that they moved all of their business over to one of Tillman's primary competitors. This was the end for the company he inherited because their revenue stream could never make up this shortfall. Within nine months, Tillman's company began to divest its assets and the creditors were knocking on their door. In order for Tillman to escape with his home and personal belongings, bankruptcy was his only option. He was a brilliant economist who lacked common sense, and his greatest downfall was his ego and lack of humility. J.R. Tillman never went back to the private sector and somehow made his way over to the academic setting, which was what his bruised ego needed in order to survive. He was now in a position to theorize what he thought should be done in the business world, and he took full advantage of this newfound authority. He despised anyone who didn't agree with him, and he made it a point to intimidate where appropriate. He was about to clearly define the rules of engagement in his classroom, and his first target was Ms. Erika Lewis. The 5'2" bombshell would soon be taught a lesson, and Tillman loved the thought of his upcoming interrogation. He was ready to clearly define his expectations; however, this was one competitor he deeply underestimated. Tillman wasn't ready for what was about to come his way.

Erika Lewis had grown up on a farm in Cedar City, Iowa. From the time she was seven years old, she spent nearly every waking hour milking the cows and cleaning out the pens. She was the oldest of five children, and it was expected that she set a strong example for her younger siblings. Erika was forced to grow up at a very early age, as tragedy came knocking on her door when she was just 12 years old. On a cold, December night, she found her father dead in the barn after an apparent heart attack. He had literally worked himself to death trying to support their family. Erika's mother, Emma, was able to keep the farm going after her husband's sudden departure, but it wasn't easy for any of the Lewis clan. Emma wanted Erika to go on to college and show her siblings that the real key to survival in this world was through an education. Needless to say, Erika felt an enormous amount of pressure to bring back the degree that would help raise the bar for the rest of her family. When Erika earned a full-ride scholarship to Central Valley State, it was bittersweet for everyone, especially her mom. Emma was extremely proud of her daughter because she was the first in the household to ever attend a college of any kind. In addition, she was the rock of the family since her dad died, and her mother quickly realized that filling her void at home would be impossible. Emma had taught her daughter to be tough and to stand up for what she believed in, just like her father would have wanted. Without a doubt, Emma would have been very proud of her daughter on that first day in Tillman's class. She had taught her little girl very, very well.

"And who do we have here?" Tillman asked in his condescending way. "Looks to me like we've been graced by the presence of a young lady who thinks she can survive my class, even after she treats me with absolute contempt and disrespect. In all my years of being a professor, the best professor in this university I might add, I've only had one student who showed up late for one of my classes, and that was the last one he ever attended. He decided it was in his best interest to attend a different university and transferred the following week. A very good move on his part, if I do say so myself. You, on the other hand, took tardiness to a whole new level and decided to test my patience on the very first day. What do you have to say for yourself, little missy?" Erika gathered her composure and stood up next to her desk. The top of her head hit Tillman just below his shoulders, but she jumped at the opportunity to respond. Her intellect was impressive; however, it was her wit that made her even more dangerous. "My name is Erika Lewis. When I found out I was in your class, I immediately became overwhelmed with excitement. I've read all of your books, and while I don't agree with all of your opinions, I do admire your work. You could say, Mr. Tillman, that my expectations for you and this class are very high. I only hope you can, in fact, meet them." And with that, she sat back down in her chair and took out her books. She was now officially ready for class to begin.

Tillman was dumbfounded, and for the first time in his illustrious teaching career, he was speechless. Although he was clearly agitated and taken back by Erika's response, he was very good at hiding his emotions. Tillman smiled at Erika and said, "Thank you, Ms. Lewis. We are very lucky to have you in our class. I'm confident you will be a strong contributor to any discussion we may have. Oh, and regarding your expectations of me…I promise I will do my best." The entire class took a deep breath. Erika had stated her case very well, and everyone in the class was impressed. Everyone that is, except J.R. Tillman. Jonathan had never witnessed anything quite like this before, as he watched the entire interaction from the best seat in the house. The tension in the classroom during their exchange made everyone want to crawl under their desk. As Erika sat back down in her seat, she glanced over at Jonathan. With a brief smile and a slight wink of an eye, she let Jonathan know that she was in full control. Jonathan, on the other hand, felt like a bowl of jelly sitting in his seat. Never in his life had he ever seen a girl like this before, and now she was sitting right next to him controlling the infamous J.R. Tillman. Jonathan's mind began to race. He had dated a few women during his college days; however, he had vowed to wait at least until he was 30 before he got serious with anyone. He had no desire to let anyone get too close, as there were still so many things he wanted to do and places he wanted to see. All those thoughts went right out the window when Erika Lewis walked through that door. Jonathan was shell-shocked, and his whole body felt numb. The dismissal bell couldn't ring quickly enough for Jonathan because he wanted to find out more about this girl. His heart began to pump wildly, his palms were sweating, and he felt like a complete dork. What was he going to say to her? He had to find out more about this Erika Lewis, but before he knew it, she was gone. Somehow, she had made her way out of class, and he lost her. Never again would he let her slip away. Tomorrow's class couldn't get here fast enough for Jonathan. In a matter of minutes, his mind was already thinking about how he was going to ask this girl out.

When Jonathan got back to his apartment late that afternoon, he couldn't wait to share his day with his roommate, Daniel Baker. Jonathan had a feeling that Daniel would have a hard time fully understanding what had happened today, but Jonathan just had to tell someone! Things like this didn't take place in Tillman's class because everyone in the university knew about the reputation he had since his arrival. Jonathan made his way into the house and yelled for Daniel, but there was no answer. Coming back to an empty house was exactly what Jonathan didn't need right now because he could not get Erika out of his mind. This girl had literally walked into class and, within minutes, she had turned everything upside down. Jonathan just had to find a way to ask this girl out on a date, and Daniel would be the one with all the answers. His mind was moving in overdrive, as he began to contemplate his next move. Suddenly, the phone rang and Jonathan found himself hoping that it would be Erika on the other end of the line. He raced over to the kitchen counter where the phone sat and quickly gathered his thoughts. The voice greeting him would not be Erika's, and without any warning whatsoever, his world was about to change forever. Reality would quickly settle in, as Jonathan reached for the phone. It was Jonathan's father, William, and the news from back home was not good.

"Son, this is your dad. I need to tell you what happened a short while ago. Your mother suffered a massive coronary, and her condition is deteriorating by the minute. If you can get home as quickly as possible, I think it would be a good idea for you to be here. She's in very bad shape, and there's no guarantee she will even make it through the evening," said William, while he tried to somehow maintain his composure. Jonathan was speechless because he wasn't prepared for this news right now. In a matter of seconds, his priorities immediately changed from a girl he just met to the most important person in his life. He couldn't even begin to think about losing his mom since there was so much he wanted to tell her. Within minutes, Jonathan was packed up and out the door. Elation over the events of the day had immediately turned to sadness. Mom had been getting worse, but she always found a way to persevere and fight on. Jonathan could tell from his dad's tone of voice that this time may be different. Going back to how things used to be would only cloud his judgment, he thought, because he needed to remain focused and positive right now. Jonathan had to make it home as quickly as possible because he needed to get back and assess the situation for himself. His mom had always been his rock, and now he had to find a way to be hers as well. The trip home would take him about eight hours, and it was just starting to get dark when Jonathan pulled out of town. Tears continually revisited him during his dark ride home, and he couldn't imagine being without his best friend. Her support and encouragement was the one true constant in his life, a given that he had grown to depend on over the years. Never before had he heard his father in such a desperate state of mind, and Jonathan knew in his heart that he had to find a way to be strong. After all, this was what his mother would have wanted...

Jonathan pulled into Rocker under a full moon, and the night around him seemed to be frozen in time. He looked up into the sky and seemed to be mesmerized by the beauty that surrounded him. The light reflected off the driveway, as Jonathan knew he had to find a way to be strong right now. No matter how much he felt like holding his mother and feeding off her comfort like years gone by, she would be the one who needed his strength. He put his head down and took a deep breath. Jonathan knew he was in for a long night based on the discussion he had earlier in the evening with his dad; however, even he wasn't prepared for what was yet to come. He got out of the car and started to walk toward the front porch. William opened the door and reached out for Jonathan and held on to his only son with everything he had. Never before had Jonathan ever seen his dad like this, as William broke down in the arms of the one he needed most right now. Jonathan always knew his mom was the rock of the family, but it became even more obvious when he saw how his dad was handling the recent sequence of events. "Glad you could get here, Jonathan. Your mother has been calling for you and refuses to go back to the hospital. I may need your help in getting her back there. Doc Adams says she needs to get to the hospital if she is to have any chance at all. She's in real bad shape, and you know how strong-minded she can be. I just can't even imagine not being with her right now. We really need to get her to listen to the doctor's instructions. I hope you can talk some sense into her. Please, see if you can get her to listen." Jonathan gave his father a big hug and started down the hallway. He felt sick to his stomach because he was afraid to think about what waited for him on the other side of the door. He gathered his strength and slowly reached for the knob...

Jessica was a battler and never complained about anything. Even after the car accident took her legs and her basketball future years ago, she always found a way to somehow focus on the positive. Her pride and joy was Jonathan, and she made it a point to make sure he was happy no matter what she was going through. William was never the same after the tragedy, but Jesse knew she had to move on. Her ability to never look back would be the key to her happiness and positive outlook on life. Hopefully, these traits had rubbed off on Jonathan because he was about to enter into a world that nobody could ever prepare for. The one he loved more than anything was fighting for her life...a life that meant everything to him. Jonathan made his way into her room and there she was, doing all she could to muster up another smile despite the pain that had taken hold of her body. Jonathan reached out and grabbed her hand. With what little strength she had left, he could feel a slight squeeze. He leaned over and gave her a kiss and whispered, "I love you, Mom. You look as beautiful as ever." Jesse smiled and slowly took a deep breath. Her body was starting to shut down, and Jonathan could sense that it wouldn't be long now. Even though the physical pain continued to latch on to her every breath, she also had a peace that was hard to explain. Somehow, seeing his mother like this had given Jonathan a sense that she knew something he didn't...and that she wasn't afraid of what would happen next.

The morning came, and everything seemed to be moving at record pace. Jonathan's life had changed in the course of one day, and now here he was holding on to the one who meant everything to him. He hadn't left his mother's side all night long and continued to encourage her to hang in there. Deep down inside, he knew that this was more than likely a futile attempt at avoiding the inevitable, but the thought of her leaving him right now was something he just couldn't accept. Jonathan's mind began to take him back to the times they had together, as she had given him something that would follow him for the rest of his life. Jesse was the epitome of absolute encouragement in everything she did and had provided Jonathan with the confidence he needed in order to survive. She absolutely refused to let others bring her down, regardless of the circumstance. Here was a woman who had everything going for her, and within minutes, the use of her legs was taken away. However, she refused to give in to the negativity that surrounded her and continued to live her life as if nothing had changed. How would Jonathan ever repay his mother for what she had done for him, for the way she always stood by him no matter what the situation entailed? What in the world would he ever do if she was gone?

Back at Central Valley State, Tuesday morning was just another day in Tillman's class, as he outlined his expectations for the day. He was one of the few professors who still took roll call for every class, and this day would be no exception. "Jonathan Gunn," he called out. There was no response; not one person in class had seen Jonathan since the day before. Being tardy on the second day of class was not the way to start out in anyone's class, especially Tillman's! Jonathan had built a strong reputation for always being on time for everything he did at the school; therefore, the concern for his unexpected absence was warranted. Not showing up for class was out of sorts for Jonathan, and Erika could sense something was definitely wrong. Since Tillman put a lot of weight on attendance and participation, she wanted to make sure he was all right. He seemed like such a great person, someone who Erika could see was different from the rest of the guys she had met at the school. When class ended, Erika immediately checked with the other students to see if anyone had seen him earlier in the day. She had always been the kind of person who just had to know everything about the affairs of anyone she knew, and Jonathan's disappearance would be no exception to her inquisitive ways. Her obsession regarding his whereabouts gathered speed quickly and, without any hesitation whatsoever, she was off and running. Erika was able to track down his phone number and address through a close friend of his, Jason Hollow, and quickly gave him a call. Erika just had to find out where Jonathan was because she knew Tillman would not take his absence lightly. The phone continued to ring repeatedly, and it became apparent to Erika that she just couldn't sit around and wait until the news of his whereabouts eventually made its way to her. She was bound and determined to get involved and help Jonathan if she could, but deep down inside, she had a sinking feeling that something terrible had happened. His disappearance just didn't make any sense at all…

William continued to pace back and forth in Jesse's room, while she continued to rest with very little activity whatsoever. Jonathan didn't move from her side and found himself hoping for a response of some kind. As painful as it was for Jonathan to look on, William seemed to be struggling even more with the turn of events that had quickly flipped their worlds upside down. William had become totally dependent on Jesse, and the possibility of her not being there for him anymore was far too much for him to handle. Jesse was the leader of the family, which suited William just fine. His relationship with Jonathan had gotten much stronger over the past couple of years, and Jesse had a lot to do with this recent transformation. Her dream was to somehow find a way to bring the two of them together and make up for lost time. As Jesse lay motionless in the bed, her mind began to race with thoughts that quickly converted her personal dreams over to nightmares. Jesse could almost feel her insides begin to shake because she could see her two men separating from each other after she was gone. How in the world was Jesse going to peacefully leave them if she believed for an instant that they would drift apart after her passing? Somehow, she had to find a way to make sure this never happened, before it was too late.

Suddenly, Jonathan could feel his mother squeeze his hand, as she slowly started to wake up. Her beautiful eyes began to open, and Jonathan's were there to meet her. Jesse tried to sit up, but her body just wasn't cooperating since the attack. Jonathan leaned over and whispered, "Don't try to move, Mom. Dad and I are here to take care of you. We're going to find a way to get you better." Jesse smiled and did everything she could to acknowledge her son's presence because this was what she needed most right now. William stood right next to his son in order to make sure Jesse could see that they were in this together. Jesse took a deep breath and opened her eyes one more time. She began to pull herself up and gathered her strength because the message she was about to deliver had been weighing on her for a very long time. "I've been blessed to have both of you in my life," Jesse said, as she began to deliver the message that she felt had to be heard. "I dream about the perfect life and then I wake up, and you're both here with me. My dream has come true. Both of you have always been perfect for me, but before I go, I have one more special request. We all know the end is near for me, but I am at peace. However, I do have one very important request from you before I leave. Please, promise me that you'll both take care of each other when I'm gone. You're only going to be strong enough to tackle what life has to offer if the two of you pull together. When times are tough, I know this is when the two of you will shine. My final chapter is about to come to a close, but for both of you, I know there are many pages left that will make this world a better place. God has been very good to me, and I'm not afraid to die. I know I'll be with Him, and someday again, I hope and pray that I'll be with you as well. Whenever you feel alone, just close your eyes and think of me, and I will be there. I promise I'll always be there for you. I want to see you hold on to each other from this point forward and be strong. Hold on to each other with everything you have. This is what I'm praying for right now."

Jonathan stood up and looked at his dad. Tears were streaming down William's cheeks because he knew his one and only love was right once again. William reached out for his only son, and all of his emotions let loose. For the first time in his life, Jonathan felt his father's true love. William sobbed uncontrollably and said, "I love you, Jonathan. I'm so sorry it took me this long to tell you. Will you please forgive me?" "I love you too, Dad. I've always loved you," responded Jonathan, as they held on to each other with every ounce of strength they still had. And with that final vision engrained in her mind, Jesse smiled and closed her eyes in peace. The dream she had prayed for had finally come true...

The man slowly opened his eyes and proceeded to look around him, as the darkness of his hospital room was beginning to suffocate his every thought. While his mind was taking him back to the events of yesterday, his body seemed to be set on reminding him of the reality of his present state. He found himself wanting to go back in time because the past was so much more pleasant than what the future had in store for him. In one breath, his mother's sweet fragrance seemed to engulf his every thought...while in the other, he could almost smell death knocking on the door outside. Slowly, her beautiful smile began to fade away, and the man could feel the reality of imminent death grip hold of his tired body once again. Oh, how he wanted to touch and see his mother and tell her how much he loved her. He wanted to tell her how beautiful she was and how proud he was to be her son. But...was she in a place now that he would never see? Would he ever smell her fragrance again, or would this be the last time his mind would tease him before his journey came to a stop? The man could feel himself try to wake up in order to somehow get answers to all the questions that seemed to be laughing in his face, but it was no use. He fell back into a deep sleep, and the sweet smell of yesterday's world was nothing more than a distant memory...

Chapter 4

"Picking Up and Moving On"

For the third consecutive day, Erika was still unable to get in touch with Jonathan. Her repeated phone calls continued to go unanswered because Jonathan's roommate, Daniel, spent most of his time at the school or the gym. Erika knew something was terribly wrong and couldn't believe that Jonathan would simply check out of his final semester when his impending graduation was riding on Tillman's class. Erika knew Tillman could care less about Jonathan's personal situation, as his tardiness was already becoming an issue. Bound and determined to find out what had happened, Erika's intuitive side was about to take over. What would it hurt if she just stopped by his apartment to check it out for herself, she thought, while she contemplated her next move. Jonathan's position in Tillman's class would be severely jeopardized if his absence continued, and this was the last thing Erika wanted to see happen. After all, he seemed like the kind of guy who would cover her back if she was in trouble. Jonathan's good looks, coupled with his youthful innocence, made Erika's journey even more desirable. After all, this could be the start of something very special…

William's inability to cope with Jesse's premature departure was consuming Jonathan by the minute. Jonathan found himself completely worn out because his sole focus was now on his dad. He never realized how dependent William was on Jesse until he experienced it firsthand. All the funeral arrangements were being done by Jonathan, and he quickly took control of everything that needed to be done. He would have loved to have had his father's help, but he knew this wouldn't be possible. William was struggling with his own loss and had very little interest in the events that were going on around him. Jonathan had to make sure the arrangements were done the proper way; therefore, he decided to just make all the decisions himself. Any personal mourning he may need would have to be put on hold because he found himself consumed with the task at hand. Oh, how Jonathan just wanted to sit down and cry. His need to release the built-up emotion that was still being sequestered from within was beginning to consume him. Jonathan's mind was moving a mile a minute, and then it hit him right between the eyes! He suddenly realized that he had left school without telling anybody. Jonathan was so concerned about the events leading up to this point that he simply forgot to tell anyone of his situation. Nobody back at school knew about his mother's situation, including Daniel and his new person of interest, Erika Lewis. Not even Tillman knew why he had left town! Jonathan began to sweat profusely, as he thought about all the things he had forgotten to do. Here he was in the middle of the saddest time of his life, and he found himself worried about his advanced marketing class. This was crazy! But then again, this was the kind of effect Tillman had on everyone around him. Why in the world did Jonathan think for a minute that he would be immune to Tillman's span of control, which was inflicted on all who came in contact with him? Jonathan made his way to the bathroom and doused himself with cold water. From the time he was a little boy, his mom was always his personal crutch. Not anymore. This time, he would be on his own.

Jonathan and William drove to the funeral with each other, and the attendees who were there in person numbered just over 150. There wasn't much for them to say to each other because the fear of Jesse leaving the two of them alone was now a reality. As they pulled up to the church, William turned to Jonathan and did all he could to somehow capture the thoughts that were racing through his mind. He knew Jonathan had to get back to school soon and move on with his life; therefore, it would be up to William to make sure Jonathan got back into his routine as quickly as possible. Jonathan's entire college career was coming down to this last semester, and William knew it would be important for him to persevere and keep moving forward. If William didn't encourage his son to go back to the life he once had, then he knew Jonathan would stay for as long as William needed him. It was time for William to lead his son down the right path, even though this was something that typically fell in Jesse's camp. His words needed to be filled with compassion and love because this was what Jonathan needed most right now. "Jonathan, before we go in, there's something I need to say to you," said William, as he began to search for the words that he felt Jonathan needed to hear. "First of all, I want to thank you for everything you've done regarding your mother's funeral. You've done a super job of getting everything ready for the day. There is no way I could have ever done it by myself. Son, I also want to tell you I'm very sorry. I am so proud to be your father. One day, I'm going to make you proud to be my son as well. After today is over, I have only one request from you. I want you to move on with your life because this is what your mother would have wanted. This is what I want as well. You must never forget that your mother loved you more than words can say. Your mother's entire world revolved around you. She did everything she could to keep our family together, and you and I are both lucky she did. Your mother would want both of us to move on and be there for one another. I just want you to know that I'll always be there for you, and you'll never be alone. I love you, and I'm so sorry I haven't lived up to your expectations. Please, forgive me for not being there for you when you needed me the most. I promise it will never happen again." Jonathan immediately felt a quietness come over him because he could sense for the first time in his life that his father really did love him. These were the words he needed to hear. This was the saddest day in Jonathan's life, yet there was an incredible feeling of tranquility. Jonathan was finally at peace with the relationship he needed the most right now. He reached over and tightly wrapped his arms around his father and told him he loved him as well. With that, William knew he had done the right thing. He was grateful for the man that Jonathan had become, and he could tell from Jonathan's reaction that he was ready to move on. Jesse would have been very proud of both of her men today. This was exactly what she had always prayed for...

Erika continued to knock on the apartment door, but her repetitive tapping went unanswered. She could hear the radio playing inside the house; however, she still wasn't sure if anyone was home or not. Erika decided to walk around to the bedroom window and see if she could get a better view of the rooms inside. Her eyes continued to scan from left to right, but there was no sign of anyone in the house. Just as Erika was about to leave and get back into her car, she heard a voice from around the other side of the complex. She ran around back to find out where the noise was coming from, but once again, she was greeted by nothing but silence. She immediately ran to the front door and proceeded to knock loudly; it was time for her to get to the bottom of this! Erika began to shout for Jonathan, hoping that someone would finally hear her request for assistance. "Jonathan, if you're in there, open the door. I need to talk with you. It's Erika Lewis from your advanced marketing class. You've been gone from class for the last three days, and I just want to make sure you're ok." Suddenly, the front door opened and there, right in front of her, stood a man Erika was not prepared to see. She had never met this guy before, and by his response, he had never seen her before either. "Can I help you?" asked Daniel. Erika was caught totally off guard. She looked up at him, caught her breath, and said, "I hope so. Do you know where Jonathan is? He hasn't been in class for the past three days, and we're all starting to worry about him." Daniel responded, "Why don't you come on in so we can talk." Erika smiled and began to make her way into the apartment. Daniel followed her in and closed the door behind him. Where on earth did this girl come from? Jonathan never said anything about her before...

Jonathan and William drove home after the funeral ceremony, and the fifteen minutes in the car together felt like an eternity. As they walked through the front door, it became apparent to both of them that everything in the house seemed to capture a small part of Jesse. She had knitted the welcome mat nearly 10 years ago, and the front door's green and white trim still looked perfect, due to her meticulous detail. Inside the front door, everything had that special touch of Jesse as well. Pictures of the family growing old together were everywhere, as Jonathan's life was chronicled from his first steps all the way through high school graduation. The pictures made it clear to any of their viewers that Jonathan's life was the focal point of the camera lens in the Gunn household. Jonathan could feel himself begin to miss his mom all over again because her beautiful smile seemed to reach out and mesmerize him. The wedding picture, William during his glory days, Jonathan in Little League, the neighborhood kids swimming in the old pond out back...it was hard to believe that these pictures were nothing but distant memories right now. The house always looked perfect, but now its life was being taken over by quiet nights, rather than youthful exuberance. With Jesse's premature departure, it was as if the life of the house had literally vanished as well. What would William do when Jonathan went back to school? Would he be able to handle his greatest enemy disguised as loneliness, which would soon sneak up on him and challenge his mind like never before? Jonathan and William sat down by the fire, both waiting for the other one to speak. The stillness of the room began to take hold of them, as they became almost paralyzed by its grip. Finally, Jonathan looked over at his father and said, "I'm sure going to miss Mom. You and I are stronger because of her, and I know she'd want us to move on and not be sad. We need each other now, Dad, because we will not survive alone. We need to find a way to help each other through this sadness right now. That's what Mom would have wanted." William could only nod his head in agreement. Life would go on for both of them, but they knew it would never be the same. Jonathan had been exposed to death for the very first time, which was something he would never forget. Although he could sense the peace that consumed his mother during her final hours, it was the finality of the situation that was taking hold of him now. Talking about death is one thing, but seeing it firsthand brings a whole new perspective to the word. No matter how hard he tried, Jonathan just couldn't shake this feeling of closure. His mom would be gone forever, and this was what he struggled with most...

"Would you like something to drink?" asked Daniel, as he sat down on the couch. "A cup of hot tea would be nice," answered Erika, while she made her way over to the chair on the other side of the coffee table. It didn't take long for her to jump right in because she felt compelled to get some answers. Up until now, she had no idea what was going on. "Do you have any idea where Jonathan is? He hasn't been in class since our first day together, and everyone is very concerned. Everyone, that is, except Professor Tillman. He could care less about anyone but himself." Daniel leaned forward and responded, "Last night, I received a call from Jonathan. He told me his mother passed away a couple of days ago. Evidently, it was a sudden heart attack that caught everyone off guard and eventually took her life. Jonathan found out about it on Tuesday and was there by her side within hours. I was at the gym so I didn't even get a chance to talk with him before he left. I feel terrible that I wasn't able to make it to the funeral, but the timing for me couldn't have been any worse. I've been trying to get ready for three big tests, and I just couldn't afford to leave town. Jonathan said he understood, but I still feel like I let him down. He's my best friend, but there just wasn't any way for me to get over there that quickly. I know he's in a lot of pain right now, and I really wish I was there with him. Everything happened so quickly that neither of us had time to react to anything. It wasn't that long ago that I saw his mom and dad. Jonathan is going to have a very hard time with her loss. They were incredibly tight, and she had become a fixture at all of our games for years. I just can't believe that I'll never see her again. I wish I would have told her how much she meant to me before she was gone. I feel bad because the last time I saw her, I really didn't say all that much to her when we were together. I guess I kind of took her for granted. I really wish I could have that day back now because I would have handled it a whole lot differently than I did." Erika could sense that Daniel truly felt terrible about Jonathan's loss and that he was in a lot of pain right now as well. It was obvious to her that Jonathan's mother was a very special lady; the kind of person she would have loved to have met.

William insisted that Jonathan go back to school immediately after the funeral, but Jonathan still had a couple of important things he needed to finalize before his departure. Jesse's personal items hadn't been touched since her passing, and Jonathan knew how difficult this would be for his dad to tackle alone. As a result, he decided to stay in Rocker for a couple of extra days. This would not sit well back at school, especially in Tillman's class. Jonathan knew his father would never get through the next couple of days alone, as the most difficult task for both of them would be going through Jesse's personal items. William had fallen in love with her a long time ago, and although he seemed to be somewhat disengaged at times, his commitment to her never swayed a bit over their 25 years of marriage. Jonathan promised his father he would organize everything for him, and he met little resistance when he made the suggestion. Why did she have to leave him so quickly? Not being able to hug his mom and tell her just how much he loved her was the hardest thing for Jonathan right now. His best friend was gone, and now he would need to find some way to regroup and move on. Somehow, Jonathan also needed to make sure his father would do the same thing. This was the part of the equation that would undoubtedly be the most difficult.

Erika and Daniel visited and exchanged small talk for about 20 minutes. Finally, Erika's curiosity got the best of her. She wanted to find out more, and this was her opportunity. "So, Daniel, why is Jonathan still single? He seems like such a great guy. Do you know if he's seeing anybody right now? I'm really surprised that nobody has him locked up by now. Why is that?" Erika asked, as she intentionally sat back in her chair. She knew that a relaxed environment typically meant more conversation, which was exactly what she was hoping for. Daniel wasn't the kind of guy who needed to be coerced into talking because he could strike up a conversation with just about anybody. Erika's desire to get a better picture of Jonathan's background was about to be satisfied, as Daniel was already feeling comfortable with his newfound acquaintance. She seemed to be genuinely concerned about his best friend, and Daniel found himself in need of someone to talk to as well. Erika could sense that Daniel had kept something inside for a very long time, and her job was to just sit and listen. For whatever reason, Erika just felt like she had to know more about Jonathan's background, and the opportunity to find out was now. Daniel's vulnerability quickly took hold of him, and without much persuasion at all, he found himself happy to delve into the past...no matter how painful it may be. Daniel took a deep breath and slowly began to respond to Erika's inquisitive ways. He was about to go down a slippery slope, one he had somehow been able to avoid for years.

"Well, Jonathan hasn't seen anyone steady since our junior year in high school," Daniel said, as he shook his head and slowly ran his fingers through the front of his uncombed hair. "I guess he just hasn't gotten over what happened." "What do you mean, Daniel?" inquired Erika, as she could tell right away that he was about to take her into uncharted waters. "What in the world could have happened that has kept Jonathan from getting close with anyone else? It had to be something pretty bad to keep him away from a relationship. I mean, the guy is such a catch. I'm here to listen, Daniel, so just take your time and get it off your chest. I'm sure you'll feel better once you get it out there in the open." Daniel knew he had set himself up. Erika wasn't going to let this opening get past her, and Daniel could feel himself going back in time to a place he tried to escape a long time ago. She could tell by the look on Daniel's face that something had happened that was still fresh on his mind. Erika was just getting started, and she poured herself another cup of tea. Daniel had done everything possible to fight off the past, but tonight would be the exception to the promises he made long ago. The combination of Jesse's death and Erika's genuine curiosity made for a dangerous combination. Daniel had absolutely no chance of keeping quiet with Erika sitting right across from him. He felt his mind start to wander back to the night that would never go away...the night that would change everything.

Packing the boxes and trying not to dwell on every memory was nearly impossible for Jonathan. Every dress, every blouse, and nearly every memento Jesse kept seemed to have a special place in Jonathan's heart. He was so proud of his mom and had the utmost respect for everything she stood for because she was always the one who exemplified joy regardless of the circumstance. She was a beautiful, young woman with tremendous athletic ability who was literally taken out of her prime in an instant, yet absolutely refused to be taken down by the negativity that surrounded her. William never got over the accident and continued to blame himself, even to this day. However, Jesse would have none of that! She was bound and determined to never look back and made sure she instilled that mindset within Jonathan as well. It would have been very easy to have blamed William for what had happened, but Jesse loved him dearly right up until the very end. Jonathan could see the peace that had come over her during her final hours, and this was what he would embrace whenever sadness crept in. Jesse's death had brought father and son together, and Jonathan would make sure it stayed that way. Even in her death, Mom had worked miracles once again. Jonathan would never forget the look on Jesse's face when she closed her eyes for good. She was at peace, and Jonathan had no doubt in his mind that she was in heaven right now. That peaceful look on her face was something he would never forget; that indescribable picture of absolute serenity would be what he would remember most. This would be the image that Jonathan would always hold on to because it would somehow get him through his sleepless nights. Without a doubt, Jesse was at home with her true Father now. She could only hope that the rest of her family would someday be with her as well.

Erika sat back in her seat and began to listen, but even she wasn't prepared for what was about to come her way. Daniel had sparked her curiosity, as his somber demeanor created an absolute stillness in the room. Erika had struck a nerve because it was visible in his face. Why was Daniel even going down this path? He and Jonathan had promised each other years ago that they would never talk about this night again. Yet, here he was, about to open up to a girl he had never even met before. His mind began to race, as his internal rationalization soon overcame the guilt that initially took hold of his every thought. He needed someone to talk to about his loss, and Erika was his only option during this time of need. Daniel could sense that he was about to enter into a world that had been off limits for years. The path he was about to take would only confuse him more; it would simply add to the guilt and pain that he thought he had buried long ago. Daniel had gone almost five years without revisiting the night that would forever link him with Jonathan. After all, keeping this secret inside for all these years couldn't be healthy, he thought, as he began to go back in time. He hoped Jonathan would somehow understand. The events of days gone by were slowly coming back to life once again...

The final gun went off. It had been a very long wait for Rocker High School, but the State A Football Championship was finally theirs for the taking. The night was cold and chilly; however, the harsh conditions had no effect on the team's execution of the game plan. The offense was led by Jonathan Gunn, the junior quarterback with the rocket arm. The defense was led by Daniel Baker, the junior linebacker who hit like a freight train. It was uncommon for any opponent to work up a strategy that didn't involve trying to stop Gunn and Baker. They were the kind of players who just didn't come around very often, and the opposition did everything possible to somehow keep them at bay. The fact that both of them were juniors made it even better because this would undoubtedly be a sign of things to come for their senior year as well. They had established themselves as the true leaders of the team back in August when training camp first got started. Gunn and Baker were looked upon by all to keep the team focused, no matter what the challenge entailed. Who would have ever thought that this would be the last time they would suit up in a game together? Who could have ever predicted the events that would transpire and change their lives forever...

Sirens blared and fire trucks raced through the city of Rocker because the team had finally won the elusive state championship that avoided them for a very long time. For the past 20 years, there wasn't a whole lot to cheer about on Friday evenings, but this night would be much different. It had been a long dry spell for the city, but the state championship trophy had finally come home. The whole city was literally on fire for the team that had brought them all together, with Jonathan and Daniel being the focal point of everyone's attention. Fans, parents, and students alike had elevated them to "rock star status" because they had somehow found a way to rally their team around a prize that was treasured by all. Jonathan and Daniel were able to inflict a positive frame of mind on the entire city, even if it was just for one evening. This was the night the entire city had dreamed about, and finally it was here. Football was the only thing Jonathan and Daniel had focused on over the past six months, but this night would be different. Tonight, they were ready to go out and finally have some fun! The atmosphere around the locker room after the game was electric, with nearly 500 students waiting for the team when they came out the front door. Roosevelt Pass was their destination, as the first keg of beer would be tapped within the hour. Both boys made a break for Daniel's car because they wanted to beat the crowd up the winding, mountain pass. Increased traffic on this dark road only added to the challenge that greeted every driver, which was not a good sign for anyone. The pass was tough enough to maneuver, even on a clear day. Their real adventure was about to begin, but nobody involved had any idea what this truly meant.

The beers were already flowing when the two of them arrived, as a number of students had gotten off to an early start. The energy around the crowd was absolutely incredible; never before had anyone been a part of something quite like this. Daniel parked his car around the side of the lot, and the two of them quickly made their way to the front of the line. The crowd was practically screaming the school fight song, and this sign of camaraderie seemed to put a smile on nearly every face surrounding the yellowish-red bonfire flame. Every face, that is, except one…Leonard Mattice. Bad attitude, bad temper, and bad intentions had found a resting place in Leonard's soul long ago. Why would he show up tonight when he knew deep down inside that nobody wanted him to be there? Why would he want to be part of something that epitomized everything that he was not? On this particular night, none of this mattered to Leonard. He had grown accustomed to this kind of treatment from his fellow students a long time ago. Leonard had been an outcast since the second grade, and the anger had been building up inside him ever since. He had been thinking about this particular evening for a very long time, and now everything was lining up perfectly for his plan to finally take place. His ultimate objective was to send a message to the entire school that would never be forgotten, to somehow take away the joy when it was truly at its apex. Tonight was the perfect fit, as Leonard could sense that his opportunity to get even was fast approaching. This would be the night that he would be the star, the night that he would finally steal the show. He watched from a distance and stood near the back of the crowd, prowling for his targets. His eyes shifted through the crowd like a hungry lion, waiting for the opportunity to pounce on his prey. Almost instantly, he spotted the perfect choice. Patience set in for Leonard because he knew it would be quite some time before he could effectively carry out his plan. His thought process was deliberate, and he knew in his mind exactly how this would play out. This was a night he wanted to savor; one he wanted to never forget. After all, he had been thinking about this night for a very long time. Jonathan and Daniel were just starting to have some fun, and this fed right into Leonard's wheelhouse. Leonard could feel the corners of his mouth begin to move upward, as a slight smile slowly formed on his face. He watched their every move from a distance and searched meticulously for the opening that would allow him to put his plan into action. He knew that before the evening was over, he would be in full control. Jonathan and Daniel would be nothing more than puppets on a string…a string that he was finally able to pull.

Jonathan had a huge crush on Leslie McPhail, who happened to be a junior as well. Leslie was one of the more popular girls in the class and was the kind of girl everyone wanted to be around. Jonathan first met Leslie during the beginning of his sophomore year, but he never had the courage to ask her out. She was gorgeous, as her dark hair and big, brown eyes made Jonathan melt in his boots whenever she was around. Leslie was the one girl who always captured Jonathan's attention, and this night would be no different. Her contagious smile and willingness to get along with all the students at Rocker High were intangibles not often seen in the typical high school teenager. The fact that she was beautiful also didn't hurt! Jonathan couldn't wait to see Leslie because his newfound confidence after the big game was just what he needed in order to finally make his move. Hopefully, the courage that had eluded him for the past two years would finally take hold. Jonathan and Daniel slowly made their way through the crowd, as they were embraced by fellow students at nearly every turn. Little did they know, they were also being watched closely by another set of eyes in the distance. However, this set of eyes had far different intentions than the rest of the crowd that hovered around them.

Leonard Mattice had always been a strange kid. He was a loner who didn't say much to anyone in his class, and he seemed to like it that way. Jonathan tried to get to know Leonard during his sophomore year, but he found himself frustrated with Leonard's unwillingness to respond to anything that came his way. None of the kids in the school wanted anything to do with Leonard because his lifeless face seemed to leave an uneasy feeling with anyone who came in contact with him. Although he never confronted or harmed anyone in school, there was a general consensus among all the students that Leonard was nobody to mess with. His physical presence was intimidating, as he stood 6'3" and weighed close to 200 pounds. He had a face that didn't respond to much of anything at all, no matter how hard those around him tried. He was the kind of kid who always seemed like he was sizing up his competition, looking for an opening to make his move. Up until now, this uneasy engagement had been harmless to those around him. Tonight, this was all about to change. The crowd fast approached 500 by 11:30 p.m., and everyone was in a partying mood. Leonard watched the festivities from afar and continued to assess the playing field in front of him. His quiet side began to subside, and he could feel his adrenaline picking up speed. He closed his eyes and slowly tapped into the darker side of his soul. It was time for Leonard to go for a walk…

Finally, there she was and more beautiful than ever before! Jonathan's heart began to beat faster and faster, as his eyes became fixated on the girl he had been thinking about all night long. She was absolutely gorgeous, and Jonathan could feel his knees begin to buckle as he thought about his next move. Jonathan tapped Daniel on the shoulder and said, "There's Leslie right over there, and she's not alone." Daniel immediately scanned the girls who were with Leslie and found himself circling back to Terri Dwyer, an attractive brunette who was one of Leslie's closest friends. Daniel actually had his eye on Terri long ago but just didn't have the time to do anything about it. Jonathan and Daniel were about to make their move, but their actions would not go unnoticed. Leonard watched the two of them work the crowd and searched for an opening, while his eyes peered from the darkness that surrounded the gathering. The laughs and cheers were deafening to him and continually pounded his head like a set of well-oiled cymbals. More than anything else, Leonard wanted to make the laughter go away once and for all. Voices in his head continued to convince him that all of this would soon disappear, and their joy would eventually become his prized possession. On this particular night, things felt very different to Leonard. For the first time ever, Leonard truly did feel like he was the one in control, that he was finally the one calling the shots. He felt like he was invisible and that nobody could stop him from what he needed to do. Everyone was having far too much fun to notice Leonard Mattice, but this was all about to change. He knew most of the kids who were at the party, and every single one of them had slighted him at some point during his time at the school. Jonathan and Daniel would be perfect targets for Leonard because they were the focal point of the entire evening. However, the timing had to be a fit for his plan to work. If for some reason, the opportunity didn't present itself regarding Jonathan and Daniel, then Leonard would have to move on to an alternate plan. After all, there were plenty of targets on this particular night, and nobody was safe. Leonard was not about to relinquish his control and slip up in any way whatsoever; therefore, his actions were calculated and deliberate. The blueprint for his plan had taken form years ago, and tonight was all about its execution.

It didn't take long for Jonathan and Daniel to strike up a conversation with Leslie and Terri, as they quickly made it over to where the two girls were standing. They were the heroes of the game, and everyone was anxious to spend time with them. Leslie and Terri were no exception and quickly moved closer to extend their congratulations as well. As a high school football star, this was the kind of night dreams were made of, and Jonathan and Daniel were having the time of their young lives. It was as if the four of them had been together before, as they laughed and talked about all the things they were going through at school. Small talk quickly evolved into their plans for the evening, and Jonathan gathered up the nerve to finally make the first move. "Hey, Leslie, do you two want to meet us down at the Broadway Café for a late night breakfast?" asked Jonathan, as he found himself stumbling through the words he had been rehearsing for the past 20 minutes. "We can get caught up on a number of things, plus it will be our treat." Leslie and Terri responded with an innocent set of giggles, even though their hearts were racing with anticipation. Suddenly, Terri felt a slight nudge from behind and quickly turned around to see who it was. "Excuse me," the dark figure said, while it slowly disappeared into the crowd. "That was strange," Terri said, as she leaned over and told Leslie what had just happened. "Leonard Mattice actually just said something to me. How strange is that...he hasn't said anything to me all year long. I certainly didn't expect to see him here tonight." Maybe, just maybe, he wasn't a bad guy after all, Terri thought, as she walked closely behind Leslie. They didn't want to lose sight of Jonathan and Daniel because both of them were eager to get away. After all, this was the night they had been waiting for since the beginning of the year...

"Why don't you go ahead of us, Jonathan," said Leslie. "Terri and I will head back down Roosevelt Pass after we use the restroom. We'll meet you there for breakfast within 30 minutes or so. You can save us the best seat in the house. After the game you guys played tonight, I'm sure they will give you whatever seat you want!" Before Jonathan could suggest they follow each other, Daniel interjected, "Sounds great, we'll see you girls there. Don't worry...we'll make sure we save the best seat just for the two of you. Jonathan and I have connections." As they were walking to their car, Jonathan was struggling with the anticipated sequence of events. "Why don't we just wait for them, Daniel?" asked Jonathan, as they made their way down the hill toward the parking lot below. "I'm not too crazy about them making the drive alone. We both know how dangerous Roosevelt Pass can be at night." "Don't worry about the two of them," said Daniel, as he was quick to rebut Jonathan's position of concern. "They'll be right behind us. Trust me. If they want to be with us, they will come. Playing hard to get is the way to win this game." Jonathan smiled and said, "You're probably right, Daniel. This is one game I'm not very good at. I just hope they show up. I really like Leslie, and it looks like you and Terri are really hitting it off. Man, what a night. This is the best night of my life!" "Me too, buddy," said Daniel, while they made their way to the car. "This is a night we're never going to forget."

Leslie and Terri made their way back up the hill to the darkened restroom. They couldn't wait to compare notes and continued to move further and further away from the crowd. The lights above the door were burned out, but they didn't even notice their absence due to their own temporary state of euphoria. Both of them were ecstatic to be together and made their way inside the room. The moon seemed to hide behind the clouds that had formed, as darkness was now settling in for the evening. Leslie and Terri had their eyes on Jonathan and Daniel for a very long time, and it looked like their wishes were about to come true. Both girls had strong morals, and they felt very comfortable with their decision to go out for breakfast. After all, what could possibly happen on such a perfect night? Jonathan and Daniel were the two boys that every girl in the school wanted to spend time with, and now here they were, living out their dreams firsthand. The night had already been one of their best ever, and they couldn't wait to see what would happen next. There was no way they could have ever prepared themselves for what was about to come their way...

Jonathan and Daniel pulled up in front of the diner at a little past midnight and quickly made their way to the front door. They were happy to see their favorite booth was still open, and their entrance immediately caught the attention of the late night patrons who were already seated. Leslie and Terri would be there soon, and Jonathan and Daniel wanted to make sure everything was in place when the two of them arrived. Jonathan and Daniel had made the trip down in less than 20 minutes, which was perfect timing regarding their plan. As they quickly approached the 30 minute mark, both of them could sense that something just didn't feel right. Leslie and Terri were nowhere to be seen, and their absence just didn't make any sense at all. They all seemed to be on the same page just a short time ago, but Jonathan and Daniel were beginning to feel legitimately concerned about their whereabouts. Maybe Daniel should have listened to Jonathan and had the girls follow them down? His idea of playing hard to get was beginning to look like a very bad idea, as they both sat in silence and waited. The night was turning out to be much darker than anyone expected, especially away from the fire. On this particular evening, that darkness had a name to go along with it...and it was Leonard Mattice.

Leslie and Terri came out of the restroom with one thing in mind, which was to meet with Jonathan and Daniel down at the Broadway Café. As they walked down the hill to the end of the parking lot, their excitement was consumed by fear in an instant. Both of them could feel the presence of someone or something in the vicinity, while they made their way toward the blue sedan in the parking lot below. As soon as they got to the car, they jumped inside and immediately locked the doors because they could sense their own vulnerability. Terri jumped in the passenger's side and Leslie took the wheel. "Let's get out of here. I think someone's following us," said Leslie, as she could feel her heart begin to race uncontrollably. Leslie began to turn on the headlights and that is when she saw it...how in the world did it ever get there? Panic set in, and it was obvious to both of them that they were not alone. They knew they had to get out of there...and fast!

Jonathan and Daniel were really starting to worry by now because there was no way Leslie and Terri should still be missing from their planned breakfast. "I think we need to go back up there and see what happened," said Jonathan. "Something just doesn't feel right. This isn't like them, Daniel. They had no reason to stand us up tonight. They could be in real trouble right now." Daniel nodded his head in agreement since he was still replaying the events of less than an hour ago. Jonathan's interest had been on Leslie for quite some time now, and he was hoping tonight would be the start of something special. He had never really dated anyone before, but she seemed so much different than the rest of the girls in the school. Jonathan and Daniel were beginning to realize that they should have waited for the girls to follow them down the pass. Why didn't they just wait like they were supposed to? What in the world could have ever happened to the girls in such a short amount of time? Unfortunately, the two of them were about to find out...

Leslie traveled everywhere with the good luck doll that her grandmother had given to her when she was just five years old. It had become an ongoing joke among her friends because she would always take out her little friend whenever there was something really important that needed an extra boost. She had brought it with her to the game earlier in the evening, as her superstitions had once again gotten the best of her. This was the biggest game in the history of the school, and there was no way she was going to take a chance on not having her good luck charm with her. She kept it in her backpack, just like she did before every big game. However, this night would turn out to be much different. As she sat in her blue sedan, she began to play back the events of the evening. She thought back on the game itself and everything that led up to the opening kick-off. Just like a number of others in the stands, Leslie had become so enthralled with the game that she carelessly left her backpack under the bleachers. When she finally retrieved it, she noticed that the zipper to the side pocket had been left open. This was so unlike her because she was borderline obsessive compulsive when it came to little things like this. As Leslie replayed the events of the evening, she did all she could to convince herself that she must have left it open by mistake. At the time, she didn't think much of it and quickly moved on to watching the next play. It seemed like the game had taken place a long time ago, and her mind was now focused on what needed to be done next. Everything was moving way too fast for her liking. The night had gone from excitement, to one of anticipation...and then to one of darkness. The events that were about to unfold had been set in motion long ago, and now one thing was obvious to all involved. There was one person who was in control right now, and he had been waiting for this moment all his life. There was no way he was about to let this opportunity slip by...

Things were starting to come together for Leslie, as she struggled to make sense of what had happened. The beam from the headlights of Leslie's car immediately brought the small figurine into focus, and their eyes became mesmerized by the hanging doll. Leslie began to shake, as she and Terri watched it slowly swing in the wind, just in front of their car. Someone had hung the doll from the old oak tree with a 16-inch piece of nylon rope, and now it seemed to be almost laughing in their faces. Both Leslie and Terri sat motionless and watched it slowly twirl in front of them. The wind was blowing at a constant pace and moved the doll in a counterclockwise rotation. Leslie and Terri were in a state of shock, as they watched the doll slowly spin around. Who in the world would ever do this to her prized possession? The doll represented a piece of Leslie's past that had somehow been violated. This sick joke belonged to the mind of someone she never wanted to meet in person, and she knew right away that she had to find a way to quickly get out of there and find some help. Panic set in, as Leslie put her pedal to the floor and quickly sped out of the lot. From behind the tree, the tall, dark figure came into view and watched the red tail lights speed away. Silently, he tapped the silver wrench in the palm of his gloved hand and stared at the car as it moved toward Roosevelt Pass. The tail lights soon became two, small red dots, as the car quickly began to pick up speed. The tall figure stood alone in the moonlight, while his pale face began to slowly crack a smile. Watching the car gain speed as it headed for the pass made him feel good inside because he knew he was finally in control. He was the only one who knew, without a doubt, that the outcome would not be good. The man then turned and threw the wrench as far as he possibly could toward the 200-foot ravine. He knew nobody would ever find it there, which was exactly what he wanted…

Roosevelt Pass was a difficult stretch of road to maneuver, even when a person's head was clear. On this particular night, Leslie was no match for the dangerous turns that were yet to come. Terri was still in shock over what they had seen and was unable to provide any guidance whatsoever. 55, 65, 75 mph…the most difficult turns were still in front of them. Leslie could feel herself lean into the first two turns, but the third was far too sharp for the tires to grab. She slammed on the brakes and closed her eyes. Nothing happened… the brakes were overmatched, and the grinding noise echoed along the canyon walls that lined the dangerous roadway. The old car was out of control and still picking up speed, as it severed the guardrail like a machete. Leslie and Terri could feel the car go airborne, while they grazed the tops of the pine trees far below. Fear suffocated the two girls like an old blanket, and their bodies felt paralyzed from top to bottom. Death was about to quickly take hold of them, as the stillness of the night crept in without warning. The old, blue car finally came to rest nearly 200 feet below, as Leslie and Terri never had a chance. Each of them took their last breath long before the car came to rest…and the help that would eventually find them would not be needed.

After waiting for over an hour, Jonathan and Daniel decided to head back up the pass to see what had happened. By the time they approached the section of the road where the accident took place, an emergency vehicle had already arrived. It wasn't uncommon to have a quick response time on the pass because the County Search and Rescue Division was located at the bottom of the hill. Jonathan and Daniel jumped out of the car and ran over to the guardrail. They could see the fiery red ball off in the distance. Both of them went over to the edge of the embankment and shook their heads in disbelief. Somehow, they just knew the wreckage at the bottom of the ravine was Leslie's. Guilt immediately began to consume both of them because they knew deep down inside that this tragic event could have been avoided. Their night had gone from excitement to darkness in a matter of hours, and now they were left behind to pick up the pieces. On this tragic evening, a piece of life was taken from both Jonathan and Daniel. No matter how hard they tried, neither would be able to erase this from their memory. Somehow, both of them would have to fight off the demons that would never go away. Jonathan and Daniel stood in the darkness, both staring off into the distance on a clear, cold autumn night that would never be forgotten. Although they would somehow find a way to press on, neither of them would ever be the same again.

"So, was there ever an investigation into the accident?" asked Erika. "Nope," said Daniel, as he fought back the tears he so desperately wanted to release. "We all knew that someone was responsible for the severed brake-line, but because the wreckage was so bad, the investigators never came to a definitive conclusion." Erika could see the pain on Daniel's face when his eyes began to tear up once again. "You know, Jonathan and I never played another football game together after that night. We tried to move on and help each other as best we could, but it hasn't been easy. College has allowed us to leave Rocker and get away, but no matter how hard we try, the events of that evening continually resurface and make it very hard to move ahead with our lives. We both still have a lot of pain and guilt regarding that night, and I have a sense that it will always be this way. I don't think the empty feeling will ever go away. It still hurts to think about it. In fact, this is the first time I've even talked about it since that night." Erika said nothing. For whatever reason, she now felt a connection to Jonathan's life. She felt numb by what Daniel had just shared with her...and very sad for both of them. She could see the genuine love on Daniel's face when he talked about his best friend, and for the first time in her life, she didn't say a word. There just wasn't anything she could possibly say that would help make the pain go away...

Chapter 5

"It's Never Too Late"

Jonathan closed the final box of Jesse's personal belongings, as the past three days had been spent getting everything together before he made his way back to school. There would never be absolute closure, but it was important for him to move on. Now that his father had released him, so to speak, the coming weeks would be easier for Jonathan. Jesse's death had already started to take a toll on William, and he was having a difficult time accepting the fact that she would never return. As Jonathan backed out of the driveway, he waved good-bye to his father and couldn't help but have a heavy heart. For the first time in his life, he was truly going to miss his dad. Unlike his trips of the past, Jonathan felt empty inside as he drove down the street that reflected many of his childhood memories. What in the world could he do for his dad that would help ease the pain? He had a thought...

Jonathan pulled into the local pet store, hoping to find the ideal gift for his dad. He made his way to the back of the store and immediately knew what he wanted. He still remembered the day he received Buck, and it was one of the happiest days of his life. Oh, how he hoped he could somehow do the same for his dad right now. Jonathan went from cage to cage, while he continued to search for the perfect gift. As he made his way around the final corner, there he was! He even looked like Buck; a 7 week-old yellow lab with a little, white spot on his chest. The dog was absolutely perfect, and although the price tag would set Jonathan back a long way, it was the medicine his dad needed right now. The big, red bow around his fluffy, yellow neck put the finishing touches on him. Jonathan had no idea when he would be able to get back and see his dad; therefore, the puppy would keep him focused on something other than the loss he just suffered.

As Jonathan pulled into his driveway, he spotted his dad out back sitting in his favorite chair under the old cedar tree. Next to him was Jesse's empty chair, where she had spent many summer evenings right alongside William. Jonathan approached his father from behind and startled him, as he covered William's eyes with both hands. "Dad, our life has changed, and it will never be the same again. But Mom would have wanted us to embrace each new day just as she did. I have a special gift for you. I really hope it helps you look at every day as a new beginning. This is my way of saying thanks to you for being my dad. You have always taken care of Mom and me. I promise I will always do the same for you too. I love you, Dad." And with that, William turned around and before he knew it, the little yellow lab with the big, red bow was licking his face. William gasped for air and began to laugh uncontrollably. Jonathan just stood back and savored the moment because he had never seen his dad like this before. Even though his happiness was temporary, Jonathan knew in his heart that this was the beginning of a long and arduous journey for his dad. For this one moment in time, Jonathan felt like he had finally become his father's hero, which was something he had hoped for since he was a little boy.

Jonathan's return back to school got off to a shaky start because his broken heart was still at home with his dad. No matter how hard Jonathan tried to focus on the job at hand, his mind continually took him back to the loss of his mother. Jonathan just couldn't seem to get Jesse's beautiful face out of his mind, and before he knew it, he became the focal point of Tillman's ire. As his level of engagement in class diminished, Tillman's frustration escalated even more. This was classic for Tillman, as he had a reputation for going after individuals who showed any vulnerability whatsoever. Just like the bully on the playground, Tillman was all about elevating his own status at the expense of others. Jonathan's personal situation had zero impact on Tillman, and he expected uninterrupted attention from every one of his students. There were a number of things that bothered Tillman about Jonathan, but one thing in particular seemed to irritate him the most. Not only did Tillman hate the fact that Jonathan never let his emotions get the best of him, he especially despised the way Erika Lewis seemed to throw herself at the mercy of his feet. For some unknown reason, Jonathan seemed to lose interest in Erika shortly after his mother's death. As is usually the case, this type of behavior increased Erika's desire to be with him even more, which did not bode well for Jonathan. Tillman had become very fond of Erika, and his jealousy was beginning to impact the way he conducted himself in class. As Jonathan's grades began to slide, Tillman made sure he found a way to bring it to the attention of his fellow students at every interval. Whenever Tillman had the chance to take a verbal shot at Jonathan in front of Erika, he would take full advantage of the opportunity. However, no matter how persistent Tillman was with his personal digs and innuendos, Jonathan would have no part of it. Jonathan's intuition told him not to go there because he knew Tillman was a dangerous man. Taking Tillman on just didn't make any sense, and Jonathan realized that one slip-up on his part was all Tillman would need right now. Tillman's time was running out, and he knew he had just two weeks to break this young man. He was accustomed to getting everything he wanted and would stop at nothing in order to fulfill his every need. Jonathan would have to be very careful; the last thing he could afford was to let Tillman break him down. Not only did his graduation ride on it, his emotional state of mind was on the verge of being exposed as well. Jonathan needed to stay focused on somehow completing his degree; he simply could not afford a hiccup of any kind.

Erika Lewis was in Tillman's crosshairs, as he had been attracted to her since the first day in class. He liked the fact that she imposed a challenge to him right from the start and felt a strong need to take full authority over his younger prey. The fact that she was the same age as his only daughter made no difference to him whatsoever. His daughter meant nothing to him right now because it had been nearly 14 years since the last time they had spoken to one another. Give his ex-wife credit...she knew early on that she had to get their only daughter away from him at a young age. Tillman was the kind of man who never put his wife ahead of his interest in other women, and his marriage was over after eight, tumultuous years. He had an eye for the younger girls, which meant the college campus provided him with the perfect environment for his greatest weakness. His plan was about to go into action, and he knew he had to move quickly. With final exams fast approaching, Tillman realized that his time was running. Erika was carrying a B+ average heading into the final test, while Jonathan was still holding on to a solid B. As Tillman began to assess the upcoming schedule, it became obvious to him that an opening for him would soon surface. Tillman was fairly confident that Jonathan's grade would be high enough to avoid failing the semester, and he knew Jonathan would do everything possible to attain a passing grade. Even though he absolutely despised the kid, Tillman could sense that Jonathan still had a strong grasp of the material being presented in class. On the other hand, Erika was a totally different story. Tillman had set her up for failure a long time ago because he had lulled Erika to sleep with inflated scores. He made sure she clearly understood that this leniency could, in fact, bring with it a heavy price to pay. Numerous times, Tillman kept Erika after class and made it obvious to her that his advances were happening for a reason. Nothing ever happened, but he had clearly defined the playing field for Erika. Without a doubt, Tillman was now in total control. That first day in class was a distant memory, as Erika could feel her confidence subside on a daily basis. As her self-esteem slowly evaporated, Tillman's advances increased even more. He was now taking Erika down a path that came all too easy for him. Although Erika was a very smart girl, her ambition and inherent pressure to succeed was getting the best of her. The degree she coveted so dearly was within her grasp, and this played right into Tillman's dangerous web. She knew how to play the game, and although this flirtatious side of her was quite harmless, she was absolutely no match for Tillman. He was setting her up for the kill, and the hunt was officially ready to begin...

William and his newfound friend, Buck Junior, or BJ for short, were quickly becoming the best of friends. There was no replacement for Jesse, but BJ was definitely helping to ease the pain. The fact that BJ looked almost identical to Buck brought back all those memories from years gone by. William could still see Jonathan's smile when they drove home from Rocker on that beautiful summer day many years ago. He found himself reminiscing about the good times they had as a family, as his nostalgic side continually visited him throughout the day. If only he had the opportunity to live those days all over again, he would somehow find a way to savor them even more. He had regrets about the way he handled his son, but Jesse was always there to pick up the slack. Jonathan was becoming the man he never was, and that made him very proud. Soon, this pedigree would be challenged like never before because Tillman was preparing to make his move. Jonathan would need to be ready for the unexpected, as the end of the semester was fast approaching. The great J.R. Tillman was on a mission to get what he wanted and anyone who stood in his way was fair game, including Jonathan.

The final exam was about to begin, and every student in the classroom knew Tillman was prepared to give them his best shot. Jonathan hated the fact that nearly half the questions would be essay because this could give Tillman the subjectivity he needed to alter the answers in his favor. However, Jonathan had worked hard to prepare himself for the exam and soon began to reap the rewards of his hard work. Erika, on the other hand, seemed to be very uneasy with the format of the test. Her continual sighs of desperation became an annoyance to Jonathan, but he somehow found a way to fight through the constant interruptions. Periodically, he lifted his head, only to catch the watchful eye of their looming professor. Tillman was looking for a reason to fail Jonathan; therefore, he made sure the lifting of his head was only temporary. Erika's eyes also began to wonder, and Tillman quickly picked up on her distracted state of mind. He could tell by her actions that she was in big trouble, as she was quickly playing right into his hand. Her uneasiness increased Tillman's confidence regarding the outcome he had desired, and he began to mentally prepare himself for what was yet to come. The more Erika squirmed, the more Tillman stared her down. For the first time since the beginning of the semester, Erika felt both insecure and vulnerable. Her bull's-eye was getting bigger in size, and Tillman was the one with the arrows. He continued to glare at Erika right up until the final bell and seemed to peer right through her inner core. As Erika approached him on her way out the door, she handed him her test. "So, how did you do, little missy? Doesn't look to me like you're quite as confident as you were on that first day of class," Tillman gloated, as he let out a laugh that brought everyone's attention Erika's way. Erika could say nothing and quickly turned and walked away. Ten steps out the door, and she could still hear Tillman laughing behind her. She could sense that Tillman would be back for more because she had a sick feeling in her stomach that he was just getting started.

Jonathan had gotten into the ritual of frequenting the local diner after every big test, and tonight would be no exception. Erika always made it a point to join him as well, but this night would be different. Jonathan arrived just after 6:00 p.m., feeling very confident about the exam they had just completed. He knew Tillman would have difficulty challenging the answers he had given, and he felt very good about the way he had stood up to the challenge. Despite everything he had been through over the past month, his preparation had definitely paid off. Jonathan was anxious to share his success with someone, and for the first time in a long while, he found himself actually looking forward to seeing Erika. Lately, he just didn't have the desire to expend any energy on the relationship because his personal ordeal regarding his mother's death had him completely worn out. For whatever reason, tonight felt different. He couldn't wait to see how she did on the test, as he was hoping that both of them could celebrate the end of Tillman once and for all. However, he had a sinking feeling that this would not be the case for Erika. Jonathan was still having a difficult time getting over his mother's death, and he knew he had to find a way to mentally move on. Hopefully, this night would help him continue to move forward with the healing process that he so desperately needed right now. 7:00 o'clock and still no sign of Erika...this was so unlike her because tardiness had never been a part of her vocabulary. Jonathan was beginning to worry about her and had an uneasy feeling that something just wasn't right. His curiosity was getting the best of him, and he found himself thinking about the sequence of events that led up to her unknown whereabouts. Jonathan kept going back to that look of absolute despair on Erika's face during the final exam. She had a look of confusion that soon morphed itself into a look of fear, which meant only one thing to Jonathan. He knew he had to find out where she was...and fast.

Tillman was not the kind of guy who missed the opportunity to bag his prey, and tonight, he was undoubtedly the hunter. He realized he had to move quickly, and his finger dialed her number via memory. "Hello," Erika said. Her voice quivered, as if she already knew who was on the other end of the line. "Hello, Erika, it's J.R. I thought you might want to know how you did on the test today. I decided to grade yours first because I knew how much you wanted to know the results. Well, if you do want the details, I thought it would be best if you saw them in person. There are a few questions that can be better explained face-to-face. Plus, if you feel the desire to challenge my reasoning, your probability of persuading me could go up exponentially if you agree to see me tonight. Otherwise, you just may have to take your chances." The phone fell silent, as Erika felt paralyzed. She could say nothing. "I interpret your silence as a resounding yes," said Tillman. "1551 Brookplace is my address. Your test results will be available in 60 minutes. Erika, trust me, unlike your first day in my class, this is one meeting you don't want to be late for." Click! Erika shook with fear and buried her face in her hands. Her farm back in Cedar City seemed so far away. She missed her family very much, and tonight, all she wanted to do was go home.

Jonathan's concern was starting to consume him, and he felt a sudden urge to find Erika as quickly as possible. He flagged down the waiter and asked for his check. Erika should have been with him by now, and Jonathan felt a strong inkling to quickly track her down. She didn't live too far from the diner, so he decided to go and see firsthand why she didn't show up. He jumped into his car and sped out of the parking lot. His adrenaline was starting to rush through his body, as he could sense that something was terribly wrong. Pulling into her driveway, he noticed the front door was wide open. This was so unlike Erika, who had a reputation for being anal retentive regarding everything she did. Jonathan ran up to the porch and yelled for her. He peered in through the front window, but there was nothing happening inside. He couldn't see any activity in the home; however, it was hard to tell if Erika was inside or not. He felt compelled to go inside and find out for himself. "Erika," Jonathan yelled, "it's Jonathan. Are you in here?" No answer. Darkness was starting to set in, as Jonathan made his way to the nearest telephone and turned on the desk lamp. Everything was in order and very clean, which was very typical for Erika's home. However, Jonathan noticed a notepad and a pen on the table, which immediately seemed to be out of place. 1551 Brookplace was scribbled on the pad. Jonathan sat down and shook his head, as the address seemed to be calling out his name. Where in the world had he seen those numbers before?

Ding-Dong. The chimes rang throughout the house. "Good evening, Erika. Come on in. I was hoping you'd make it in time. Class is about to begin." Erika looked up at Tillman and showed no emotion. The door closed behind her, while she stood in the rotunda. This was a very cold house, as the pictured walls seemed to be screaming out with voices from the past. How many other young college girls had been in this same room over the years? How many other young girls had fallen prey to this sick man? Erika had a feeling that the number was probably too large to count. "Let me take your coat, Erika. There is a beverage for you over on the counter. We need to have a drink to clear our thoughts. You know wine has a wonderful affinity for clearing the senses. You will enjoy my wine. I carry only the best."

Jonathan could feel his heart begin to race. He knew Daniel was still back at home, and for a split second, he wanted to get a second opinion regarding what to do next. He also had a sinking feeling that Erika needed him now. Even though he had been preoccupied recently and hadn't paid much attention to her, she still meant a lot to him. He also knew Erika was not one to fall out of touch like this unless something was terribly wrong. The fact that she didn't show up at the diner earlier that evening was something she would have never done without the involvement, or coercion, from someone else. Jonathan ran out of Erika's house and quickly jumped into his car. 1551 Brookplace... the numbers and address were like voices ringing in his head. For whatever reason, they were calling out his name, and he had no idea why. Maybe he should call Daniel for backup, Jonathan thought, as he contemplated his next move. Jonathan had no idea what was in store for him; however, he had no doubt in his mind that Erika was in big trouble...and it had to do with that Brookline address. Tracking down Daniel may impede his ability to make it in time, and this was something he could ill afford to have happen. As much as he wanted to get his help, he was afraid of what may happen to Erika if there was any further delay. Being alone was not by choice, but he really had no other alternative.

"Erika, you know I've had my sights set on you for a very long time now. From the very first day you set foot in my class, I had this evening planned out in my mind. You are scheduled to graduate this spring, and fortunately for both of us, you need a passing grade from me in order to receive your degree." Erika said nothing. She felt her hands start to shake and her lips begin to tremble. She felt frozen in time, as she closed her eyes and opened them quickly, hoping the nightmare would somehow go away. Unfortunately for Erika, this nightmare of hers had developed into a reality, and the game was about to begin. Tillman was just getting started and was savoring every moment of this interaction. His confidence was sky high, as he began to explain the rules of the game. "Erika, I have some good news and some bad news. Since I am such an optimistic guy, I will end with a positive. First, the bad news; I graded your test, and it looks like your final score is a 60%. As you know, anything under 70% is considered failing, so it doesn't look too good for you and your graduation plans for this year. The next time the advanced marketing class is offered is next spring. I will be teaching the course that semester as well. This means you'll need to wait at least another year to celebrate, since our graduation ceremony always takes place after the grades are officially turned in. Of course, this would be assuming you do better next year than you did this year. Based on your rapid deterioration regarding performance over the last half of the semester, assuming you will do better next year is, quite frankly, a real stretch. By the way, I have a tendency to be even tougher the second time around." Tillman smiled and could sense Erika's self-confidence disintegrating by the second. The tear in the corner of her eye gave him even more pleasure because he knew he was in full control now. Iowa seemed so far away to Erika, as she knew she was outmatched by Tillman when it came to this particular interaction. She was playing on his turf now, and he was very accustomed to house rules. "Now, do you want to hear the good news?" Tillman whispered, while he leaned closer to where Erika was standing. The fun was about to begin.

Boom! Jonathan's car began to swerve. He could feel the tire deflate in a matter of seconds and did everything possible to keep his car from flipping over. Pulling over to the side of the road, Jonathan knew he had to get to Erika as quickly as possible, but now he was in big trouble. There was no way he would make it in his car because it was definitely done for the evening! He started to run along the dark pathway, as the rain continued to pound on his wet face. The Brookline address was a good 12-15 miles away, and Jonathan realized the only way he would ever make it in time would be to flag down the next vehicle that came his way. He also knew the chances of getting an immediate ride were slim at best because he was literally out in the middle of nowhere right now. The night was dark, cold, and lonely…and Jonathan could almost hear Erika calling out to him. She had nobody else, and he knew her hopes rested on his ability to find out where she was as quickly as possible. Jonathan was running as fast as he could, and his heart felt like it was going to pound right through his chest. His only hope right now was to somehow find a ride and rescue Erika from whatever trouble she was in, before it was too late.

"I do have some possible good news," whispered Tillman. "I say possible good news Erika because it's all about how you respond to my questions. If you respond in a positive way, you just might see your graduation day this year after all. If you play games and disappoint me, there's a very high probability you will never see that little, white piece of paper you so desperately long for. I would strongly recommend that you play this game with the energy and passion that I would come to expect from you. I hope I make myself clear. Otherwise, the game will end abruptly, and your grade will be recorded as is. The choice is really up to you. Now, are you ready to get started?" Erika choked back her tears and reluctantly nodded her head yes. "Good decision, Ms. Lewis," said Tillman, as his smile began to slowly consume his weathered face. "Let the games begin."

Tillman set his drink down and motioned for Erika to follow him, while he led her down the large hallway. He had accumulated a considerable collection of art over the years, and pictures lined both sides of the corridor. Tillman proceeded to walk into the last room on the left. Erika followed him from approximately ten steps behind. For a brief moment, she felt compelled to turn around and run away. However, the pressure to make her mama proud still consumed her and she continued to press on. Like so many other young college students, she had defined her success by attaining that little, white piece of paper, and Tillman knew it. There was no way she could go home a failure because this would be far more than Erika could ever handle. Entering the darkened room, she immediately noticed the chair in the middle of the seating area. Tillman was about to conduct his own class, and it was evident that she would be the only student invited. Erika could feel her knees begin to buckle, while thoughts began to run rampant in her mind. She was all alone, and she could tell that this particular night had been played out in Tillman's sick world for days, or possibly weeks, by now. Tillman had disappeared into the darkness, and the only light that was on brightly engulfed her seating area. "Sit down in your chair, Erika," Tillman said softly. "Your real education is about to begin."

Jonathan was beginning to lose hope, when suddenly, he heard a loud sound coming from about 200 yards away. The semi was racing toward him at an alarming pace, and Jonathan knew he had to somehow quickly stop the driver. Jonathan took his sweater off, ran out into the road, and began to wave his arms frantically in the air. He knew he was hard to see, but this may be his only chance to hitch the ride he so desperately needed. The horn blew loudly because the driver had spotted Jonathan with less than 100 yards to spare. Jonathan wasn't going to move, as he was bound and determined to somehow find a way to stop the oncoming box of metal. The truck finally came to a stop, and Jonathan quickly ran up to the driver's side. "I'm very sorry, sir, but I have a very close friend of mine who's in immediate need of my assistance. I must get a ride to a location that's only about 10 minutes away. Please, help me," Jonathan begged, while the rain continued to pelt the top of his head. "Get in, son," the voice responded, as it seemed to echo in the darkened cab. Jonathan ran around the back and jumped up on the platform, just above the wheel-well. "Now, where do you need to go?" Jonathan looked over at the man and said, "1551 Brookplace. Straight ahead, just as fast as you can. I'll give you specifics as we get closer." The man stared over at Jonathan, as his raspy voice responded, "No need for directions, son. I know that location very well."

Erika felt her knees tremble, while she sat down in the chair. How did she ever get herself into this position? She could see Tillman's dark figure standing near the corner of the room. "What do you want from me, Mr. Tillman? You told me to come here tonight because you wanted to discuss my final exam. And now, here I am sitting in this chair feeling like there is some sort of interrogation about ready to take place. Why are you doing this to me?" There was no answer, and silence filled the room. Erika could feel her heart begin to race faster and faster. "That's it, Mr. Tillman. I've had enough of this silly, little game you want to play." Erika began to stand up, when suddenly, she heard Tillman's voice say very directly, "If you leave this room and forfeit your position in my class, I will flunk you. I will make sure you never see your college degree…ever! Do you understand me? This is not kindergarten here, Ms. Lewis, and this certainly isn't Iowa. You are in my classroom now, my court of law so to speak. Now, sit down, unless of course you want to be a failure to your loved ones back home." Tears began to swell in Erika's eyes, as she contemplated her next move. She was afraid of both choices that were in front of her. However, the fear of failure had consumed her since she was a little girl, and she just didn't think she could bear to see the look on her mother's face if she showed up without her degree. Erika sat down and took a deep breath. Class was ready to begin…

"Name is Bill. What brings you out in the rain on a night like this?" the old man said, while he maneuvered the 18-wheeler up the hill toward Brookplace. "My name is Jonathan, sir. Thanks again for picking me up. I have a friend who may be in some serious trouble tonight. Long story short – I need to get to 1551 Brookplace and reach her before something terrible happens. I have absolutely no idea what's going on with her tonight. I just know something isn't right. Please, take a left up here and drop me off. I don't want to go right up to the address, if that's ok with you." "Sounds good to me, Jonathan," Bill said, as he maneuvered his way around the corner toward Jonathan's destination. "Do you need any help tonight, son?" asked Bill, as he slowly brought his truck to a stop. "Thanks Bill," said Jonathan, "but I think I'm going to be just fine. You've done more than enough already. I don't want to put you out. I'd ask you to call the police, but I just don't have any idea what I'm walking into. Got to go, Bill. Drive safe, and thanks again." With that, Jonathan reached his hand out to say thanks to his newfound friend. However, Bill's right hand rested near his side because it had been crippled in the war years ago. Without hesitation, Bill extended his left hand out to Jonathan and squeezed his cold, dwarfed fingers with a grip that felt like a vice. "Be safe, Jonathan. You be careful up there near that old house. Rumor has it that there've been some strange things happening around here for a very long time," said Bill, as he peered through the wiper blades that methodically removed the rain from his view. Jonathan jumped off the platform and began to sprint as fast as he could. Bill watched Jonathan very closely, while Jonathan disappeared into the darkness. The street took a sharp, left turn and seemed to lead to the old house tucked away on the side of the hill. Jonathan could barely see anything, as the stillness of the night seemed to overshadow all objects around him. He ran up to the mailbox located just outside the cast iron eight-foot fence surrounding the tree-lined property. 1551 Brookplace…JRT was engraved on the side of the box. Jonathan needed to slow down and gather his thoughts. Those initials looked very familiar to him. Somewhere, he had seen them before…

"Very good, Erika," said Tillman, as he continued to explain the rules of the game. "You don't look like you're having any fun right now. You need to relax. You're about to play a game that will have a huge impact on your future. I don't want to put any additional pressure on you; however, I need to be honest with you. The next 30 minutes will have a dramatic impact on your life. Everything you've worked for will undoubtedly come down to the game we're about to play. Here's how it works. I have your test results. Your score was disappointing to both of us, but there are five essay questions that I could be persuaded on. Your current score is 60% and you know what that means. Nobody passes my class if they flunk my final exam. However, let's get back to the five questions. I'm willing to give you another shot. Each question is worth four points and every correct answer will be added to your final score. You can walk out of here tonight with an 80%, which would mean your final grade this semester would be a very respectable "B". However, for every question you miss, there will be negative consequences. You see, there has to be something in this for me. Each time you miss a question, you'll lose the opportunity to improve your final score. This means Erika that if you miss three out of the five questions, you belong to me. Pure and simple. If you only miss two questions, you'll be able to walk out of here with a 72%, which is a passing grade for the test and for the semester. You could say there is some significant pressure here. You only need to get three questions correct, and let's be honest, this should be a "gimme" for you. Oh, and the best part for you is these questions will be multiple choice – which means no subjectivity. Based on your poor performance regarding the final test you took earlier today, you should be grateful that I've eliminated any essay questions moving forward. You see, Erika, at the end of the day, I really am a nice guy. However, I hate to lose at anything and, quite honestly, I don't plan to lose at this little game either. You're either right or wrong. I'll have absolutely no say in your final result. Your success or failure will be determined by your ability to perform in adverse conditions. Let's not forget just how confident you were on our first day of class. I hope you can somehow capture that same mindset right now. Both of us would agree; however, that the circumstances and ramifications are much different here tonight than they were on that very first day of class, when you waltzed into my room late and proceeded to insult me in front of your peers. However, I have no hard feelings whatsoever. I'm only trying to help you get a better grade…that's all. Like I said before, I really am a very nice guy."

Jonathan began to climb the iron fence and felt a tremendous sense of urgency to get inside and find Erika as quickly as possible. He knew that time was running out, but he was still uncertain as to what he might find once he got inside. Erika had been acting out of character lately, and Jonathan knew she was under an enormous amount of pressure to get through school and ultimately attain the degree she and her family dearly coveted. Her mother was very proud of her oldest daughter, but with that pride, came a huge set of expectations. Erika wasn't going to fail in her quest to get what she came to school for, no matter what the cost. Jonathan knew this obsession could one day become problematic for her, but he had no idea that this moment of truth was now here. Tillman was pulling the strings, and his puppet was in real trouble. Nothing could have ever prepared her for what was about to happen.

Tillman smiled and handed Erika the five questions. She glanced down at the test and felt her pulse begin to race uncontrollably. She felt helpless and vulnerable. She had been without her father for a very long time, but she still remembered what it was like to sit on his lap and just hug him. Oh, how she longed for those days right now. As she somehow tried to gather her thoughts, Erika realized she was in big trouble with nowhere to hide. She took a deep breath and flipped over the test. Once she began this process, she knew there would be no turning back. This was the part of the game that Tillman enjoyed the most. His sense of superiority and control was what he relished more than anything. His mind was racing, as he pictured the rest of the evening. He had no intention of letting Erika win this little battle. Erika Lewis was about to be taught a valuable lesson. Now, J.R. Tillman was in absolute control of her every move, which was just the way he liked it. "Why are you doing this to me?" asked Erika, as she fought back the tears. "Oh, that's an easy one," laughed Tillman. "It's because I can! You have five minutes to answer the questions, beginning right now."

Chapter 6

"Cat and Mouse"

William had become a regular at Murphy's Diner since Jesse's passing, as he and B.J. would get up every morning and walk the mile and a half together. He had become very active in the real estate community, with his primary focus being on the commercial side of the business. His competitive drive had been funneled into this area of the market, and his hard work was beginning to pay significant dividends. Each day, he would arrive at Murphy's at around 6:30 a.m., and then he would be back at home in his office by 8:00 a.m. William loved the breakfast at Murphy's, but even more than that, he really looked forward to the daily conversations he had with their waitress in charge, Maggie Delaney. He missed Jesse more than he could ever imagine, but he found himself longing for someone to spend his mornings with…Murphy's Diner provided him with the perfect fit. Maggie seemed to fill this void nicely, even if it was for just an hour or so each day. Their conversation every morning turned out to be the highlight of William's day, and even though nobody would ever replace Jesse, he wasn't the kind of guy who was good at being alone. Jesse had taken care of him for most of his life, and now all the little things that she typically did were being left up to him. Although William was truly struggling with his newfound independence, his intentions at this point in his life were focused on conversation only. However, Maggie Delaney's aspirations were much different. She had her sights set on William immediately after Jesse's passing, and she knew he was all by himself. William was quickly falling into her trap…

Erika could feel her whole body start to quiver, while she began to open the envelope with Tillman's questions. Tillman had positioned himself directly behind the pillar in the corner of the room and watched intently with bated breath. How could an intellect like Tillman allow this sick game of cat and mouse to continue? This was the ultimate chess match; a beautiful young naïve girl at his fingertips with little or no control over his actions. Why he chose

Erika was no secret. She imposed the greatest challenge for him because her wit and beauty made for the perfect combination regarding Tillman's desires. As he stared over at Erika in the chair, he found himself getting restless while he contemplated his next move. The anticipation phase was over. Tillman's heart began to race, and it was time for the game to officially begin.

Jonathan rolled down the side of the hill and found himself on the west side of the house. He had no idea what he was looking for, but he was certain Erika was in the building somewhere. None of the lights were visible from where Jonathan lay; however, he could see a reflection near the back of the structure. He ran around the corner of the house and proceeded to look in each of the main level windows. As he got closer to the light, it became apparent that all the other rooms in the house were completely dark. He couldn't tell if there was any activity in the room that was lit because the rain from the storm had significantly blurred the window. If it wasn't for the initial reflection he saw from the hill, it would have been very easy for Jonathan to assume that nothing was happening in the house. However, he knew this wasn't the case, and he had to move quickly. He could feel the pit in his stomach start to swell, and his adrenaline was officially kicking into overdrive. Jonathan carefully approached one of the darkened windows and peered inside. He was able to catch a glimpse of the light on the other side of the wall, which happened to be the same light he had seen from the side of the hill. The reflection extended upward, as the roof was designed with solar panels intended for maximum lighting. However, on this particular night, maximum lighting was not the objective. The room was full of darkness, and Jonathan could feel an uncomfortable presence while he contemplated his next move. This was an odd room; it was as if the design of the room was intended for some kind of secluded activity. Jonathan had to get inside and see what was happening. He surveyed the area and noticed the old cotton tree extending up near the solar panels of the room. If only he was able to climb the tree, he could probably see what was happening inside the house. Quite possibly, this just might allow him the port of entry he so desperately needed in order to get to Erika. He saw no other way of getting in, and he knew that time was running out. Jonathan jumped as high as he could and grabbed on to the first limb available. Quickly, he began to climb and made his way to the top of the tree. He positioned himself approximately 30 feet off the ground and rested on the branch closest to the panel. Jonathan took a deep breath, as he prepared to look inside.

Maggie Delaney grew up in Northern Ireland and moved to Rocker with her parents at the age of 16. When she was 24, she decided to move to New York City and pursue her lifelong dream of hitting it big on Broadway. Unfortunately, as it turned out, her dreams were squashed early on when she found herself involved with the wrong agent. His name was Joseph Galante, and he was bad news from the very start. He made promises to Maggie with absolutely no intention of keeping them. The result was tragic for her because she ended up spending her entire life savings on a couple of worthless gigs. Joseph eventually got Maggie pregnant and then dumped her when the money disappeared. Her innocence was gone and bitterness quickly set in. Her dreams had vanished and now it was just a matter of finding a way to survive. At age 30, Maggie and her five-year-old son, Anthony, picked up and moved back to the Rocker area. For the next 20 years, Maggie had nearly a dozen jobs, mainly working as a waitress or cleaning hotel rooms. She had relationships with a number of men in the area but couldn't find anyone willing to marry her. Maggie was a real gold-digger, but she was running out of options. She was on a mission, and now William was dead in her sights. Her blue eyes still had that youthful twinkle, but she desperately needed to find a way to discard the hand she'd been dealt. Although Maggie's reputation preceded her wherever she went, William had no idea what he was getting himself into. His focus over the last 30 years was on his Jesse and nobody else. Maggie could sense this, and his naivety made her want him even more. William Gunn was vulnerable and alone, with the bull's-eye clearly painted on his heart. Maggie had been down and out for a number of years, and she needed to change her life right now, before it was too late. She knew William's loneliness was her ticket to entry, and she wasn't about to let this opportunity slip by. Deep down inside, she had a feeling it might be her last.

The bright light extended from the corner of the room adjacent to the solar panel. Jonathan positioned himself on the overlaying branch and had a perfect view inside. Jonathan began to peer through the window, but there was no way he could have ever been prepared for the picture that awaited him. He felt like he was watching some kind of bad movie, as he peered into the window and contemplated his next move. He immediately felt the rage consume his body, while he watched Erika in the center of the room. Tears were streaming down her face, and she sat aimlessly staring off into the distance. She was holding a white envelope and seemed to be shaking her head in disbelief. Jonathan couldn't tell who else was in the room, but he could sense from Erika's facial expressions that she wasn't alone. He had to find a way to get inside fast, but he also realized that he needed to maintain his self-control. Whoever was doing this to Erika clearly had a sick mind and was probably capable of far worse. Jonathan surveyed the room, but he could see no other activity except for Erika. She seemed to be conversing with somebody in the corner of the room; however, Jonathan had no idea who it was. He needed to get a better view and made his way out to the end of the branch. Suddenly, Jonathan heard a loud crack and felt himself start to fall! The branch he was resting on was unable to hold his weight any longer, and he could feel himself heading straight down.

He felt helpless, as his body crashed through the solar panel and on to the floor of the room. Jonathan landed approximately 10 feet from where Erika was sitting and glass from the panel scattered everywhere. Erika screamed in disbelief and gasped for air. She was in shock and started to shake violently, while Jonathan's body lay motionless on the floor of the room in front of her. The glass from the panel had severely cut his body during the fall and blood began to flow profusely from the exposed wounds. Erika jumped to Jonathan's side and felt her heart sink. She reached down and gently shook him, hoping that he would wake up from the fall that nearly broke him in two. Erika turned to where Tillman was standing and screamed, "Do something, Jonathan is hurt real bad. We need to get some help. Look what you've done now!" Tillman immediately gathered his thoughts and began to think about how he could possibly get himself out of this mess. His last concern was Jonathan, and his mind began to race. He could care less about the kid right now. This disruption only made him angrier than before the evening started...

"Hello, William, don't you look good this morning! What'll you have, honey, the regular I'm sure," said Maggie, while she welcomed William to the restaurant with a smile once again. "Sounds wonderful," responded William, as he settled himself into his favorite booth. "I've been thinking about this breakfast all night long." William's best friend these days was B.J., but oh, how he loved his breakfast at Murphy's Diner. William wasn't ready to get involved with anyone right now, but he found himself really looking forward to the mornings just talking with Maggie. This was all he really needed, but Maggie had additional ideas in mind. Little did he know, Maggie Delaney was already planning for much more than just being his friend. Soon, she would be making her move. William had been away from this game for a very long time, and his exposed vulnerability would soon be targeted by one of the best.

Tillman peered from behind the pillar near the corner of the room, just to make sure Jonathan was unconscious before he stepped out. Erika turned to Tillman and shouted, "Aren't you going to do anything, you sick old fool!" Tillman began to laugh uncontrollably and responded, "What an idiot this kid is, now look at him. He should have minded his own business. I ought to just leave him here to die; however, that wouldn't look too good for me, now would it?" Tillman knew he had to think fast and find a way to spin the events of the last hour or so. The last thing he needed right now was a blemish on his academic record because this type of scandal would undoubtedly place a black eye on his record for good. He had his sights set on much loftier goals at the university, and he wasn't about to let a couple of kids get in the way. Tillman was being considered for the vacant "Dean of Business" position at Central Valley State University, and he could ill afford any detour in his presumed climb to the top. He had visions of running the entire school within the next three years, and nothing was going to stop him now. His mind began to race, as he thought about his next steps and how he could once again take control of the situation at hand. This dumb kid who fell through the roof was definitely in bad shape, he thought, but this was the least of his concerns right now.

"William Gunn, today is the day I'm going to ask you out on a date. I'd love to have you come over to my house this weekend for dinner. I make a wonderful Irish stew and my blueberry pie is to die for. You can't say no to an offer like this now, can you?" asked Maggie, as she began to make her move. "Well, Maggie, you do drive a hard bargain. I've never been known to turn down a home-cooked meal. Plus, I'd love to have the company. What can I bring?" Maggie just smiled and said, "Just bring yourself, sweetheart. Oh, and why don't you bring that beautiful dog of yours as well? I'm sure we can set aside a few bones for him, and maybe I can even put together a little treat as well. I have a perfect place on my porch for him to rest on while we visit. Let's plan on Saturday night at around 7:00." Maggie was smooth, and William hadn't played this dating game since he was in high school. He was beginning to feel like a kid all over again. Maggie was ready to eat him alive because he was no match for her cunning ways. She had William right where she wanted him...

"Good evening, officer. I'm calling to report a break-in at my home this evening. I've apprehended the perpetrators, but I don't know how long I can hold them. They're two students of mine at the university and one of them, Jonathan Gunn, has been injured pretty badly. You better send the paramedics over as well because I'm not sure how long he can withstand the injuries he suffered during his entry. His accomplice, Erika Lewis, who is also a student of mine, is hysterical and completely out of control. I feel so badly for these kids, and I really need your help. Please, get someone over here right away." Tillman hung up the phone and proceeded to walk over to where Jonathan lay facedown in the debris. He reached over and snatched the envelope from Erika and began to rip up the questions inside. His eyes seemed to pierce right through her body, as he whispered directly into her right ear, "I'm not through with you yet, little missy. Now quit your crying and don't even think about changing my story. You're making me sick."

William adjusted his blue blazer and red tie in his attempt to look and feel as young as possible once again. He had already convinced himself that Maggie was nothing more than just a close friend; however, the combination of loneliness and denial can do that to a guy. Maggie was attractive and William was available, a lethal combination that would soon be tested. Although she was now approaching fifty, she still had a way with the guys. Her accent was far removed from her earlier days in Northern Ireland, but there was still enough of one to immediately catch the attention of her next target. The only reason she worked at Murphy's was because she was currently on the rebound from a recent relationship gone awry. She had been dating a man named Tom Quinn, who had made a fortune in the insurance industry. Unfortunately for Mr. Quinn, he also liked the bottle. One evening, after a long night of drinking and playing cards with his buddies, Quinn found himself wrapped around a tree 15 miles outside of town. By the time the police got to him, it was too late. Whiskey and a wind chill factor of 25 below zero don't go too well together and hypothermia quickly set in and shut his body down for good. When Maggie was called in to help identify his remains, she was hopeful that old Tom would have at least recognized her in the trust fund that was left behind. Unfortunately for Maggie, the document made no mention of her existence and everything went to his sister who lived in California. On that day, Maggie promised herself that this type of oversight would never happen again. She had learned a valuable lesson, one that literally cost her millions. Her next target would be handled much differently...

Tillman walked over to the chair and pulled it out from Erika, and she promptly fell to the floor. He moved it back to its resting place, which was right next to the mahogany desk just outside the door. Tillman knew he had to move quickly. He ran to the back of the house and proceeded to go outside, closing the door behind him. He searched the patio for a large rock, found what he was looking for, and subsequently moved forward with his plan. He threw the rock through the panel of glass just above the doorknob. Glass crashed through the door and landed inside the house. This would provide Tillman with the means to effectively explain how Erika was able to get inside the house. His cunning mind began to race, as the story he would tell was starting to take shape. Tillman thought through the possible sequence of events and needed to build a believable story as quickly as possible. His mind began to race, as the puzzle pieces quickly fell into place...

Erika would enter through the back door, while Jonathan searched for an entrance on the roof. How could he realistically explain this? Why wouldn't they both just enter through the back? Then it dawned on him! Oh, this was going to be very easy. He thought through the dialogue that he would soon implement. The trap door just on the other side of the solar panel would represent Jonathan's initial entry point. Unfortunately for Jonathan, his devious plan failed, and he found himself on the receiving end of a terrible fall. When Erika heard him go crashing through the glass, she responded just like any ordinary girl in love would do. She came running through the back door in order to save her man. Tillman, on the other hand, was frightened to death when he heard the loud crash. When he saw Jonathan face down on the floor, he realized he needed to quickly get help for the young man. Erika was distraught and in no condition to help her lover; therefore, it would be up to Tillman to come to the rescue. Tillman responded quickly and comforted these two students of his, despite their ill-fated attempt at stealing his valuable art collection. Tillman smiled and rehearsed his upcoming lines. This would be an easy story to spin; one that he believed would pass the litmus test with flying colors. Suddenly, Tillman heard a noise from outside the door. "Mr. Tillman, are you all right?" said the voice. "It's Officer Bradford from the 23rd precinct." "I'm in here, officer," responded Tillman. "I'm so glad you're here. Thanks for getting here so quickly. I was getting extremely nervous being in the same room as these two criminals."

"Hello, Maggie, B.J. and I are a little early, but you know how excited dogs can get when they understand they have a free meal waiting!" said William, as he made his way through the front door. "I told him you make a wonderful dinner, and he has been anxious to get here ever since." Maggie smiled and said, "William, you're always welcome here and so is B.J. Plus, I just love a man who shows up early for his first date. It shows me there's excitement, and that's a very good sign. Now, it will be expected for you to keep this up on all future dates as well. Mr. William Gunn, you're always welcome in my home." William just smiled, while B.J. seemed to shake his head in disbelief. Even B.J. could see where this thing was heading! William, on the other hand, was clueless. He was just happy to be there. B.J stood more of a chance of blocking Maggie's advances than William did, which was a scary thought for all involved.

The ambulance arrived shortly after Officer Bradford, and the two paramedics immediately raced into Tillman's home to assess Jonathan's condition. As they carefully began to move him, it became apparent to both of them that Jonathan was in very bad shape. Unfortunately for Jonathan, when he fell through the panel, he landed on a razor-sharp sliver of glass nearly four inches long. The glass entered his left side and broke off just under his rib cage. In addition to the visible cut from the glass, the fall had caused significant damage to his left shoulder and collarbone as well. The issue for the paramedics wasn't so much the breaks and contusions that were visible. Their biggest concern right now was what may have happened on the inside. Internal damage couldn't be determined until they got him back to the hospital, but both of them were convinced there would be major problems to address. "Is he going to make it?" asked Tillman. "I'm absolutely shocked to see him in this condition tonight. He's always been one of my favorite students. My only concern right now is the health of this young man. How can I help?" Michael Heath, the lead paramedic, responded, "Why don't you and the young woman ride down with Officer Bradford, and we'll meet you there. When things settle down a little, I'm sure one of the officers will want to take your statement. This young man needs to be surrounded by calm individuals at a time like this.

His girlfriend will only create confusion and panic during the ride if she goes with us. Will that work for you?" Tillman thought for a minute and couched his response in eloquent fashion, knowing full well that all eyes would be on him regarding his feedback. Everyone present would be a potential witness down the road, and Tillman knew it. "I think I'd rather take my own car. While I've always enjoyed Ms. Lewis in my class, my safety was at risk tonight. Obviously, I'm still a little shook up over what could have happened to me had they been successful in their break-in. I'm sure you understand." Officer Bradford overheard the conversation and interceded. "Absolutely," he said. "I understand what you're going through. We'll leave, and you can follow us." Bradford turned to Erika and said, "You need to come with me. You're being placed under arrest for your role regarding this break-in. You better hope your boyfriend recovers or the charges will be much worse than just breaking and entering. Now, get in the car so I can read you your rights." Tillman watched while Erika was led to the backseat of Bradford's car. He was having a very difficult time keeping a straight face.

Bradford and the ambulance pulled out of the driveway, with Tillman's black Mercedes not far behind. Tillman still knew he had some important work to do, but things were coming together just as he had planned. As Tillman adjusted his rearview mirror, his adrenaline began to take an unexpected rush. In the blink of an eye, Tillman swore he spotted a 6½ foot silhouette standing near the back row of trees just outside the scene of the accident. He jumped out of his car and yelled, "Who are you, and what do you want? I see you standing over there." Tillman rubbed his eyes in disbelief. After all, it had been a very long day. For the first time in a long while, Tillman's heart seemed to skip a beat. For whatever reason, he felt out of control and tried to gain his composure. This was a far cry from how he felt just minutes before, when he was in full control of the situation. As Tillman's eyes made their way back into focus, the shadowy figure was gone. Tillman did his best to chalk it up to fatigue and made his way back into his car. He let out a slight chuckle and did all he could to convince himself that his eyes were simply playing tricks on him. However, deep down inside, he was certain he had seen something near the back of his yard. As he pulled out of the driveway, he reached down and hit the door locks, which was probably a very good idea after all that had happened just a short while ago.

Maggie was the kind of woman who had no boundaries. The evening was barely getting started when she imposed the question she had been wanting to ask for quite some time. "William, this is really a special evening and one I will remember for a very long time. You and I've had the opportunity to talk a little bit about the passing of Jesse, but I've never had a chance to hear about your son. What's he like, William, and when do I get to meet him?" William wasn't ready to bring Jonathan into the picture quite yet. He knew how close he was to his mother; therefore, he had to be very careful about rushing into any formal introduction. After all, Maggie and Jesse were about as different as they come. Jesse was a good listener and kept her words close to her vest. Maggie, on the other hand, didn't even know she had a vest! William knew Jonathan would have a difficult time with her aggressive style and had to be very careful with how he handled the next steps. "My son, Jonathan, will soon be finishing up his degree at Central Valley State in Washington. He's a very special kid, and I'm not just saying this because he's my son. I'm so proud of him. I'm sure he'd love to meet you when he gets back from school. I hope he stays in this area when he graduates because I could really use his companionship right now. He and I have become very close since Jesse's passing. We've both realized that through the pain of our loss, we've become closer than we ever were before." Maggie knew right then and there that her greatest challenge in locking up William would be to get by this son of his named Jonathan. She also believed that the pot at the end of the rainbow was well worth the ride, and she was willing to put up with just about anything to land her prize. William was much better off financially than he wanted anyone to believe, and Maggie knew it. He was an easy target, but this son of his could turn out to be a real fly in the ointment for her. Maggie wanted to move quickly, but she realized she had to be very careful regarding her next steps. William's sincere admiration for his only son was obvious by the spark in his eye when Jonathan's name was mentioned. After his loss of Jesse, Maggie would need to tread lightly to at least neutralize his son. She had her work cut out for her, and her plan of action would need to be deliberate and mistake free.

The ambulance pulled up in front of Bridger General Hospital, as Michael and his team of paramedics quickly wheeled Jonathan inside. Dr. Monte Clark, one of the top surgeons in the Pacific Northwest, was already waiting for him. Jonathan's body temperature was down to 95.6 degrees because he had lost a significant amount of blood due to the fall. The large pane of glass had done a lot of internal damage, and this kind of trauma was what concerned Dr. Clark the most. "Let's get him inside quickly. He needs an IV run immediately, as his body is starting to go into shock," shouted Dr. Clark, while he quickly moved his team into their respective positions. "I want to see how much damage has been done. I don't like what I see. Let's move right now, people." Dr. Clark was an incredible physician, who demanded the respect of everyone around him. He had been in charge of the surgery department at Bridger General Hospital for the past 20 years. Everyone on the team knew Clark's expectations were high, and he had zero tolerance for mediocrity. This was the type of accident that was the most alarming to him because he had seen the human body simply shut down from this degree of trauma. The internal organs were delicate, and in most cases, irreplaceable. Jonathan had lost consciousness, and his body was now officially in defense mode. Dr. Clark had seen this happen many times before and realized his window of opportunity would be closing soon. He had to get that glass out of Jonathan and restore his normal blood flow as quickly as possible. Dr. Clark took a deep breath and closed his eyes. He needed to be strong because this kid's life was literally in his hands. Dr. Clark learned long ago that there was no way he could tackle this responsibility alone; therefore, he continually relied on his undying faith to give him the strength he needed to press on. This case would be no different, and he needed to gather his senses and move quickly. Jonathan was in critical condition with time running out. His condition would warrant perfection from everyone on Clark's team…there was absolutely no margin for error.

Chapter 7

"Steady Hands"

Tillman pulled into the parking lot, gathered his thoughts, and immediately put his game face on. Who was that person by the house? Where did he go? What did he want? Maybe he was just seeing things? Tillman needed to regain the composure that had been his trademark for years. If Jonathan was able to recover, Tillman knew it would be his word versus both Jonathan and Erika's. However, if Jonathan didn't make it through surgery, Tillman was confident he would easily persuade the authorities to see everything his way. While Erika was typically a strong person, she had been through far too much over the course of the last twelve hours. In addition, she was overcome with guilt, and her self-confidence had been shattered. Jonathan never would have been in his condition had it not been for her decision to go to Tillman's house. Tillman knew deep down inside that his own fate would be directly impacted by Jonathan's outcome, and he found himself hoping for his quick demise. This would solve a lot of his potential problems and allow him to take on Erika's word with very little trouble. Erika felt helpless and weak in the company of Tillman, and he knew it. Tillman entered through the ER doors and, within a few seconds, he ran into Officer Bradford once again. "Good evening, Officer Bradford," said Tillman, "I'm here to help with whatever you may need. What can I do to assist you with your case?"

Just as he did a thousand times before, Monte Clark knelt and asked God for strength. He knew he would need it once again because Jonathan's body had literally retreated and gone into shock since the fall. Dr. Clark closed his eyes and tried to separate himself from the emotional side of his profession. However, the fact that he had three children close to Jonathan's age didn't make this particular procedure any easier. He walked through the first set of doors to the operating room and could see Jonathan's motionless body waiting for him. The staff surrounded his 6-foot frame, as they were prepared and ready to go. Dr. Clark immediately demanded their respect, and they knew he meant business. The confidence he exuded instantly transcended over to everyone in the room because they all realized this was the moment of truth regarding Jonathan's outcome. Without a doubt, his strong leadership made the entire team stronger, which was exactly what Jonathan needed right now. The surgical team realized they had a job to do, and they needed to move quickly. Jonathan's eyes were closed, as Dr. Clark lifted the dressing on Jonathan's left side. He was about to make his first incision. "Scalpel," Dr. Clark uttered, and the blade began to enter Jonathan's exposed side. His mind was razor sharp, as he approached every surgery with absolute focus. He knew Jonathan was bleeding badly from the inside out, and he realized very quickly that he would need to be at the top of his game. As Dr. Clark began to make the incision, he realized the injuries Jonathan had sustained were far worse than he originally expected. Everyone on the team was in for a very long night...

Erika was transported to the city jail and felt her heart sink as they brought her in for questioning. The local authorities wanted to get to her before she secured legal counsel because they knew she was vulnerable right now. This was the time when individuals typically spilled the beans and talked; therefore, their job was to get to her as quickly as possible. Nobody was better than Officer Bastion when it came to breaking down her target and exposing the truth. She was known as the "Queen of Interrogation", a title she dearly coveted. Officer Bastion was relentless and ruthless in her approach; she was already waiting for Erika upon her arrival. "Hello, Ms. Lewis. I need to speak with you about the events of the evening. Seems you got yourself into a little bit of trouble now, doesn't it?" asked Bastion, as she made her way over to Erika the minute she entered the room. Erika took a deep breath and nodded in agreement. "Go ahead and have a seat, Ms. Lewis. There are a couple of questions I'd like to ask. Please relax…this shouldn't take too long, assuming you cooperate."

"Does this young man have a family? If so, someone needs to notify them about what's happened." asked Dr. Clark, as he quickly glanced up toward his team. "We're very fortunate that he's in such excellent physical condition or he would have never survived the fall. This wound has caused a significant amount of internal damage, so we'll need to move very quickly once we get inside. The next 48 hours are going to be touch-and-go. Each of you will be expected to have your "A" game today. He's going to need it." "I'll make sure someone notifies his family, Dr. Clark," responded Rose, the head nurse. "He'll need all the support he can get right now." With that, Rose got on the phone and told her contacts in the Emergency Department to quickly find Jonathan's family. Rose immediately came back to the room and looked over at Dr. Clark. With a slight nod of the head, she was ready to help him in any way possible. He felt very fortunate to have the best nurse right by his side, as they had become the top surgical team in the hospital. While the two of them stared down at Jonathan's body, they knew they were in for a very long night.

William and B.J. arrived back home shortly after 10:00 p.m., and William was feeling like a high school senior all over again. Maggie was very good at making him feel much younger than his age, something that hadn't happened in a very long time. As William started to change his clothes, the phone rang and seemed to echo throughout the house. He ran downstairs hoping to get one last word in with Maggie before he went to bed. Unfortunately, the phone call he received was about to change all that. "Mr. Gunn, this is Elaine at Bridger General Hospital in Washington. I'm sorry to bother you tonight, but I have some bad news. Your son, Jonathan, was in a terrible accident earlier this evening. He's in surgery right now and will probably be there for a couple more hours. He's in very good hands, but his injuries were quite severe. He's going to need a lot of support, so I wanted to let you know about his condition as soon as possible." William's heart sank to his stomach, as he dropped the telephone and fell to the floor. B.J. lay down next to him and began to whimper as well. William had just lost his Jesse, and now his mind began to race at the thought of possibly losing Jonathan as well. What would he do if his only son was gone too? He frantically searched for Maggie's phone number. William had nobody else right now...maybe she could help him figure out what to do next.

"Now, Mr. Tillman, explain to me one more time why these kids were at your place. We've searched their backgrounds and have absolutely no history of any similar behavior. I'm having a hard time understanding why they would take on such a risk when the danger was so great," said Officer Bradford. "As I said before, Officer Bradford, these kids nowadays are difficult to figure out," responded Tillman, as he quickly went into defense mode. "I see it all the time in my class. You've got one kid who has influence over his or her peers, and pretty soon, you have others who want to get in on the action as well. Jonathan was obviously trying to impress Erika, and I just happened to be the target. As bad as I feel for Jonathan due to his fall, it's Ms. Lewis who is the real victim. Her life will never be the same, just because she decided to give in and go along with him. I wish there was something I could do. If only I would have known, I would have reached out to both of them a long time ago." Bradford studied his notes carefully. For some reason, something just didn't add up. Hopefully, Jonathan would recover, and he would find out why he would do something so foolish. Without Jonathan's recovery, the answers Tillman had given would go undisputed, as Erika was in no state of mind to credibly challenge them. Officer Bradford knew that if anyone could uncover additional information regarding the events of the evening, it was his counterpart, Officer Bastion. Her interrogation was about to begin. After all, this was the kind of case she enjoyed the most...

"Maggie, it's William. I just received a phone call from Bridger General Hospital in Central Washington. My son, Jonathan, was in a terrible accident this evening and is in surgery right now. I'm going to get my things together and drive over there tonight to be with him. I've got to be there when he wakes up." Maggie thought for a minute and responded, "William, you're in no condition to make that drive yourself. I'll come over and get you and we'll travel together. I'll be there for you in about 20 minutes." William didn't have time to say no. Maybe it would be nice to have the company, he thought, as he quickly began to gather his clothes for the trip. On the other end of the line, Maggie hung up the phone and smiled. This was just the opening she was looking for...

Rose reached over and wiped the perspiration from Dr. Clark's brow. He had just entered Jonathan's left side and immediately began to close off the internal bleeding that had started over an hour earlier. Monte Clark was a master tactician with nerves of steel. Rose had worked closely with him now for over five years, and she continually found herself awestruck during every surgical procedure he performed. For whatever reason, she felt especially close to this case. Jonathan's face looked innocent and peaceful, as he lay motionless on the table. Rose had seen injuries like this before, and she knew he could go one way or the other at any moment. Rose made herself a promise that she would stay in close contact with Jonathan if he were to recover because she knew he would need a lot of support. She didn't even know this man; however, she felt a strong desire to see this thing through. He just seemed like the kind of guy who needed someone right now, Rose thought, as she contemplated her next move. The truth of the matter was that Rose needed someone as well because work had consumed her life since the day she joined Dr. Clark's team. Rose had made it a policy of hers many years ago to never get involved with a patient, but for whatever reason, this one felt different. Dr. Clark took a deep breath and maneuvered his way around the delicate spleen. He really didn't like what he was seeing.

Officer Bastion shut the door behind her and walked over to Erika. Bastion was in total control of the situation and could sense Erika's vulnerability by the look in her eyes. Reaching into her pocket, she took out a pack of cigarettes and dropped one on the table. "I think you're going to need these, Ms. Lewis. I'm not going to hurt you, and I'm not going to try to intimidate you. I will; however, make you one promise. You have one shot with me. If you lie to me, I'll feed you to the wolves. I have a number of very dangerous women in the slammer right now who dream of young things like you every night. I will protect you from them as long as you are honest with me. If you're not, you will belong to them. Your days in prison will be your worst nightmare. You will not last long. Do I make myself clear?" Erika was speechless, as all she could do was nod in agreement. "I can't hear you, Ms. Lewis," whispered Bastion.

Erika took a deep breath and said, "Yes, ma'am." "Good choice of words," responded Bastion. "Now, let's get started."

William and Maggie drove as fast as they could to Central Washington but didn't say a lot along the way. William had only one thing on his mind, which was the condition of his only son. As they pulled into the parking lot at Bridger General Hospital, William reached over and put his hand on Maggie's. "Thanks for coming, Maggie. I don't think I could've made the trip alone. I'm really scared right now, and I need your support. Jonathan is all I have left." "Not true, William," said Maggie. "You have me too. You just let me know what I can do to help, and I'll make it happen. Now, let's go up and see your boy. He's going to need us right now." William got out of the car and started to walk toward the front door of the hospital. Maggie ran up behind him and grabbed his hand. She squeezed his fingers and seized the moment. William was falling into her trap, and she knew it. This Jonathan kid was the last thing on her mind right now. She had a plan for William, but she knew Jonathan was the key element regarding her outcome. She had her game face on, and her web was starting to form. If Jonathan was able to somehow survive the accident, Maggie realized she would need to make sure he was in her corner right from the start. On the other hand, if Jonathan didn't make it, William would be hers without any threat whatsoever. Deep down inside, she knew exactly what she was hoping for...

Jonathan was approaching the fourth hour of surgery, and the delicate nature of his wounds required precision and patience. Dr. Clark was satisfied with the way the operation had gone so far; however, he knew Jonathan's condition would now be out of his hands. He had done everything he possibly could to put Jonathan in a position of recovery, but only time would tell. With these types of injuries, he had seen some of his patients recover quickly, while others were dead within hours. The outcome was dependent on a number of factors; most specifically the individual's physical condition upon arrival. This would work in Jonathan's favor. As Dr. Clark examined his work one last time, Rose leaned over and notified him that Jonathan's family had arrived. He nodded and knew they would be waiting for an answer. This was always the part of his job that was the least favorite. He walked through the operating room doors and into the waiting room. William and Maggie were waiting. "Hello, Mr. and Mrs. Gunn, I'm Monte Clark. I just performed surgery on your son." Before William could speak up and correct the good doctor regarding Maggie's official title, she was off to the races. "Nice to meet you, Dr. Clark. We're so grateful for your help regarding Jonathan. Now, let's cut right to the chase. Is he going to make it or not?" Dr. Clark was a little caught off guard by the direct nature of her initial question, but he maintained his composure nonetheless. He had been around a long time and had heard just about everything in his day.

"I'm satisfied with the way the surgery went. Only time will tell. The next 24 hours will tell us a lot," said Dr. Clark. "And what exactly does that mean... they will tell us a lot?" snapped Maggie. "We just drove most of the night for some answers, and you're talking like a politician. William and I would appreciate the straight scoop. We feel like we deserve it. Isn't that right, William?" William reached out his hand and said, "Thanks for saving my boy, Dr. Clark. It's a real pleasure to meet you." Dr. Clark nodded his head and said, "Thanks. I'll be watching him closely. It's a pleasure to meet you as well." Dr. Clark slowly turned his back and walked away. Maggie shook her head and turned toward William. "I can't believe you let him get away with that. He didn't even answer my question. You embarrassed me, William. That will never happen again." William looked at Maggie in disbelief, as he felt both angry and embarrassed at the same time. "I want to go see my boy," said William, and he made his way out of the waiting room. Maggie smiled and said, "Me, too. I'm really looking forward to meeting him." William knew that if Jonathan came to, he would immediately wonder about this woman. How would he react? William had no idea; he just wanted to hold his son right now. He was beginning to wonder if having Maggie there was a good idea after all, based on what he just saw. The way she went off on Dr. Clark was an absolute embarrassment to William and what he stood for, but he couldn't ask her to leave now. After all, she seemed like she really did want to help. William's internal rationalization regarding Maggie's purpose in being there was working overtime, and he felt his mind spinning with absolute confusion and fear. What if Jonathan didn't make it? How in the world would he ever go on?

"Now tell me, once and for all, why were you at Professor Tillman's house this evening? What did he have that you wanted so badly?" prodded Bastion, as she pressed Erika for answers. Erika could feel her face begin to turn red, while Bastion's sheer presence made her shake with fear. She was no match for this woman; however, she was not about to compromise the truth. She knew the story regarding Tillman's predatory nature was hard to believe, but what else could she do? She had to trust her instincts and began to tell Bastion everything from the test score to the 1:1 tutoring session Tillman had prepared. As Erika finished with her explanation of the evening and everything that led up to it, she assessed Bastion's facial expression to determine whether there was empathy or doubt. This woman was nearly impossible to read, and her listening skills and cunning nature were impeccable. Bastion leaned back in her chair and took a deep breath. After about 30 seconds of stone cold silence, Bastion yelled out, "Smitty, I'm finished with Ms. Lewis. Could you please open the door and let me out of here?" With that, the door opened and Bastion stood up to leave the room. "Officer Bastion, what do you want me to do in here? I really need to get in touch with my family. I did nothing wrong. Please, help me." Bastion turned, walked back to Erika, leaned over, and whispered in her ear, "The wolves in here are getting hungry. Dinner will soon be served, and I know for a fact they're going to enjoy the main course." Erika fell to her knees and grabbed Bastion's leg, "Please, don't do this to me. I did nothing wrong. Please, don't leave me." Bastion shut the door behind her and proceeded to walk back to her office. Smitty just stood there and shook his head. He had seen this act before, far too many times.

William made his way to the intensive care unit since Jonathan had been moved to the floor immediately following his procedure. ICU was a different place within the hospital, as there was a stillness in the air that reflected the serious nature of its inhabitants. In many cases, the patients on this floor had crossed the transparent boundary between life and death. Families had been taken through an emotional roller coaster and were still holding on to their loved ones with everything they had. William would be no different. His stomach began to turn on the inside, while he made his way to the quarantined visitor area just outside the doors to the unit itself. The room was quiet and seemed to immediately captivate William when he sat down. Maggie made her way through the doors as well, seemingly oblivious to the environment around her. William was beginning to question why she was with him, as her lack of class was about to rear its ugly head once again. Her reaction to Dr. Clark just a short while ago had provided William with a glimpse of her other side, and he didn't like it one bit. William sat down and took a deep breath. Sitting next to them in the chairs by the window was a father consoling his 10-year-old daughter. "Why did she have to leave us, Daddy?" inquired the little girl, while she looked up at her father for much-needed answers. "What are we going to do without Mommy here? Who's going to take me to school and help me with my homework?" she asked. Her father could say nothing. He had no answers that would take away the pain. William could hear the cries that seemed to penetrate through his soul. The screams were something he would never forget; so much pain and so much sadness. "Let's go find a nurse or someone to help us, Maggie," said William, as he began to make his way out of the confined room. "I want to be with my son right now. I just can't wait any longer."

Tillman finished his discussion with Officer Bradford and felt rather uncomfortable hanging around the hospital any longer. All of these questions were beginning to irritate him because he was growing tired of the insinuating nature and aggressive tone of the inquiry. Bradford was a rather coy individual, not near as naïve as he pretended to be. Tillman realized this from the start, and he knew he had to be very careful with the responses he provided. He knew nothing constructive would come from any more conversation, but he could not afford to create any enemies at this critical juncture. "Officer Bradford," said Tillman. "I'm really tired and need to get back home. I'm in dire need of some sleep. Hopefully, we are through for the evening." "Absolutely," responded Bradford. "Just make sure we can get in touch with you if need be. Obviously, we'll be speaking with you soon regarding additional events of the evening. I'm also very interested to hear what Ms. Lewis has to say about the night." "I understand, Officer Bradford," responded Tillman. "I just hope she's going to be all right. As I said before, her life will never be the same due to the acts of Mr. Gunn. I really do feel sorry for her." With that, Tillman walked out the front door of the hospital and across the street to his car. He looked in the rearview mirror and caught a glimpse of his own rage staring back at him. Although he was very confident regarding the discussions that had just taken place, there was just one slight problem…his night with Erika had been cut short. Tillman needed to find something to replace the evening he had planned because his dangerous appetite for women had not yet been quenched. He pulled out of the parking lot and stopped his car at the end of the dark alley. Tillman proceeded to get out of his car and opened the trunk. He grabbed the cardboard box that lay under his old flannel jacket and brought it back into the car with him. Within minutes, he had transformed himself into a bearded man with shoulder length salt and pepper hair. He popped his contacts out and put on the wire framed glasses that were only used for these special occasions. Tillman sped out of the alley and on to Main Street. Within 15 minutes, he had arrived at his home away from home. "Good evening, Mr. Frizell," said the bellman. "Good evening, son," said Tillman. "How are the girls looking tonight? I hope we have some new additions to the family." "Absolutely," said the young man. "Only the best for you, sir." The stench of the enemy consumed the air, and it quickly strangled all who entered the front door. Tillman had been living a double-life for a number of years now, teaching kids during the day and visiting young women at night. You see, as bad as Tillman was, he was nothing compared to Frizell. It had been a long day, and Frizell was ready for some fun.

Jonathan slowly opened his eyes and there was William at the foot of his bed. An immediate sense of calm seemed to consume Jonathan, as he did everything he could to somehow welcome his dad with a smile. He tried to say hi; however, his body was far too weak to conjure up enough strength to do anything right now. Jonathan had no idea where he was and began to scan the room in search of something familiar. Nothing in the room looked like anything he had ever seen before. The wall was painted a different color than his bedroom. The plant in the corner of the room looked far too green for something that belonged to him. And the television was attached to the ceiling…what was that all about? As Jonathan turned his head to search the rest of his surroundings, he heard a voice coming from the other side of the bed. It was a voice he had never heard before. There it was again! Not quite as bad as fingers on the chalkboard…but close. "William, does he have any clue who we are right now? He seems like he's really drugged up or something," said Maggie, while she continued to project her voice with zero compassion for anyone around her. "I think he looks incredibly good for what he's gone through," William retorted. "The fact that he's even responding to us right now is an absolute miracle." "If you say so, William," responded Maggie. "As for me, I can't wait to meet him when he knows who in the world I am." Although he was unable to speak, Jonathan could sense an uncomfortable presence in the room. His curiosity was getting the best of him. Who was this woman with the voice that only a mother could love? His initial impression was not a good one. With that, Jonathan closed his eyes and fell back to sleep. Hopefully, that voice would be gone the next time he woke up.

Frizell was surrounded by a number of women near the dance floor, and he continued to buy rounds of drinks for anyone who would listen to him. Eventually, he made his way back to the bar. He was ready for a stiff drink, one for the road that would bring an end to the perfect evening. "How has your evening been, Mr. Frizell?" asked the bartender. "Terrific as usual, my boy. But…I'm ready to go home. This has been a very long day. Give me the usual for the ride." The bartender poured him a tall drink, a whiskey and seven, and Frizell was out the back door. The tension in Frizell's back began to subside, as the recent events of the evening had seemed to calm his nerves. He pulled out of the parking lot and soon made his way back to the main drag. The drive home would take him approximately 30 minutes because traffic was nonexistent at 2:30 in the morning. He wanted to get home to finally get some rest and made it back more quickly than he anticipated. By now, he had taken his wig off and had slipped it into the box in the back seat. Frizell was done for the evening, and now it was time for Tillman to get some rest. As he entered his garage, something seemed out of place. He was very meticulous about the way he organized his lawn tools and immediately noticed that one of them was missing. Where were the trimming sheers? Suddenly, Tillman recalled the dark figure he had seen earlier that evening when he was pulling out of his driveway. He had forgotten about what he had seen, but now it was all coming back to him once again. Maybe he was just tired, or quite possibly, the individual had actually made it inside. Tillman did everything he could to gather his thoughts, but it was difficult as total exhaustion was beginning to set in. He punched in his security code and entered through the adjoining door that led him into the utility room. As Tillman approached the kitchen, he noticed a notepad sitting out of place on the table as well. He slowly made his way over to its location, as the pad seemed to be calling out his name. The handwritten note was meant for him. "Dear Mr. Tillman…I know everything. Your little secrets are no longer safe." Suddenly, Tillman was no longer tired, and his adrenaline kicked into high gear. He took a deep breath and tried to maintain his composure. The game was ready to begin, with Tillman finally finding out what it was like to be the hunted. He could feel the sweat begin to form on his top lip, and all he could do right now was shake his head in disbelief. How in the world did this happen, he thought, as he began to think about his next move.

Jonathan could feel the warm cloth on his forehead and suddenly felt a strong sense of security come over him. He began to open his eyes; however, he was completely disoriented by the environment he was in. As his vision cleared, there she was…the most beautiful woman he had ever laid his eyes on. Her back was turned to the side, while she gazed out the window; a perfect silhouette reflecting the morning sun. Jonathan found himself speechless and almost reluctant to say anything. He simply didn't want her to move. Who was this angel, and what was she doing in his room? If he was dead and this was heaven, oh, what a special place it was! He wanted to freeze time and never forget the picture in front of him right now. Slowly, he began to come to and realized that this was, in fact, not a dream. She was real. Jonathan looked around the room and suddenly realized where he was. However, nobody was there with him, except this beautiful woman. He couldn't tell what she was wearing since the sun's glare made it difficult to see her clothes. The only thing he did know was that she was gorgeous. Just then, the door opened and in walked William and Maggie. Jonathan's eyes were still fixated on the woman near the window. "Jonathan," said William. "I see you've met your nurse, Rose. How are you feeling, son?" With that, Jonathan responded, "I feel great." He looked over at Rose and smiled. Their eyes met and she knew just what that smile meant…and so did he.

"Hi, I'm Maggie. I made the trip over here with your father. We were so concerned about you; we just had to get over to the hospital and see you. It's a real pleasure to finally meet you." Before William could say anything, Rose intervened. "Ma'am, Jonathan has been through an incredibly difficult procedure and needs to get his rest. I'd like to see him go without any visitors for the next couple of hours. He really needs to be left alone." William agreed, "Let's wait outside, Maggie, so Jonathan can try to get caught up on his sleep." Rose could sense the uneasiness Jonathan was feeling; however, before Rose could whisk Maggie out of the room, Jonathan responded, "Who are you?" Maggie's response ripped Jonathan's heart out because she was not about to couch any words. "I'm your father's girlfriend, Maggie Delaney. We've been together now for quite some time. I'm surprised William hasn't told you about me. We're in love." Jonathan looked over at his father and shook his head. He slowly turned away and closed his eyes. All he wanted right now was to be left alone. He needed this nightmare to go away, and he longed for his mom to come back. Why did she have to leave him in the first place?

Chapter 8

"Someone is Watching"

The ink had barely dried, with the words carefully thought out. "Dear Mr. Tillman…I know everything. Your little secrets are no longer safe. I know all about the web you've spun over the last couple of days. I have pictures of you and your sadistic little world. I know all about the accident last evening and the chain of events that led up to it. You may have caught a glimpse of me when you pulled out of your driveway, and you should know I'm telling the truth when I say I know all about you. Do not take me lightly. I will only say this once. If you do not meet my demands, my tape will be handed over to the school. Your career and your life will never be the same. This tape will be sent to every member of the university board and the press if my demands are not entertained. For you, it is quite simple. $1M delivered to me in small bills. You will need to get them ready as quickly as possible. I'll let you know where you can make the drop. If I don't have my money within 48 hours, I'll assume you think I've bluffed. This would be a big mistake." Tillman's stomach began to churn on the inside, as he sat down on the chair and quickly tried to gather his thoughts. Tillman examined the note very carefully, looking for clues to see who had composed it. He was perplexed and confused, and his mind began to race a hundred miles an hour. When did this person start to watch him? Tillman started to think back to the events of the evening, which seemed like days long ago. He also knew he needed to find out who this person was before irreparable damage to his life and his career set in. He walked up the stairs in search of anything that was out of place. Nothing seemed to be moved or missing. He went into the bathroom and noticed a few drops of water on the side of the sink. The intruder had been in his bathroom. Tillman needed to remain focused. Was the person still in the house? His entire world could cave in if this message was accurate. Tillman knew he had to find this person quickly and derail their request. He sat down in the corner of the room and started to meditate about what to do next. His mind began to race, and he wasn't tired anymore.

"Do you think Ms. Lewis is telling the truth, Officer Bastion?" asked Smitty. "It's hard to tell," responded Bastion. "She absolutely refuses to change her story. I know she realizes that her friends right now are very limited, so I see no reason for her to lie. However, you know me, I trust nobody. I have one more little exercise for Ms. Lewis that will indicate once and for all whether she is, in fact, telling the truth. Why don't you go ahead and let her know that I'll be visiting with her in about 15 minutes, but I will not be alone. I'm going to bring along a friend who will assist me in my session." Smitty thought for a minute. Who in the world was she going to bring with her? Bastion was the best at uncovering the truth, even though her methods were highly questionable. Smitty knew Erika would be taken to task regarding her side of the story, and Bastion would do whatever it took to get the real story out of her. If Bastion thought there was any chance that Erika was holding back the truth, she would be punished. Bastion was very connected on the inside, and all of the inmates were terrified of her. She had been given unlimited access to the ins and outs of the system and did everything possible to use that information to its fullest. Smitty got up and headed toward Erika's cell. Erika had better be ready for this final phase of questioning because it would be unlike anything she had ever been through before. If she didn't pass this particular test, her life would be changed forever. Bastion and her accomplice would undoubtedly make sure of that…

William and Maggie spent the evening at the hospital with very little sleep. Maggie was extremely upset with William because she was hoping to stay together at the hotel located just two blocks down the street. William, on the other hand, recognized that disappointing look in Jonathan's eyes when Maggie shared with him her interpretation of the relationship. William probably should have said something to Jonathan about Maggie, but he never really thought of Maggie in that way. She was just a good friend who was there for him to talk to, but obviously, she had other plans. How was he going to get some time with Jonathan alone to straighten things out? He had an idea. William needed some help from one of the staff members. Somebody there needed to keep Maggie at bay, so William could be a father once again. "Maggie, I'm going to take a walk down to Jonathan's room and see how he's doing. Why don't you stay here and rest. It's been a very long night," pleaded William, as he began to make his move toward the door. Maggie was quick with her response and said, "William, I get the feeling you're tying to get rid of me or keep me away from your son. Why would you do that after all I've done for you?" William was taken back with the insinuating nature of her questioning. "Maggie, you and I need to talk about a lot of things later, but right now, I don't want anything to get in the way of Jonathan's recovery. I need to be with him as father and son…you should understand." "Oh, I understand, all right," shot back Maggie.

"You needed a ride from me, and I was there to help. But…now you want to neglect our feelings for one another because you're embarrassed to have me in your life. Well, just so you know, I'm not going to let that happen. I didn't drive all this way to be ignored. Let me go find my purse. It's important for me to get some time with Jonathan as well." William was confused. Who was this woman that somehow crept into his life? William turned his back on Maggie and started down the hallway toward Jonathan's room. Just as he turned the corner, he spotted Rose at the nurses' station. "Rose, I need your help," pleaded William, as he practically ran over to where she was standing. "Could you take Maggie down to the lounge for a cup of coffee? I've got to get some time with my son to explain a few things. Having her with me will make that very difficult." "I understand, Mr. Gunn," responded Rose. "Not a problem." Rose immediately made her way back down to where William and Maggie had spent the night. Maggie was in the process of gathering her things and had started to make her way down the hallway to where William was heading. William moved as fast as he could toward Jonathan's room. He had some explaining to do, and he wanted to do it alone.

Tillman contemplated his next move. He had access to the $1M…that wasn't the problem. The legitimacy of the ransom request; however, was a whole different story. His disadvantage right now was the urgency of the situation because he knew he needed to move quickly. The clock was definitely ticking, and there were moving parts materializing from all different directions. For the first time ever, Tillman truly felt like the mouse, and he didn't like it one bit. The most difficult part of this game though was that he had no idea who the cat was. Someone may have been watching him for a very long time, which could turn out to be a major problem for him. Tillman had a lot of enemies; therefore, it was extremely difficult for him to accurately identify his opponent. There were a number of different possibilities, but it was important for him to narrow it down to a handful of likely sources as quickly as possible. Everything could come crumbling down if this so-called evidence did, in fact, exist. He searched the entire house but nothing seemed to be out of place. How could this person have seen anything that evening? Tillman was confident his tracks had been covered; however, was he willing to take that chance? He thought about his next move and felt paralyzed as he waited for the caller to reach out to him once again. It was now close to 8:00 a.m., and Tillman hadn't slept for over 24 hours. Tillman started a new pot of coffee and hoped this additional jolt of caffeine would allow him to somehow focus on the task at hand. Suddenly, the phone rang and Tillman made his way over to the ringing that seemed to be playing with his mind. "Mr. Tillman, listen very carefully. This will be the only time you hear from me. At 5:00 p.m. today, I want you to go to the old mill just north of the frontage road. You'll need to bring a duffle bag with you that contains $1M in small bills. On the southeast corner of the mill, there's a cement block that runs adjacent to the ground, extending out about 18 inches. That block can be removed very easily. I want you to place the bag in the open section and then put the block back. I'll then expect you to leave quickly and go back home. I'll be calling you at home at precisely 5:30 p.m. If you don't answer the phone, I'll immediately go to the authorities with my tape and expose your sick mind to all. If someone else answers the phone, I'll go to the authorities as well. Don't play games with me, Tillman. Your world will either be safe, or it'll be turned upside down, based on the actions you take in the next 12 hours. I hope you make the right decision. I'm very impatient, and I will not tolerate anything but total adherence to my request. Don't play games with me, Tillman, or I'll crush you." Click. Tillman could feel his heart begin to race. There was a part of him that wanted to call this person's bluff, but he knew this was a dangerous position for him to take. If he called his bluff, and he was right, everything would turn out fine. However, if the intruder actually did witness the events of this evening and others as well, his life as he knew it would be over. The skeletons in his closet were abundant, and the noise from their rattling laughter was getting louder and louder. He would have nothing much to live for, and his career and academic reputation would be in severe jeopardy. Both would completely unravel if this story leaked. He thought for a moment and then made his way back to his office because this was where he kept his safety deposit key. The thought of possibly using it for the request that had been made was turning his stomach, but the thought of being exposed was even worse. He needed to make a decision…and fast. Time was quickly running out.

"Dad, who is she? Why didn't you tell me about her before? It's not that I want to get involved in what you do, but I guess I'm just disappointed in the way it came out," whispered Jonathan. "Son, you're right," answered William because he knew the chain of events really upset his only son. "I'm very sorry. But…I'm not in love with Maggie. She's just a friend. Obviously, she's under the impression that our friendship is much more. I need to have a discussion with her when we get back home and make sure she understands where I stand regarding this relationship. I'm just very surprised that she would even think there was more. I'm very sorry, Jonathan. I loved your mother with all my heart and soul. I'm not ready to even think about someone else. Right now, I just want you to recover and get well." Jonathan was still very weak and didn't have much else to say. He simply nodded and began to close his eyes because his body had been badly beaten by the fall. William turned to walk back to the chair he had occupied earlier when suddenly, he heard Jonathan speak out to him once again, "Dad, be careful. She's a very dangerous woman." Jonathan fell back to sleep and left his dad standing there to think about what he just said. William could see the frightened look in his eyes, which was unlike anything he had ever seen before. He sat down in the chair and began to think about what Jonathan had just told him. His son had a gift that most only dream of, as his intuitive side seemed to always be a step ahead of anyone else. What did Jonathan see that gave him this feeling about Maggie? William wanted to know more, but Jonathan was in no condition to talk right now. He would need to wait until he was stronger because he was certain the discussion would not be an easy one.

"Erika, I want you to meet my close friend," said Bastion, as she slowly began to enter the cell. "Her name is Casey, and she has been in and out of the big house for the last 15 years. Her rap sheet is seven pages long, and she will more than likely never see the light of day again. However, Casey has been given full reign on activities that go on in here. She basically gets anything she wants, assuming she makes herself available to me when needed. This means that when I need help getting the truth from troublemakers like you, I call on Casey. You are her next assignment. I won't leave you alone with her, unless you force me to do so. I don't think you'll survive if I do. You see, Casey has a real disdain for young women like you. You fit the profile she dreams of every night. Now, let's go over this story of yours once again." Erika took a deep breath and felt a tear swell in her left eye. Casey began to laugh uncontrollably. "This is going to be a lot of fun," she said. "I kind of hope she does hide the truth. I'd love to have a little time with her alone. Officer Bastion, what would it take to get about 15 minutes with this sweet little thing? That's not too much to ask for, now is it?" Bastion shook her head and responded with a smile, "We'll see. It all depends on the answers we get."

Tillman arrived at the bank at around 12:30 p.m. and went straight to his safety deposit box. He had accumulated considerable wealth over the years; however, the most significant portion of his portfolio was tied up in his art. In his safety deposit box, he had also saved approximately $1.3M in corporate bonds and stock certificates that could be cashed out immediately. This was going to be very difficult for Tillman because his frugality had been established for many years. He didn't want to part with this money, and he would do just about anything possible to keep it from happening. He needed to establish a solid plan that could be implemented quickly. Tillman had plenty of enemies over the years and had burnt numerous bridges on his road to the top. The chain of events that transpired over the last 24 hours was just the tip of the iceberg. If he was exposed now, there was a strong possibility that everything would crumble around him like a deck of cards. Tillman knew he would raise suspicion with his huge withdrawal, but he really didn't have much of a choice. He filled out all the necessary paperwork and was out of the bank by 1:30 p.m., with $1M in his briefcase. He needed to get back home, so he could plot out the rest of his day. He was thoroughly exhausted, but he realized he had to keep moving forward. Tillman knew he was dealing with a very clever individual, and he somehow needed to stay focused and find a way to be at the top of his game. The fact that he was being told to be back home at 5:30 p.m. was making it very difficult to devise a plan that would work. He sat down in his study and began to write down every possible option he could think of right now. Tillman had to find the one person in his life who could help him, but this was nearly impossible. Tillman was in big trouble and mentally went through his personal rolodex of contacts. His friends were few and far between, and his enemies were extensive. He needed to find someone who wouldn't be recognized by anyone; someone who could slip in and out of what needed to be done. Then it hit him! He knew the perfect person for the job…Frizell. His plan was officially set in motion. This was the one friend he knew best…

By the time Maggie made it to Jonathan's room, William was sitting in the chair just inside the door. Due to the pain medication that had just started to set in, Jonathan had fallen into a deep sleep. "Why didn't you wait for me, William?" asked Maggie. "That nurse, Rose, practically insisted on having me join her for a cup of coffee. I told her I was going to catch up to you, but she wouldn't have anything to do with that. She is, without a doubt, the pushiest little nurse I've ever seen." William had a very difficult time not cracking a smile because he knew how difficult it was to actually control Maggie. He was beginning to really like this Rose since she seemed to always be there when she was needed the most. In addition, William could see the way his son was looking at her when he first entered his room…and he could see why! Rose was beautiful and intelligent, which was the perfect combination for any young, single man like Jonathan. "William, are you listening to anything I'm saying to you?" said Maggie. "No, actually I'm not," responded William. With that, Maggie turned and stormed out of the room. William was still focused on his son and wasn't about to get distracted by Maggie. Her continual need for attention and desire to control the situation was really starting to grate on his nerves.

Tillman began to initiate his plan at around 4:00 p.m., as he knew it would take him at least 20 minutes to get changed and ready to go. He would be handing the baton over to the only friend he had right now, but he was confident Frizell was up to the task. He had no doubt in his mind that he would be more than ready to move forward with the next phase of the plan. The more Tillman thought about the possibility of actually giving someone $1M, the more it became apparent to him that there was no way he could let this happen. He would rather risk everything than part with his small fortune. Fortunately for Tillman's plan, the night was clear and lit well by the full moon that was just starting to creep over the horizon. This would allow Frizell the opportunity to get a better look at the caller when it became necessary for him to carry out his portion of his scheme. He pulled out of the driveway and on to Main Street. Within minutes, he was on the frontage road and heading straight toward the old mill on the outskirts of town. He knew this area very well for a variety of reasons, none of them very good. He reached into the glove compartment and took out his serrated 10-inch knife with the wooden handle. Frizell was very good with the blade because of his love of hunting over the years. Tonight, his objective would be different though since his primary goal would be to inflict one direct, fatal wound. Frizell thought through his anticipated sequence of events. He decided that he would place the duffle bag near the corner of the mill and then wait for his victim to claim the prize. When the caller made his move for the bag, he would launch a surprise attack and take care of him, once and for all. The more he thought about the 5:30 phone call, the more he questioned its legitimacy. He started to believe that it was just a stall tactic to get him away from the mill once the drop had occurred. Transforming himself into Frizell would allow him to create a critical element of surprise for the caller, which was exactly what he would need when everything went down. Frizell wanted to see who this man was; plus he knew the caller would be on the lookout for Tillman, and this would undoubtedly be his edge. If the caller ever got ahold of the money, his savings would be gone forever, and Tillman knew he could not afford for this to happen. It was important for him to stop this lunacy before it got out of hand, which meant the caller would have to be eliminated. Tillman's ultimate fate depended on it...

He could see the mill off in the distance, as it was closing in on 4:45 p.m. Frizell pulled the car off the side of the road and gathered his thoughts. There was zero activity around him, and the caller was nowhere to be seen. However, Frizell was still confident the caller would show up to claim his money and that would be it. The minute he was within striking distance, Frizell's plan was to catch him off guard and get rid of him once and for all. Frizell took a deep breath and played out the anticipated plan in his mind once again. For the first time in the last couple of days, he felt like he was finally back in control of the situation. At the end of the day, the caller would be nothing more than collateral damage and he would move on with his life. Tillman and Frizell were about to team up once again and this made them both very happy. Life would soon be back to normal for the two of them, which was exactly what was needed right now.

Officer Bastion continued to question Erika regarding the events of the evening. The answers were the same as the first, second, and even the third time around. Erika made a few mistakes along the way; however, she had always been truthful in her assessment of the events that led up to the evening in question. Tillman had set her up, and she didn't realize the dangerous mind of the individual she was dealing with. Once he realized she was in trouble, Jonathan came to save her from potential harm. He wasn't there to steal anything but instead was trying to help a close friend in need. Bastion's questions continued in rapid fire. "Why were you attracted to Professor Tillman? Did you have a physical relationship with him? Did you use that relationship to infiltrate his home, hoping that it would soon result in a big payoff for you and your other lover, Mr. Gunn?" Erika was able to maintain incredible composure throughout the interrogation. Her answers remained consistent with the version she gave early on in the process. However, Bastion had one more test for Erika before she let her off the hook. In came her secret weapon named Casey, who had been waiting for this moment since she first laid eyes on Erika. "Erika, I'm going to turn this interview over to my partner here. I'll be back in about 15 minutes. Casey, she's all yours." Casey looked over at Erika and smiled. "Smitty, can I get some help over here. I need to step out for a minute," signaled Bastion. "Open the door to the cell. Casey is going to be taking over for me now." Smitty approached the cell and opened it for her, letting her out into the hallway. Casey was now alone in the cell with Erika, as Bastion turned her back and walked away. The door slammed behind her, and the echo seemed to polarize Erika. She sat motionless in her chair and took a deep breath. Casey, on the other hand, just sat and smiled.

Frizell got out of the car and made his way over to the old mill. He was careful not to raise his head, keeping the collar of his jacket up over the side of his face. He knew he was being watched; therefore, it was important for him to make sure he didn't tip off his disguise. The caller would be looking for Tillman, so it was important for Frizell to remain an unknown, at least for now. His plan would only work if the individual suspected that Tillman was, in fact, the person dropping off the duffle bag. Frizell reached down and removed the cement block that would soon be the temporary home for his drop-off. While he had no intention of ever giving the money to the caller, he had everything appear as though he did. Frizell put the bag in the open space and soon covered it up with the 18-inch slab of cement that would hide its identity, at least for the short-term. Again, Frizell was careful not to lift his head and soon made his way back to the car. He turned on his headlights and drove away. As he approached the curve that led away from the mill, Frizell spotted the dirt road he had scouted out earlier that evening. He turned off the engine and lights and parked the car about 30 feet off the main frontage road. He immediately jumped out of the car and began to run back toward the mill. He stayed close to the tree line, and within minutes, he was well-positioned above the back of the structure. He could see the side of the mill where the duffle bag rested, and he carefully contemplated his next move. For now, he would simply wait for his bait. Hopefully, his gamble would soon pay off and he would have his life back once again. He wasn't going to be at home when the phone rang at 5:30; therefore, he was banking on his assumption that the phone call would never take place. He kept his eyes glued on the old mill and had a strong feeling that his adversary would soon make his move. Frizell reached into the side pocket of his jacket and slowly removed the knife. The blade was razor sharp, and Frizell's mind was as well. His plan had to work. There was far too much on the line for it not to…

From the time she was 10 years old, Rose Doliak always wanted to become a nurse. Born and raised in Western Kansas, her family depended on the land for their living. Nursing was something that nobody thought of in her little world. Everything revolved around the price of grain, pork bellies, and cattle. Rose was the oldest of three children, and she was looked upon by her siblings for guidance ever since they were kids. Rose's father had positioned her for full control of the farm, but Rose had her heart set on taking care of kids instead. Initially, this would be her primary focus at the hospital. However, everything changed when Monte Clark decided to recruit her to assist him in surgery. He spotted her abilities early on and then made sure she was in a position to really put her talents to work. He was never attracted to her physically because he had been happily married now for over 25 years. Clark was in dire need of someone he could rely on, and Rose was the perfect choice. Their respect for one another was genuine, as both were consistently at the top of their profession. Rose was simply the best and most talented nurse in the hospital, and Dr. Clark was the top surgeon. Together, they made the perfect team.

Rose's family still lived back in Kansas, and she was pretty much on her own in the Central Valley. She missed them dearly; however, her job was the primary focal point of her life. She had been involved with only one man two years ago, but they decided to break it off when it became obvious to him that she wasn't going to cut back on her hours for anyone. From the moment she first laid eyes on Jonathan, she knew there was something different about this young man. She was three years older than he was, but his level of maturity just seemed to give her strength. She had seen him when he first came into the hospital, and quite frankly, she didn't think he was going to make it. Rose had never been attracted to a patient before, but she knew in her heart that this man was different. She found herself stopping by his room a number of times each day just to see how he was doing. Most of the time he was asleep, but there were times when he found a way to gather up enough strength to give her a smile. This was more than enough for Rose, but what would happen once he recovered? Rose had read the stories in the newspaper about Jonathan's rumored involvement with Erika and the twisted web that was spun at the Tillman house. Rose really didn't know what to think. She just knew this man seemed different to her, and she wanted to find out why. He didn't come across as the kind of person who would do all those awful things that Tillman said he did, and Rose would have to be proven wrong. Oh, how she wished her intuition about him was right...

Frizell stared at the old mill, as the clock was fast approaching 5:30 p.m. Maybe he had made the wrong decision? There was absolutely no movement in the wooded area just behind the mill, and it looked like his presumed intuition may have cost him everything. If the caller decided to phone him in order to make sure he had held up his end of the bargain, he would be exposed, and his life could quickly come crashing down. Suddenly, Frizell heard something move about 100 yards to the north of where he was sitting. Frizell could hear movement from behind the trees, but he couldn't tell exactly where the noise was coming from. Just then, out came a tall, dark figure. This had to be the caller because he methodically moved toward the mill, looking behind him the entire way. Frizell took a deep breath and felt his pulse begin to ramp up speed. He was certain his identity had not been revealed, and he could see the dark figure move closer to the front of the structure. Frizell positioned himself so he could get around the side of the building as quickly as possible. He knew the person would not be looking for Frizell, and he could catch him off guard before he realized what happened. The dark figure's back was turned to Frizell, and he moved closer and closer to where the money rested. Out came the blade, as Frizell started to move toward his target. He was not going to let this man get away; soon this silly, little game of cat and mouse would be over for good. He wanted to wait until the timing was perfect because it was critical that he dispose of this man with one fell swoop. The dark figure reached into the opening and out came the duffle bag. Frizell could see the man, and he started to zip open the bag. His hands began to reach into the bag, as if he was checking to make sure everything was included and nothing was missing. Frizell positioned the blade and began to move toward his victim. He still couldn't see his face, but that wasn't necessary. This was his man! One slice to the throat was all he needed, and then he would be home free. Frizell maintained his composure and was now only about 20 feet away. His hand began to elevate...he could feel his adrenaline start to rush. Two more steps and this silly, little confrontation would be over. He was already thinking about where to dispose of the body. Frizell felt his heart race and began to lunge toward his nemesis. His plan was working perfectly, as he pulled out the knife and moved toward his defenseless victim. Suddenly, the caller turned around, and Frizell seemed to freeze in his tracks. Their eyes met, and Frizell slowly felt his body go numb in disbelief. There was no way he could have ever prepared for what he was about to see...

Chapter 9

"Surprise"

Frizell was in shock, as his eyes met with the unknown caller. This wasn't the caller he expected! The man turned around, and Frizell quickly recognized the outline of his sunken face. It was Officer Bradford; Frizell gasped in disbelief! Frizell lunged toward Bradford and began to thrust the knife downward toward Bradford's exposed neck. Bradford reached up and blocked Frizell's outstretched arm because he could see the blade shining in the moonlight. Frizell immediately felt the strength in Bradford's forearm and tried with all his might to bury the blade into Bradford's throat. Bradford let out a scream and proceeded to push Frizell back into the side of the hill. Bradford was well-trained in hand-to-hand combat from his former days in the military, and he quickly took Frizell down to the ground. He reached around Frizell's face and grabbed hold of his salt and pepper wig, and he pulled it off before Frizell had time to react to what was happening. Tillman's identity was exposed because Bradford had full control of him now. "Well, look what we have here! If it isn't Professor Tillman. Now, what would you be doing out on a night like this dressed in this garb?" questioned Bradford, as he scraped Tillman's face along the dirt and pulled his right arm up behind his back. The knife fell to the ground, and Tillman's hands were immediately locked in handcuffs. Bradford felt the urge to give Tillman the beating he so rightly deserved; however, he decided to hold off for now. Tillman was going to be the subject of numerous inquiries back at the precinct, and Bradford wanted to make sure he would be able to participate in the line of questioning that would undoubtedly take place. Bradford walked Tillman to the car and threw him in the back seat. He proceeded to read Tillman his Miranda rights because he wanted to make sure everything was done according to policy with absolutely no room for error. Tillman turned his head in shame, as his life had totally imploded over the last 30 minutes. Deep down inside, he knew it would never be the same.

Getting out of this one would be highly unlikely because Tillman could sense the police had been waiting a long time for this day to finally take place.

Casey looked over at Erika and smiled. "So far, you've been consistent with all your answers, sweet pea," she said, "and that's a good thing for you. You see, I have this agreement with Bastion that I'll never break, because if I do, I know she'll find a way to get rid of me. Our deal is, I'm used during the interrogation phase, and if I uncover any inconsistencies regarding the information Bastion receives, I'm afforded one night with the inmate in question. However, I've given Bastion my word that I'll never turn someone in who has told me the truth. As much as I'd love to tell Bastion that you're lying to me, I've come to the conclusion that you're telling the truth. I'm not going to harm you. I'm going to get Smitty now to let me out. I honestly hope things go well for you. Good luck." With that, Casey stood up and walked over to the cell door. "Hey Smitty. Let me out of here. I'm finished with this little princess." Smitty came from around the corner and unlocked the cell. Casey would be going back to her cell, and for the moment, Erika would be left alone in hers. Smitty smiled at Erika, as he let Casey out. "Ms. Lewis, would you like anything to eat right now?" asked Smitty. "No, thank you, sir. I'm not real hungry," responded Erika. "I totally understand. If you happen to get your appetite back, just give me a shout, and I'll get you whatever you need," said Smitty, as he genuinely felt sorry for Erika because of what she had been through. Erika shook her head and made her way back to the corner of the cell. She knelt down and felt her stomach start to rumble. She placed her head over the 6-inch opening in the floor that doubled as a toilet and began to throw up profusely. Her nerves were shot, and all she wanted to do was go home where she felt safe.

Bradford's squad car pulled into the precinct's parking lot and continued to drive around back. Bradford had his man, as he had been skeptical about Tillman right from the start. However, he knew he was dealing with a very cagey individual, and catching him was not going to be an easy task. Tillman had been living a double life for nearly 20 years, and nobody had any idea just how sick this man really was. Bradford jumped out of the car and opened the back door. Tillman ran with him into the side door of the precinct, keeping his head down the entire time. He felt total humiliation and knew his world was about to be exposed. The media would definitely have a heyday with this one because this was the kind of story that sold newspapers and improved ratings. As Bradford began to bring Tillman into the main hallway, Tillman reached over and tugged at Bradford's side. Tillman felt a strong desire to know where he messed up and what had given him away. "So Bradford, how did you know I'd be there tonight? You've got to tell me. It's the least you can do." Bradford was dying to tell him; however, the last thing he wanted to do right now was give Tillman any kind of satisfaction. "Mr. Tillman, now why would I tell you that? Let's just say I had a little help from a source I hope to meet one day. Who knows, maybe he'll come by and introduce himself to you as well." Bradford grabbed Tillman by the back of his jacket and led him into the main lobby area. There were a number of other officers gathered around the conference table in the corner of the room when Bradford and Tillman made their entrance. "Well, look what we have here. I think the rest of our inmates are going to be real happy to have some company tonight," chirped Officer Davies. "What do you think, Smitty?" "Oh yeah, there's going to be some serious partying tonight," responded Smitty, as laughter quickly filled the room. Tillman shook his head in disbelief. There was nothing he could say. His little game was over, and now he had to somehow prepare for the fallout that would be coming his way. Bradford, on the other hand, needed to get to Jonathan as quickly as possible. He had something very important to talk with him about and something to show him as well.

Bastion made her way down to Erika's cell. "Ms. Lewis, wake up!" yelled Bastion. "Unless, of course, you want to stay here and keep us all company." Erika slowly picked herself up from the mattress lodged in the corner of the room. "What are you talking about?" asked Erika, totally oblivious to the chain of events that had unraveled over the past 24 hours. "Well, it looks like Tillman's little game has come to an abrupt end. What happened to you may have been just the tip of the iceberg. We have a lot of questions he'll need to answer. In the meantime, I think it would be in your best interest to go home and get some rest. Please, make sure you leave us a number where you can be reached. We still have a lot of questions that need to be answered by you as well. However, our primary focus right now will be on Tillman. I want to get to him before anyone else does." Erika let out a scream and said, "Oh, thank you, Officer Bastion. Thank you, thank you!" For a moment, Bastion actually felt happy for this young girl. As usual, she was very careful not to show it because her reputation was at stake. "Get out of here, kid," Bastion quipped, "before I change my mind." Erika ran down the hallway and stopped at the front desk to pick up her valuables. She had one place she needed to get to right now, and that was the hospital. Jonathan had been on her mind ever since the accident. She had developed feelings for him before the incident, but they were even stronger now. This man had risked everything for her, and nobody had ever done that before. She knew he was in bad shape after the fall, but she had received very little information since she was taken to jail. Was he even still alive and, if so, would he ever forgive her? Her heart began to race, as she made her way out of the building. She just wanted to put her arms around him and tell him how she felt, once and for all. Up until now, she had never really done this, and she wasn't sure why. She knew in her heart that it was time to speak up and tell him the truth. Over the past couple of days, one thing was certain. Erika had fallen in love with this man, and she needed to tell him now... before it was too late.

Jonathan was starting to feel better and was finally beginning to get back some of his strength. The hospital staff insisted on keeping him there for at least another day or so before letting him go home because they knew how uncertain the next couple of days could be. Internal injuries had a way of fooling their victims, and they didn't want Jonathan to revert back to his previous condition. By now, Daniel found out about his best friend's accident and had been with Jonathan over the last couple of days. Although Jonathan was still very weak, he seemed to respond well to the support he was getting, with the exception of Maggie. She was more of a nuisance than anything else; however, Jonathan could sense she was not going away easily. His dad really needed to see the light quickly, Jonathan thought, before she clawed her way into the family. Jonathan just didn't have the strength to address this situation right now, but he would find a way to get it done in due time. The idea of having Maggie as a stepmother caused him even more pain than the fall, as Jonathan couldn't help but have a real disdain for the woman. He would do everything in his power to make sure their relationship never made it that far, and this would be one of his top priorities as soon as he was up to it. He smelled a rat, and he was usually on target with these things. Soon, he would make sure she was stopped, and his dad wasn't hurt. After all, this is what his mom would have wanted him to do.

Erika arrived at the hospital late that afternoon. Her nerves were starting to get the best of her, and she had no idea what Jonathan's response would be upon her arrival. She was certain he had a number of questions, but she didn't care. Through the course of the incredible events that had just taken place, she had fallen deeply in love with this man, and it was time to tell him once and for all. Her silly, little crush had evolved into something incredibly special, as her heart nearly skipped a beat in anticipation of seeing him again. When she was in jail, her thoughts weren't on her family back home. Instead, they were on Jonathan. He was the only one she wanted to see; the only one she wanted to hold, and the only one she needed right now. Erika ran into the hospital and went straight to the reception desk. "Jonathan Gunn, please. Can you tell me what room he's in?" asked Erika. "No problem, ma'am," said the woman at the desk. "He's in Room 406. Just take that elevator over there up to the 4th Floor and then take an immediate left when you get off. 406 is down the hallway on the right side." "Thank you very much," said Erika, as she quickly made her way to the elevator. She took a deep breath because she had no idea what kind of reception she was in for. Erika's excitement started to build, and she felt like a little kid all over again.

Tillman heard the cell door shut behind him. "This could be your home for a very long time," chuckled Bradford. "I have a feeling your life is about to change forever. Officer Bastion will be paying you a visit very soon. Best of luck with her. Trust me; you're going to need it. She's unlike anyone you've ever been up against before, much different than your naïve college students, that's for sure." Bradford turned his head and started to walk away. Tillman could hear him laugh, as he strolled down the hallway. How did this happen? Just 24 hours earlier, Tillman was in full control of the situation. He knew it would be very difficult to escape this one, and he could sense his world was starting to crumble around him. Bradford had him dead to right, and his story and reputation were unraveling by the minute. One thing was certain for Tillman...there was no way he would allow himself to go to trial to face public humiliation. Not only would the embarrassment be overwhelming, but his entire life as he knew it would be over as well. His career had evolved into his only purpose in life, and now it was quickly evaporating. He had no family at home and very few friends. He was not about to let anyone have an ounce of satisfaction at his expense. Tillman needed to put a stop to this three-ring circus once and for all, and in his mind, he felt like there was only one option. He looked around the cell for an out of some kind, and there it was. Near the ceiling was an old water pipe that extended into the side of the wall. It was approximately 12 feet long and about 2 feet from the actual ceiling itself. He thought for a moment and decided it was time. He slid the bed over to the side of the room, directly under the pipe. He took his belt off and fastened the buckle. He spun the belt around in figure-eight style and wrapped one of the loops around his neck, the other end around the pipe. The belt tightly gripped his throat, and he took one final swallow. Without any hesitation, Tillman jumped off the side of the bed and could actually feel his neck begin to snap. His eyes felt like they were coming out of their sockets, as his teeth began to sink deeply into his bottom lip. He felt his mind seize the moment, but this was not turning out to be what he expected. Wasn't this supposed to be an easy and quick way to die? He could actually feel his feet begin to shake because his body was slowly going into shock. Why was it taking so long? He wanted to die right now, but his body wasn't cooperating. As he hung in his cell, his final seconds were consumed by distinct memories from the past. He could still picture his father, who was his coach, screaming for him to slide as he rounded third and headed toward home. Tillman could still see the catcher holding on to the ball, as he barreled down on him with all his might. Tillman closed his eyes and slid, hoping to jar the ball free. "You're out!" screamed the umpire. The umpire was right, as Tillman's body came to rest. His sad story, and his life, ended with one final breath. Just like 35 years ago during that championship game, there would be silence once again. Tillman, the man who thought he was bigger than life, hung dead in his cell. His game of arrogance and deceit was officially over…and no one would ever be hurt again.

Erika felt the elevator come to a stop, as she had finally reached the 4th floor. She could sense the presence of Jonathan just down the hallway, and her nervous excitement kicked into overdrive. It had been far too long since she had seen him, and she felt like a little kid once again. What would she say? How would he react to her visit? Most guys would be bitter, due to the sequence of events that took place over the past couple of days. Hopefully, Jonathan wouldn't be one of those guys, Erika thought, and he would embrace her with open arms. Had it not been for Erika's little visit to Tillman's house, none of this would have ever happened. She gingerly walked toward his room and could see the number 406 outside the door. Erika took a deep breath and closed her eyes. The door was closed. Erika knocked and waited. "Come in," said the voice on the other side of the door. Erika proceeded to walk in, and there he was. Jonathan looked remarkably well for what he had gone through, and a smile soon consumed his tired face. "Hello, Jonathan," said Erika, hoping for a positive response. Jonathan was not the kind of person who held a grudge. In due time, he would have ample opportunity to ask Erika what she was doing at Tillman's house in the first place, but this was not the time or place for that discussion to occur. All he could do was smile. Erika made her way to Jonathan's bed and reached out to touch his arm. Jonathan reached out with his hand and intercepted hers in mid-flight. "It's so good to see you. I'm so sorry about what happened," whispered Erika. "I understand," said Jonathan, as he put his arms around her. "I'm just happy you're ok." They embraced each other, and Erika could feel her entire body go numb. Her feelings for this man were real. In the meantime, Rose had also made her way down to Jonathan's room. Her timing was impeccable, as she stood by the door. Jonathan and Erika had no idea she was there. Rose watched as the two of them held each other for what seemed like an eternity. Rose could feel her heart begin to sink, and she slowly backed away from the door. As she turned away, she made sure nobody could see her eyes. Tears slowly trickled down the side of her face, and she made her way back to the nurses' station. Although she had never met Erika, she knew this was the girl who had been in the newspaper headlines for the last couple of days. She was afraid of this day because her feelings for Jonathan were starting to quickly gain momentum. She went back behind the desk and immediately put her head down. She took a deep breath and somehow found a way to get back into her work mode. She reached for the charts she was working on before her ill-timed visit to Jonathan's room and buried her head into the dictation that meant nothing to her right now. Maybe it was best for her to just move on and forget about him, she thought, as she wiped her tears away once again. This may, in fact, be the best solution for all.

"Officer Bastion, it's time for you to start your interrogation of Mr. Tillman. Would you like me to go down to his cell and bring him back here?" asked Officer Bradford. "That won't be necessary," responded Bastion. "I'd like to visit him there myself. I want him to feel comfortable in his new surroundings, so I can get as much out of him as possible." Bastion started to make her way down the hallway toward Tillman's new home; little did she know what was waiting for her on the other side of the sliding, steel door. As Bastion began to enter Tillman's cell, she soon found herself face-to-face with the twisted corpse. Tillman had only been hanging for about twenty minutes; however, his body had already started to stiffen like a board. His eyes were staring directly at Bastion's, as she reached over to check his pulse. Typically, this kind of scene had little impact on her, but this one was much different. Bastion reached over to untie the knot in the belt when suddenly; Tillman's body began to shake violently. Bastion could feel her heart begin to race, while she backed away from this evil man. Suddenly, without notice, a smile began to form on Tillman's swollen lips. It was as if something, or someone, had already taken over his body. Tillman was now being transformed into the true definition of death itself, right in front of Bastion's eyes. Bastion backed out of the cell and yelled for Smitty, as she turned her head away from the mangled flesh. As Smitty approached the cell, he could see Bastion on her knees in the corner of the hallway. She was throwing up and seemed to be gasping for air. Smitty looked into the cell and could see why Bastion's state of mind had been compromised. Smitty yelled for the rest of their team because he needed help getting Tillman down from his resting spot. Bastion sat back and watched, while the body was untied and fell to the floor. This had never happened to her before because she always maintained absolute composure no matter what the circumstance entailed. Oh, how she wished she had never touched this man. Her hands felt like ice, and she rubbed them back and forth as fast as she could. She needed to somehow bring them back to life because she felt like Tillman's inner being had started to consume her as well. She turned her head away and continued to throw up. Somehow, she needed to find a way to get a grip on herself. She had to get out of that cell, before it was too late.

"So, Jonathan, when do you think you're going to be able to get out of this place?" asked Erika, hoping the answer would be soon. "The doctors still want to run a few more tests to make sure my internal injuries are healing, so I'm hoping to get out of here in the next couple of days," replied Jonathan. "That's awesome," responded Erika, as she really wanted to spend some quality time with him as soon as possible. Unfortunately, the excitement for both would be short-lived. Jonathan's smile soon disappeared from his face. He could see Maggie entering the room, as she was directly behind Erika and moving fast. Jonathan could sense there would be trouble because Maggie seemed to be on a mission. After all, this woman had absolutely no class at all. He would try to nip this one in the bud as quickly as possible. "Erika, I want you to meet a friend of my dad's; her name is Maggie," said Jonathan. "Well, well, well… what do we have here?" questioned Maggie. "I'll bet this is the little missy who caused us all these problems; the one who was having the affair with that old goat, the professor. How can you even show your face around this hospital right now?" Erika was speechless, while Maggie was undoubtedly in her element. She could feel her face begin to go flush, and she turned to Jonathan for help. Jonathan didn't know what to say! Maggie had caught him totally off guard with her inflammatory remarks as well. Unfortunately for Erika, she was just getting started. Just then, Jonathan spotted Rose through the doorway. Maybe she could help the situation before things got too far out of control? "Hey, Rose," inquired Jonathan, "could you please take Ms. Delaney down to the lounge for a soda or something?" Maggie could sense what was going on and responded to this brush-off before it occurred once again. "I don't want a soda. I want to spend some time with this little troublemaker. She has a lot of explaining to do. Somehow, she thinks she can just waltz right in here and make herself at home. She practically killed my future son-in-law, and now she wants to seduce him as well." With that, Rose had heard enough. "Let me explain something to you right now, Ms. Delaney. If you refuse to leave, as per Mr. Gunn's request, I'll call security and have you thrown out. If this happens, the only way you'll ever set foot in this hospital again is if you're admitted here as a patient. If you'd like, I can arrange for that as well! Do you understand what I'm saying?" asked Rose. Maggie had met her match, and so had Erika. Jonathan looked over at Rose and smiled. Maggie walked over to the chair and grabbed her jacket. "Don't think for one minute that I'm through with you," said Maggie, as she glared over at Erika. "This family is very, very close, and we won't be fooled by anyone, especially you. Don't be surprised if we decide to sue you for what you've done to us!" All Erika could do was shake her head in disbelief, her eyes welling up with tears. Jonathan nodded to Rose, and she proceeded to whisk Maggie out the door. Rose looked back and gave Jonathan a smile that said everything, and Erika's heart began to sink. Suddenly, Maggie's remarks were irrelevant to Erika because the pain they caused were dwarfed by Rose's smile. It was her smile that cut Erika the deepest.

The body felt much heavier than 200 lbs., as death has a way of settling in quickly. Smitty and his three colleagues untied the belt from Tillman's neck. The room was silent, and all four of them could practically feel the inner soul of Tillman slowly begin to seep through the cracks in the floor. This was not a man who would rest in peace, and they could feel it. It was as if his soul had already made its way into the dark confines of the earth, where others would be slowly feasting on the remnants left behind. His life had been riddled with deceit and dishonor for many years, and now it was time for him to pay the ultimate price for a life gone mad. Finally, the truth would be revealed. For some reason, Smitty felt compelled to reach out and close Tillman's eyes, as the dark red circles were almost too much to bear. After the hanging, Tillman's body had gone through a number of contortions, and now the 23rd precinct was left with the remains. Smitty's hand reached out to shut his eyelids once and for all because he felt like this would somehow help bring this violent act to closure. He couldn't help but think about the man's life and how it had gotten so messed up. How could a thing like this happen, and what would they uncover at the house that may help with the explanation? Smitty felt compelled to be on the team that searched Tillman's home for answers because he wanted to learn as much as possible about this case before it was quickly swept under the rug. For whatever reason, he felt a strong desire to be on the investigative team that made its way to Tillman's premises. "Officer Peters," said Smitty, as he put his cell phone to his ear, "Smitty here. We have a dead body in the jailhouse. Professor Tillman just hung himself. The word's going to spread quickly, and the media will have a heyday with this one. I'm certain his home will be inundated with all members of the press as soon as they find out. I'd love to get over there beforehand, so we can take a look at his possessions prior to the feeding frenzy. Maybe we can find something that will help us better understand what triggered his irrational behavior. Can you get ready and make the trip with me?" "No problem," answered Peters. "I'll pull around the side of the building and get you in five minutes." "Sounds good," responded Smitty, "I'll be ready." As Tillman's body lay motionless on the cold cement, Smitty noticed a piece of paper in his left front pocket that seemed to be rolled up in a ball. He reached into Tillman's shirt and took it out. It was a phone number with an out of state area code, and next to it was the name, Angie. Smitty pulled out his cell phone and dialed the number. "Hello," said the voice. "Is Angie there?" asked Smitty. "This is she," responded the woman. "Who is this?" Smitty felt compelled to cut right to the chase. "I'm Officer Smith at the 23rd precinct. Who am I speaking with?" The young woman responded, "This is Angie Tillman, is there a problem?" Smitty said with a slight sense of hesitation, "Yes, there's a problem, but I'm not sure you can help or not. I just want to ask you a quick question." "No problem, sir. What is it?" asked Angie. "Do you know J.R. Tillman, Professor at Central Valley State University?" Silence interrupted the conversation, as Angie's voice immediately retracted. "Yes, I know him. He's my father. What did he do now?" This was the part of the job Smitty hated the most. How in the world was he ever going to explain this one?

Erika could feel a stillness in the room, as Rose escorted Maggie out the door. Jonathan seemed to be fixated on the door, and his mind was racing a mile a minute. "So, is she the nurse who's been taking care of you since you arrived?" asked Erika. "Yes, she's really been wonderful," responded Jonathan. "I don't know what I would have ever done without her. As you can tell, her strong approach with my father's newfound friend, Maggie, is exactly what I've needed here. I'm really sorry about the things she just said to you, Erika. Don't pay any attention to her. I never met her until I got injured. Suddenly, out of nowhere, she shows up with my dad. I really need to make sure she doesn't hurt him in any way. I just don't trust that woman. I have a very bad impression of her already." "I totally agree with you, Jonathan," responded Erika. "I've never seen anything like her before. Where does she come off saying the things she said to me? Maybe I should have waited before I came to see you. My visit today has created unnecessary tension, and I'm sure this is the last thing you need right now. I just couldn't wait any longer. Jonathan, there's something I need to tell you, something that's been on my mind for quite some time now." Erika's eyes began to tear up, as her heart felt like it was about to be exposed for the first time in her life. Jonathan could see in Erika's eyes that her words were genuine. He braced himself for the unexpected. Erika took a deep breath because it was time for her to finally tell Jonathan the truth.

Bradford needed to get to Jonathan and let him know about Tillman's demise before the media tracked him down. He had a few questions he wanted to ask Jonathan regarding the chain of events that eventually led to Tillman's capture. Bradford was on his path for quite some time; however, he had recently received an unsolicited tip that quickly set the wheels in motion. Bradford had no idea how dangerous Tillman was until he read the note that was waiting for him in the parking lot, just three days before Tillman's arrest. The note had been left by someone who knew full well that Bradford, in fact, would be the recipient. On the night he found the note, Bradford had noticed an old soup can in the middle of his regular stall with a piece of paper taped to the top. He could see the note attached because it was blowing in the wind when he stopped his car. The handwritten message read as follows:

"You have a very sick man in this community. His name is Professor Tillman, and he has been hurting young girls for many years now. In fact, I saw him tormenting the young girl, Ms. Lewis, just a couple nights back. Stay close to him, and he will eventually mess up. He's been getting away with this because nobody has had the guts to go after him before. Please get this man before he hurts another innocent young girl. If you don't get him soon, then I will. And if I do, it aint gonna be pretty!" The note was composed by someone who was left-handed, as the words were written with a distinct slant from left to right. This had been confirmed by the handwriting experts who were called in to analyze the words left for Bradford; however, this was about the only thing anyone knew about the author. Bradford was hoping that maybe

Jonathan had an idea of who it may be, since he and Erika were supposedly the only individuals on Tillman's property the night of the accident. Up until now, this was what everyone had suspected. However, someone else must have been at Tillman's house as well, but who in the world could it have been? Bradford wanted to talk with Jonathan before the word leaked out regarding the note because he knew what the media would do with this kind of information. Innuendos and numerous questions were already being asked about the bizarre sequence of events that transpired over the past week; therefore, Bradford needed to quickly derail this dangerous rumor mill. He needed to take it one step at a time because he knew it would be important for him to concentrate on the true facts of the case. Inaccurate information would do nothing but distract the entire investigative team, and Bradford wasn't about to let this happen. Whoever left that note was the key to the real story behind Tillman's sick mind. More than likely, this left-handed author knew of others who had been hurt by Tillman as well; others who may be willing to step forward now that he was gone. Bradford had to identify the person who had written the note as quickly as possible. Soon, the feeding frenzy would begin, Bradford thought, and this would only make matters worse.

Bradford ran as fast as he could to the front entrance of the hospital, jumped into the elevator, and took it straight to the 4th floor. The unit was quiet because most of the visitors that day had already gone home for the evening. Bradford went straight to Room 406 and peeked inside. Erika was sitting next to Jonathan and seemed to be in the middle of a very serious discussion with him. Bradford couldn't wait for them to finish, as it was important for him to get to Jonathan before someone else did. This was far too important for Bradford to wait. With a firm knock on the door, Bradford walked in before getting the official invitation. He was hoping it was enough to gain Jonathan's attention because he could tell their discussion was getting pretty deep. Erika seemed to be teary-eyed and turned to see who had interrupted their conversation. "I'm so sorry, Mr. Gunn. I had no idea you had company," said Bradford. "Oh, that's ok," responded Jonathan, "can I help you?" "I certainly hope so," said Bradford, as he made his way over to the bed where Jonathan was lying. "I need to speak with you alone." With that, Erika stood up and walked toward the door. She turned to Jonathan and said, "I'll try to get by and see you tomorrow, Jonathan. Hope you have a good sleep." Jonathan had no time to respond, and Erika made her way down the hallway and out the door. Jonathan turned to Officer Bradford, obviously irritated with the timing of his inquisition. "What is it now?" Jonathan asked. "Professor Tillman has just been found dead in his jail cell," answered Bradford. "He hung himself about an hour ago when it became evident that his life was about to take a dramatic turn for the worse. You see, we know all about Tillman's activities over the past week that ultimately impacted you and Ms. Lewis. However, I don't think any of us had any idea just how sick this man really was. I'm sure we'll soon find out, but I'm going to need your help. The media will be here soon, and I can help you deflect their questions if you'd like. I think you're going to need my assistance because I know just how ruthless they can be." Jonathan found himself in shock since it was hard to believe that Tillman was actually gone. "Wow! I never thought the great Professor Tillman would go down like that. I'm trying to understand why he did what he did, but I'm sure none of us will ever know. He hid his secret for a very long time, but I saw just how dangerous he was the other night before the accident. He was a very troubled man." Bradford responded, "I'm sure you're right, Jonathan, but I do think there's one person who knows far more than you or me. You see, I don't think we would have ever caught Tillman had it not been for the tip I received just after your fall. I'm receiving all the credit for bringing Tillman to justice, but I was merely following the details that were given to me from someone who was really the key to this case. This individual needs to be recognized for what he did, but I have a major problem. I have no idea who it is!" "What are you talking about, Officer Bradford?" asked Jonathan. Bradford sat down in the chair next to Jonathan and began to shake his head. "The notes have been right on target. It's as if this person has been watching Tillman for quite some time now and really wanted him put away. I have no idea who it is because the information given to us has been totally anonymous. Do you have any thought who it might be, Jonathan?" asked Bradford. Jonathan considered Bradford's question for a minute and said, "I have no idea who it is, not a clue! Erika and I were the only ones there that night; at least I think we were. Have you received anything that would indicate someone else was actually there?" Bradford rubbed his chin and said, "Not really. The only clue I have is that our informant is left-handed. We've confirmed this through our internal experts who've analyzed his handwriting. Other than that, we have no idea who it is." Jonathan thought for a moment and felt numb. Who did he know who was left-handed? Nobody, at least for now, came to mind…

Erika walked in the front door of her house and slowly made her way over to the couch. Her visit to see Jonathan had ended in disarray because she knew he was slipping away right before her eyes. Erika couldn't help but remember the first couple days in Tillman's class when Jonathan seemed like he was the only student who had it together. Her feelings for Jonathan started out slowly; however, it wasn't long before she found herself wanting to see him on a daily basis. What did she do wrong? Maybe she should have told him a long time ago how strong her feelings were…maybe this would have made a difference. Erika picked up the remote to the television set and began to randomly search through the channels. Suddenly, she heard the name Tillman being referenced, and the fear that had consumed her just hours before began to quickly settle in once again. Her body began to quiver, while she listened to the special news report. "Professor J.R. Tillman was found dead today hanging in his jail cell," said the reporter. "He's apparently taken his own life. Professor Tillman had recently been taken into custody following a bizarre sequence of events that had taken place. Tillman had been under investigation for his involvement with a number of former students, most recently Ms. Erika Lewis. Lewis and Tillman were found together last month at Tillman's estate, subsequently leading to an additional inquiry by the local police department. Jonathan Gunn, an acquaintance of Ms. Lewis, was critically injured after an apparent break-in at the estate went awry. Lewis' involvement in the incident is still under investigation. Authorities are not releasing their findings; however, one anonymous source has indicated that Tillman was involved in some very questionable events over a number of years. More details will be released as they are gathered and verified."

Erika leaned back in her chair and took a deep breath. She had no idea how to feel. On the one hand, she was relieved that Tillman was gone and would never bother her again. On the other, she felt like a tramp, and she knew it was only going to get worse as rumors would undoubtedly gain momentum at her expense. She would be at the center of attention regarding Tillman's sick, little web and her name would never be the same again. Jonathan was slipping out of her grasp as well, and this was the part that bothered her the most. Her only true friend undoubtedly had his eye on someone else and the thought of him turning elsewhere for a relationship right now was more than Erika could handle. Maybe Tillman had the right idea, she thought, as facing her problems alone seemed incomprehensible. For the first time in her life, she didn't want to live anymore. After all she had been through, Erika just couldn't imagine living her life without Jonathan. Voices began to race through her mind and consume her every thought. Unfortunately, she didn't seem to have the strength to fight them off, as her demons were beginning to win the battle they coveted the most. Erika's mind was their initial target because they knew it represented the gateway to her soul, which was their ultimate prize. Her confidence and will to live were beginning to crumble, and this made her demons want her even more. Wouldn't it be easier for Erika to just close her eyes and say good-bye, she thought, as she contemplated her next move? Family and friends would always look at her with trepidation and confusion from this point forward. She would be thought of differently because of what happened with Tillman, and the idea of being the focal point of this unwanted attention was far too much to bear. Erika got up and made her way over to the kitchen, as her mind began to race. Her car keys hung on the nail next to her refrigerator, just like they did every day. However, on this particular day, it was almost as if they were calling out her name for a much different task. She reached out and subsequently deposited the key chain into her pocket and turned toward the garage. Her eyes began to tear up, as she thought about her next move. The garage was dark; however, it lit up when she opened the door and let herself in. She slowly made her way over to the car and heard the door to the garage close behind her. Without any advanced warning, darkness quickly set in, and loneliness seemed to capture her every thought. The air seemed to close in around her, while Erika put the key into the ignition. She could feel the tears streaming down her cheeks, and she began to turn the key slowly to the right. She clutched her teddy bear, just like she did when she was a little girl back on the farm...but even those memories seemed to fade like a comet in the night. Her mind had become the ultimate battleground, and the demons did all they could to take Erika back to the task at hand. The engine turned over on the first turn. With that, Erika lay her head down on the front seat and closed her eyes. It wouldn't take long...

Chapter 10

"Wake up"

The exhaust quickly began to fill the room; however, this silent killer would be seen by nobody. Erika's eyes began to roll back in her head, while she curled up in the fetal position with her little bear snuggled tight. The path she had chosen was supposed to be an easy one, she thought, and she found herself waiting to fall asleep. It wasn't like she jumped off a bridge, shot herself, or even took an overdose. This seemed like the easiest way to go; the quickest way to leave this world before she caused any more pain. Deep down inside, Erika really didn't want to hurt herself and never had thoughts of suicide before this particular day. She just wanted out and, more than anything, she wanted to be loved again. Her mind began to race, and she thought about the reaction her passing would cause. Suddenly, she could see the image of her family and friends looking down at her in that old, pine box. Oh, how she hoped they would think she looked beautiful! Her body began to grow limp, and she could tell it was getting close to the end. Soon, she would be able to rest with no interruptions whatsoever, and the name Tillman would never haunt her again. It was almost as if she was now beginning to play out her demise before it actually happened. Her dream was ready to begin, and now the real question would be how long would this play last? The darkness would soon have a message for Erika; however, there was no way she would be ready for the deliverer. Nobody ever told her about him…

Out from the floor they came, slowly moving in single file. Their bodies were hunched over, and they walked low to the ground with their heads cocked at an angle. Their faces were clear in texture, and there eyes were bloodshot. They came one-by-one and gathered around Erika's body. There were 12 in total, and each of them stopped and stared at the motionless body. It was as if they were waiting for someone, or something, to join in this sadistic ritual. The air was very still, and Erika could feel her subconscious state of mind begin to set in. The 12 dark visitors began to slowly chant, "Sleep will bring you peace, sleep will bring you peace." As the chanting became louder, Erika began to feel the pain subside and slowly go away. She closed her eyes and waited…

From behind the old closet door he came, and the chanting immediately stopped as he entered the room. He was known in his dark world as Selera, and his soldiers obediently followed his every move. Selera walked over to Erika's body and began to rub her eyebrows. He slowly caressed her forehead and softly whispered, "Soon, you will be with me; your pain and suffering will forever be in my control. I will not harm you." His hands were dark blue and his fingernails were reddish-orange. He smiled and looked over at his 12 assistants and said, "It is time…let's take her with us." Erika's body would soon be lifted slowly from the vehicle; not her physical body but only her soul. This was all Selera really wanted. In due time, she would experience pain unlike anything she could have ever imagined, but for now, a deep sleep would be their primary goal. She thought it was the easy way out, but oh, how Erika was wrong. Selera had her right where he wanted her, but he needed to move quickly. Her soul was within his grasp, and he wanted it all for himself.

Suddenly, an old tree branch came crashing through the only window in the garage, and the noise was deafening. Erika's eyes slowly opened, and there he was! The smile on Selera's face was gone because he knew where the interruption had originated. Erika was well within his grasp, but now he could feel her getting away. She was starting to wake up and began to twitch violently. Without notice, the thought of death became frightening to her, and she found herself not wanting to leave this world anymore. Erika gasped for air, as she reached out and touched his face. She screamed and felt his flesh begin to melt in her hands. She looked up and saw the broken window, and somehow, she knew she had to find a way to get to the light. She reached over and pulled the handle toward her. The car door became ajar, and she fell onto the cold, garage floor. Erika pulled herself up and kept her eyes focused on the light. She knew that the light was key and she could not, under any circumstance, look back at her uninvited guests. She staggered over to the work bench that was directly under the broken window. She could hear the 12 creatures below begin to chant her name in hypnotic unison. Erika knew she couldn't look back and had to find a way to get to the light. She pulled herself on to the bench and slowly reached up for the window. She knew it was critical for her to get some air and do so as quickly as possible. The temptation to look back was consuming her, even though she knew it would be a big mistake. As she gathered her last bit of strength, she felt compelled to look back one last time…and that is when his eyes met hers! They pierced through her inner being, and she could feel her body go numb once again. The old serpent began to slither over to the workbench and wrapped his body around the leg of the chair. It was time to end this game once and for all because he wanted Erika all to himself.

He began to slither up to where Erika lay and slowly began to enter her mouth. Erika was beginning to feel tired once again...

Selera knew he had to move quickly in order to end this game and take her back to his home. He wrapped his coils around her throat, as Erika began to gasp for air. By closing off her windpipe, the suffering would soon be over. Erika leaned her head back and took one last look at the light. The tree branch that had broken through the window seemed to be taking on an identity of its own. As Erika focused on the smaller pieces of the branch that were closest to her, it was as if the branch was reaching out for her hand. She began to pull herself closer and closer to its smaller components and finally, with every ounce of strength in her body, she grabbed on with both hands. As she began to pull herself up toward the light, a face began to form right in front of her. Erika became fixated on the eyes that developed, and tears began to flow profusely down the side of her face. The image of God became clear and beautiful, and for the first time in her life, Erika knew she was not alone anymore. Never before had Erika felt this sense of peace, as she stared into the loving eyes that convinced her everything would soon be ok. She closed her eyes and whispered, "I am so sorry. You've shown me once again just how beautiful life can be. I don't want to die, I want to live! I want to live again. I want to live for You!" Before she knew it, God's face slowly faded away, and she felt total peace. She turned and looked back to see what kind of activity hovered around the car, and there they were...the 12 creatures and Selera protracting back into their respective holes. Selera knew he had been defeated, and for now, he and his followers would leave Erika alone. They would never give up, and if the opportunity presented itself again, they would return for Erika's soul. She had escaped self-inflicted death and would be forever grateful because she knew she was one of the lucky ones. The serpent and his followers would simply move on to their next victim. Somehow, this one had gotten away, and Selera would need to regroup once again.

Rose reached for Jonathan's personal items and slowly helped him into the wheelchair. This last push out the door was something he had been looking forward to for a very long time. Finally, Jonathan was getting out of the hospital, and he would never be the same again. Over the course of the past week, he had come face-to-face with death and had somehow broken free. At the same time, his mind had been captivated by a woman that had only existed in his dreams. Rose was brought into his life when he least expected it, and now she was right there with him when he needed her the most. Neutralizing Maggie would not be easy; however, Rose had clearly proven that she was up to the task. She knew just how important it was for Jonathan to slowly get back on his feet again, and the last thing he needed right now was any additional undue stress. The road to recovery would be a long one, but Rose knew in her heart that Jonathan was going to make it. She also realized that William would need to soon take a position regarding Maggie's interference. Her personality was not conducive to Jonathan's recovery; however, this would need to come from William himself. He was the one who brought her out to the hospital. Now, he would also need to be the one who somehow made her go away...

William realized he had to make a move regarding Maggie because he couldn't afford for her to create any more friction between Jonathan and him. After Jesse's passing, their relationship had somehow been strengthened, but this could all change if Maggie had her way. William was convinced that her behavior at the hospital was inexcusable, and that he needed to distance himself from this woman before irreparable damage was done. He planned on letting Maggie know it would be best if they quit seeing each other, but he knew that delivering this message wouldn't be easy. His desire was to wait until they got home; however, Maggie's current frame of mind was making this very difficult. It became obvious to William that keeping her around would only prolong the inevitable and hurt others in the process. Once again, she stormed her way into the hospital, bound and determined to get the answers she felt she so rightly deserved. Just like her behavior since Jonathan's fall, Maggie had no reservations about when or where she spoke her mind. Maggie was heading straight for the three of them when she was intercepted by William...it was time for him to put a stop to this once and for all. He had seen enough, and he would have no part of her little game anymore. Before he addressed Maggie, there was something he just needed to say to Jonathan. He built a wedge between Maggie and Jonathan and turned to face his only son. Maggie could only stare at the backside that was quickly right in front of her.

"Today is a great day, son. You've come a long way, and I'm confident you'll get better and better each and every day. We really need to be careful that you don't push it, so I'm hoping you'll agree to come home with me where I can take good care of you," pleaded William, as he slowly pushed Jonathan toward the hospital exit. "Dad, I really appreciate the offer, but I'm going to need to be here to wrap up any loose ends with school," responded Jonathan, as he looked up toward his dad. "The semester just ended, and I want to make sure everything is in place for graduation. The ceremony is coming up in a couple of weeks, and I really don't want to miss it. I'm going to be just fine here, and Daniel will be around if I need him." Rose continued to walk closely behind William as he pushed his son, with Maggie now standing directly behind Rose. Maggie felt like she was being left out of the conversation, and she would have no part of it. She had heard enough. "Jonathan, you need to listen to your father," exhorted Maggie, as she pushed her way in front of Rose to where Jonathan was sitting. "We've been cooped up here for the past week waiting for you to recover, and now he's asking you to spend time with him. If you ask me, I think you're being very disrespectful by saying no to him. I plan to be there with him at the house, and

I can take care of you as well. Come on, Jonathan, we're a family and I say you need to be with us and not here waiting for some silly graduation. Your health, and your father's peace of mind, is a lot more important than a little piece of paper that will probably get lost anyway." Jonathan looked up at Maggie and began to respond to her; however, William knew it was time for him to clearly state his position before his son got dragged into this mess. "Maggie, I've patiently listened to you now for the past week, and you've continually taken shots at my family and their friends. I want you to know that I don't appreciate this whatsoever. In fact, I'm quite frankly embarrassed by the way you've behaved ever since we got here. I'm not heading back home with you because I'm going to purchase a bus ticket and travel alone. You and I are not an item, and I don't expect my son to miss graduation. I'm going to ask you to leave now because I want to spend some quiet time with Jonathan and Rose. This is my family, and I don't want you to take these cheap shots at their expense anymore. As of right now, you and I are finished, even though there never was anything between us to begin with. I wish you all the best." With that, William reached out and started to push Jonathan toward the car, with Rose right by his side. "William Gunn, you get right back here," screamed Maggie. "I'm not through with you yet. You can't get away with this. I'm not going to go away. You just made one big mistake, mister. You'll be alone back in Rocker, and I'll be waiting for you. You would have been lucky to have me, you old goat!" William continued to push his son away from the dreadful noise that disguised itself as her voice. It had been another eventful day for all, but William knew he did the right thing. Jonathan looked up at Rose and smiled. Finally, they could both breathe a much-needed sigh of relief.

Jonathan made his way into his house and was shocked at what he found. The place was spotless, as Daniel had everything looking better than when they moved in at the beginning of their junior year. Jonathan just laughed and stood in amazement. "Man, I've seen everything now," said Jonathan, while he went straight to his favorite chair. "My roommate actually cleaned the place. I don't think this has ever happened before. He must not be feeling well or something." William and Rose laughed along with Jonathan, and it felt good to be happy once again. All of them knew this was a special day for Jonathan because he was very fortunate just to be alive. William was grateful to have his son back, as he knew just how close he had come to losing him. Never again would he take anything for granted because the helplessness he felt as Jonathan lay in his hospital bed was something he would never forget. Rose was also feeling grateful for what had transpired and could feel herself falling in love with this man. From the time he was admitted into the hospital, Rose knew there was something different about him. He made her heart skip a beat, and she found herself thinking about him all the time. To have Jonathan out of the hospital and resting at home was truly miraculous, considering the condition he was in just a week ago. She had never felt this way about anyone before; however, she had no idea where their relationship would eventually lead. The excitement she felt in her heart right now was something she embraced, and she didn't want it to go away. Jonathan and Rose had been brought together by a series of events that started with Tillman, one of the most despicable men on earth. Now, here they were together, each of them forever changed by the bond that was created in Jonathan's hospital room. Jonathan sat back in his chair and felt his mind race with thoughts of where his world may go now that Rose had somehow made it in. How could his feelings be so strong for someone he just met? This was so unlike Jonathan, but he wasn't about to fight the change that was happening from within. His heart had been stolen by the woman who captivated his every thought. His recovery time would be lengthy, but Jonathan knew that Rose would be there with him every step of the way. On this particular day, the peace of knowing that she was with him was all that he needed. Never before had he ever been so grateful for what he had because Rose had brought him peace and happiness, and he knew he would never be the same again.

William knew it was time for him to get back to Rocker because his extended visit had undoubtedly left things in disarray back on the home front. When he got the word that Jonathan had been injured, he left town as quickly as possible. Now, it was time for him to return and try to put everything back together once again. As William made his way down to the bus station for the long ride home, BJ was right by his side. With an extra $50.00 tip, William was able to bring BJ along for the ride, which was exactly what he needed. William was leaving his son behind, and soon he would be walking into the empty house that awaited him. However, things were much better now for him than they were when he got the call. Other than the loneliness that had taken up residency in William's heart since Jesse's passing, he was now at peace with Jonathan's physical condition. The past week had been such a mixture of emotions for him that it was nice to finally have a sense of relief. Knowing that Maggie was out of his life also helped with his mental state of mind, but what would be her next move? There was no chance of her just going away, William thought, as he reflected back on her irrational behavior since Jonathan's fall. William had a feeling that Maggie wasn't getting a lot of offers these days and, more than likely, this would only add to her bitterness toward William regarding the way things ended between them. As much as he hoped she would simply disappear, he knew he would have to be on the lookout for her when he got back home. He really needed to be careful with this woman...

Jonathan's recovery was almost hard to believe, as he went from very little activity to an almost normal routine in just a few weeks. One of the primary reasons for this quick turnaround was the help he received from his constant companion. Rose made sure he did everything by the book and quickly took control of his daily activities. Jonathan had no problem with this and loved every minute of it! He had fallen hard for Rose from day one, and his desire to be with her had escalated ever since. Jonathan had no doubt in his mind that she was the one for him because of the way he felt every time she was near. While Erika Lewis had captured his attention in Tillman's class, his interest in her quickly subsided after his mother's death. His infatuation with Rose, on the other hand, only grew by the minute. Jonathan just couldn't imagine ever losing interest in Rose, as her beauty seemed to mystify him more and more every day. He still thought about Erika often, but only because he was deeply worried about her well-being. She had been through a lot with Tillman, and he knew she would never be able to erase that night from her memory. Jonathan had done everything possible to get rid of those memories as well, but there was still one thing that continued to haunt him on a daily basis. Who in the world was the person who exposed Tillman, the person who left the note, the person who revealed Tillman's sickness in the middle of his own little game? Jonathan continued to wrestle with the events that led up to the infamous evening at Tillman's house, but he just couldn't put his finger on it. If someone else was at his residence that evening, then why didn't Jonathan or Erika notice? Hopefully, something would trigger his thought process and someday it would all make sense.

Bradford was coming up empty-handed back at the precinct, but he still continued to work on the Tillman case. Tillman's death almost went unnoticed by all because he really didn't have any true friends in the community. His list of enemies was huge, as he had trampled on nearly everyone in his path to get to his position. His daughter, Angie, quickly made her way in and out of town and subsequently sold all of his possessions at auction for pennies on the dollar. She had absolutely no interest at all in anything of his, and the opportunistic pack of wolves quickly gathered around the old mansion when the sale took place. Once the frenzy had ended, Angie immediately put the structure up for sale and left town. Every night when he went to bed, Bradford would think about the tips he received regarding Tillman and his ongoing, maniacal act. He knew deep down inside that he would have never busted this case wide open had it not been for the information he received. The person responsible for this act of justice never did step forward, and Bradford knew the chances of it happening now were highly unlikely. Who was this person, and why did he or she not own up to such an admirable act? Bradford just wanted to personally thank the person because he knew that Tillman's ongoing escapades would have never been stopped had it not been for the information he received. Thankfully, someone was finally able to stop him. Bradford just wanted to know who that someone really was...

Erika's life was slowly getting back together again, as she was finally able to move on from the terrible events that had rocked her life just a short while ago. Graduation had been a special time for her, as her mother, Emma, and all her siblings made the trip out to Central Valley State for the ceremony. Erika was looking forward to spending time with her family and getting away from the events of the past couple weeks. Tillman nearly ruined this young girl, and Erika knew it would be very important for her to move on with her life as quickly as possible. She would be forever grateful for her escape from Selera, but Erika knew he would be back again if she let her guard down. Her faith had been elevated to a level she only dreamed of before that gray afternoon in the garage, as God's grace had changed her heart forever. She would never forget the vulnerability she felt while lying on that cold, garage floor. Getting back to the farm would be the best medicine for her; however, losing Jonathan would only be healed by time. She knew his heart belonged to someone else right now, and despite her pain, she was happy for him. More than anything else, Erika wanted to remain close friends with him because of what he had done for her. She knew she would have never made it without him since he was the one who stopped Tillman from carrying through with his plan. Erika realized that she may have never recovered had it not been for Jonathan's willingness to come after her, and for this, she would be forever grateful.

The man could feel his entire body go numb, and he felt like it was slowly being consumed by the enemy that had worked its way inside his door. He looked over to see if he could make out its face, but instead, the figure just stared back at him with eyes that were only a blur. The man began to think back on one of the events that he just couldn't shake free, and then it hit him like a two-by-four right across the face. He quickly played back his life and became fixated on the fall that almost cost him everything. His mind kept taking him back to the man who seemed to come out of nowhere, soon after his car came to a screeching halt after the unexpected flat tire. He could still see that big left hand reach over and shake his, just before he got out of the truck and headed up to the old house at 1551 Brookplace. And then it dawned on him that the big left hand held the key to one of his greatest mysteries! That hand belonged to the same person who had left the notes for Bradford and exposed Tillman for good. The man lay in bed and desperately tried to remember the driver's name, as he continued to play back the ride through the pouring rain. He found himself reaching for names of the past, hoping to prove to himself that he hadn't lost his mind. He lay in desperation and found himself racing against time, hoping the name would somehow work its way to the forefront of his thoughts. Slowly, he felt a smile start to form on his face, as his eyes began to drift off with recollections from the past. "Bill... you old son of a gun you," he whispered, "hope to see you again someday soon." The man closed his eyes and fell into a deep sleep; however, this time he had a smile on his face that wasn't about to break free. Not yet anyway...

Chapter 11

"The Answer, Please"

The months seemed to move by very quickly, and before he knew it, Jonathan had been out of college for almost a year. His relationship with Rose had blossomed into his primary reason for existence, and he was convinced that she was the one he wanted to be with for the rest of his life. Now, it was time for him to see if the feeling was mutual! He was ready to move forward with the most important event of his young life, and he needed to make sure everything was in place. He wanted his proposal to be different than all the rest, unlike anything a girl could ever imagine. He thought about all the ways he could deliver this question, but it needed to be perfect, just like his Rose. Jonathan's stomach was in knots, while he began to think through all the details that would need to be in place in order for him to pull this off. He had finally found the woman who came to his rescue during one of his darkest times, and now it was time for him to show her just how much he truly loved her. Just as he was fighting for his every breath, Rose was brought into his life when he least expected it. He still remembered that first day he laid eyes on her, while resting in his hospital bed. Her perfect silhouette would be forever engrained in his mind, and he never wanted to forget that beautiful smile of hers when their eyes first met. Rose's beauty had captured his heart ever since, and his love for her continued to grow stronger each and every day. She was the one he wanted to be with right now, more than anything he could ever imagine. He never wanted to let her go…

Back in Rocker, William had fallen into a steady routine with his best friend, BJ. He hadn't heard from Maggie since their trip to be with Jonathan, and that was just fine with him. He stopped eating breakfast down at the diner because he was afraid to have any contact with her after what had happened during Jonathan's recovery. She was a problem waiting to happen, and his interest in her had completely disappeared. Over the past couple of months, William felt himself missing Jesse more and more every day. He didn't realize just how truly special she was until she was gone, and now his nights were filled with nothing but distant memories. Even though BJ was his constant companion and seemed to make the days much easier for him, the pain of losing Jesse was still suffocating at times. William could sense that things were getting more and more difficult, as his old baseball injuries were finally starting to take their toll on him. Although the physical challenges seemed to grow on a daily basis, it was his mental aptitude that was digressing the fastest. There were days when William could still remember specific pitches that were thrown to him years ago, but he couldn't remember where he set his shoes from the night before. He kept telling himself that he would somehow find a way to fight through it, but deep down inside, he was scared to death that his symptoms would only get worse. He couldn't imagine being forced out of his home right now because this was where his life was made whole, the place he never wanted to forget. William continued to hide his mental challenges from Jonathan and didn't want to burden him with anything right now. For the first time in his life, Jonathan was truly in love, and William couldn't allow anything to get in the way of his happiness, especially himself. His greatest fear was that he would soon become a burden for Jonathan, which was something he dreaded the most. No matter what the cost, there was no way he would ever let this happen.

"Hello, Mr. Whitney, this is Jonathan Gunn," said Jonathan, while he gathered his breath and spoke into the phone from his apartment. "I've been talking with a lot of people about an idea I have regarding the most important question I'll ever ask. I'm going to ask my girlfriend to marry me, and I have an idea that I hope you can help me with. If I've got any shot at pulling off this plan, I'm going to need to hire the best. Let me tell you what I'd like to do, and then you let me know if you're up to the task. I need the best person available, and everyone has indicated to me that you're the one I need to see," inquired Jonathan, as he waited for Whitney's response. "Son, I never speak poorly about my competition; however, I truly am the best for a job like this. After all, this will be one of the most important days of your life. You can cut corners and take a risk, and things may just work out. However, if you fail, the result could be devastating," said Whitney, as the cagey veteran began to tap into his lifelong experience. There was no way anyone else was going to secure this client, and Whitney would make sure of that! He'd been around forever, and he knew exactly what to say regarding these kinds of discussions. Jonathan could tell Whitney knew what he was doing, which was exactly what Jonathan was looking for. "Whitney, let me walk you through my plan, and then let's see if the date I have in mind is open for you," said Jonathan. "If your date is open, then we have a deal," responded Whitney, as he thought about what Jonathan had said. "I'll move things around to help you out, son. It's been a long time since I've been able to have this much fun on one of my trips. Count me in… just let me know when, and I'll be there." Jonathan took a deep breath and closed his eyes. His big day was getting close, and he felt good about having Whitney on board. Jonathan was confident about one thing…Rose was about to be blown away!

The sun had yet to peek over the horizon, but Jonathan had already been up for nearly two hours thinking through the events of the upcoming day. The weather report was absolutely perfect, as there were no clouds in the forecast. Jonathan would soon be leaving to pick up Rose; however, she had no idea what was in store for her. His only instruction to Rose was to be ready at 5:00 a.m., and he would be there to pick her up. She needed to bring a warm jacket and some sunglasses, but other than that, the only thing needed for the day was her beautiful smile. Jonathan lived for her smile and couldn't wait to make it wider than he had ever seen it before. He pulled up in front of her place; however, the combination of excitement and anxiety was almost more than he could handle. As he made his way to the front door, he could see Rose sitting in her chair. Through the window, he just stared at her while she patiently waited for him to arrive. Before he knocked on the door, he found himself in awe of the most beautiful woman he had ever seen. Oh, how he loved this girl so…she was absolutely gorgeous. Her eyes were the kind that mesmerized her target, and Jonathan was grateful that he had been that benefactor for well over a year now. Jonathan took one more deep breath and reached out for the door. One thing was for certain. This day would change his life forever…one way or the other.

"Hello, Mr. Gunn. Nice to see you this morning," said Whitney, as he watched Jonathan and Rose make their way over to his station. Jonathan gave Whitney the thumbs-up sign, while he slowly led Rose over to where she would be standing. Rose had to be careful because she had never walked this far under such difficult conditions. Being blindfolded was not something she was accustomed to doing! She felt almost helpless, as she gingerly made her way into the compartment that waited below. Jonathan had difficulty helping her because it was still dark outside, and he needed to make sure she got settled in without any incident. Whitney watched from a distance and made sure everything was in place. Jonathan maneuvered his way over to the other side of the platform and waited for Whitney to give him the sign. Rose's smile extended from ear to ear, and she had absolutely no idea what Jonathan was up to. "Rose, I'm about to take you on a journey you'll never forget," said Jonathan, as he reached out and slowly caressed her glowing cheeks. "Please, be patient with the blindfold because I promise that when you take it off, it will be well worth the wait." Rose extended her hands toward Jonathan's face and returned his touch with one of her own. "I love you, Jonathan," responded

Rose. "Thank you for making me feel so special. I trust you with my life, and I always will. I promise I won't take the blindfold off until you tell me to." With that, Jonathan gave Whitney the green light and off they went! Whitney slowly began to turn the valves to the helium cylinders, and almost immediately, the balloon began to rise. Within seconds, the platform was separating itself from the ground below, and the balloon was well on its way to their destination. Whitney signaled over to Jonathan and said, "Well, Mr. Gunn, I do believe we're in for a truly spectacular time here this morning. I'll be taking us to the most beautiful place you and Rose have ever seen. Please, enjoy yourself and let me know if you need anything at all. My job today is to create an experience that neither of you will ever forget. I have no doubt in my mind that you will not be disappointed." Rose reached out and clutched on to Jonathan's right arm, as she felt the canopy begin to rise. Periodically, she could hear the sound of helium shooting up toward the sky, and her heart almost skipped a beat as the balloon was climbing by the second. The blindfold made her pulse race even faster because she had no idea where they were going. Even Jonathan wasn't quite ready for what was yet to come.

As the balloon continued to climb over the outline of the canyon below, Jonathan's entire body became numb as he looked out toward the direction they were going. Whitney had maneuvered the balloon into the most spectacular view imaginable, as it seemed to hit its apex just as the sun began to fully extend over the horizon. Jonathan found himself hypnotized by the view in front of him and, almost in slow motion, he looked over at his beautiful Rose as well. On one side of him was the most spectacular view he had ever seen, while the balloon seemed to almost stop in mid-flight. With the canyon of the Columbia River on his left side and the most beautiful woman he had ever seen on his right, the timing was perfect for him to move forward with his plan. He signaled over to Whitney and took a deep breath. Jonathan's hands began to sweat, and he felt like his heart was going to pound through his chest. He smiled over at Whitney and gave him the nod he had been waiting for…everything was in perfect position for him to move forward. Jonathan reached over and began to untie the blindfold, and Rose slowly opened her eyes. She wasn't ready for the view that was waiting for her, as tears began to well up with no warning whatsoever. Rose was speechless and looked over at Jonathan, while he began to reach up into the balloon. Gently, he tugged on the string that had made its way to the bottom of the opening…and out came the ring. The setting could not have been more breathtaking, as Rose watched Jonathan clutch on to the most beautiful ring she had ever seen in her life. Slowly, Jonathan fell to one knee and began to ask the most important question of his life, "Rose, from the first day I saw you in my hospital room, I've been in love with you. You came into my life when I needed you the most, and I've never been the same ever since. Every moment of every day, I dream about you and what life means to me now that you're here. I can't imagine not being with you, and I want to spend every waking moment with you by my side. In my hand, I have my mother's ring. Growing up, my mom was everything to me. She was always there for me, and I'll never forget all the sacrifices she made on my behalf. I wish she was here now to meet you because I know she'd fall in love with you just like I did. I know she'd be honored to have you wear her ring because of all you stand for...you truly are the most remarkable woman I've ever met. I'm so in love with you, and I want to spend the rest of my life with you. I promise I'll never leave you, and I'll always be there for you, no matter what. Rose, will you marry me?" Rose gathered her thoughts and looked into the eyes of the man she loved with all her heart and soul. "Jonathan, it would be an honor to be your wife. I want to spend the rest of my life with you. Yes, I'll marry you! I love you! I love you!" Jonathan wrapped his arms around Rose and held her with all his might. Whitney watched on and felt a tear begin to form in the corner of his eye as well. Quickly, he turned his head and wiped the tear away, hoping not to be seen. He had never been married before, but this would be the way he would want it if it were him. The sun's warmth seemed to reach out and grab Jonathan and Rose, as if it were comforting them on the first official day of their journey. The proposal was absolutely perfect, Jonathan thought, as he and Rose continued to embrace each other above the canyon below. His dream had finally come true...and he would never be alone again.

The wedding took place eight months later on a beautiful, September day. Pictures started at 10:00 a.m. that morning, while the marriage ceremony was scheduled to begin at 11:00 a.m. William came by himself, but he did have BJ accompany him on the drive to the much-anticipated event. His best buddy was with him no matter where he went, and the wedding would be no exception. BJ wasn't too happy about sitting out in the truck during the festivities, but William really had no other choice. He knew BJ could cause quite a disruption if he was given free rein on the place. Rose's family would be present as well, and her father would be giving her away. He absolutely loved Jonathan and felt grateful that his daughter had picked such a terrific, young man to accompany her through life. The pictures were taken quickly, and everyone proceeded to the church. Jonathan had never been this nervous before, but he knew without a doubt that Rose was the perfect woman for him. He watched from behind the alter, while everyone started to make their way into the church. Jonathan could see all the familiar faces that he grew up with, friends that went all the way back to Little League. It made him think again about all the great times he had playing baseball and all the support he got along the way. He couldn't help but remember his mom and how much he loved her when he was a kid. Oh, how he wished she was here with him today. He would have loved for her to meet Rose because they were very much alike. Back then, his dad was a much different man than he was today. Jesse's death had brought the two of them together, and Jonathan felt closer to William than he ever had before. He watched his dad mingle through the church and slowly get settled in. William would be Jonathan's best man on this special day. Through thick and thin, he had become his closest friend and his biggest supporter. Having him stand by Jonathan's side was what Jonathan wanted most, and he was proud to have him there.

The wedding march slowly started up, and Jonathan could hardly maintain his composure. He stood and watched Rose enter the church, the most beautiful sight he had ever seen. She was gorgeous, and her radiant smile captivated every set of eyes in the church. Jonathan just watched in amazement, as she made her way closer and closer to where he was standing. He felt tears begin to form and quickly tried to divert his attention by thinking of something else. However, this just wasn't possible. Rose was absolutely breathtaking, and he simply didn't want to take his eyes off of her. Her father slowly reached out to Jonathan with Rose on his arm and said with tears in his eyes as well, "Please, take care of my Rosie always, Jonathan." Jonathan responded, "I promise I will, sir. Thank you for trusting me with her." And with that, Rose's dad made his way back to his seat. Now, her heart officially belonged to Jonathan, and Rose reached out and held on to his arm with everything she had. The transition over to her new life was officially set in motion. Jonathan and Rose stared into each other's eyes, while their vows were read. Jonathan was ready to make their marriage official by putting the ring on her finger, and William handed it over to him. As Jonathan looked down at the beautiful diamond, he remembered seeing this ring on the finger of his mom when he was just a kid. He couldn't help but remember how happy his mom was when she wore that ring. She was always so proud to be William's wife, regardless of the circumstances. Oh, how Jonathan longed for that same feeling with Rose. He reached for the ring and then slowly put it on Rose's finger. It was a perfect fit, and Jonathan and Rose were officially husband and wife. Years later, Jonathan would always look back at this moment in time as his best ever...the day that he was officially made whole.

The years went by quickly, and Jonathan and Rose settled into their new life. Rose continued to work at the hospital; however, the long hours and time away from Jonathan had taken their toll on her. Jonathan worked himself into a director's role at the local Teen Rebuilding Center, as his heart was still with helping kids who had gone down the wrong path. He and Rose had wanted to start a family for quite some time, but numerous fertility complications continually got in the way. Although they were cautioned that a pregnancy could impose a significant risk, they continued to remain optimistic that they would someday be able to raise a family together. Their desire was to become happy parents, just like so many of their friends. That day of optimism finally became a reality for Jonathan, as Rose was waiting at the front door after a long day at the office. "Honey, I have some terrific news. Doctor Radtkey's office called today and said I'm pregnant. The tests just got in this morning, and it looks like I'm right at the eight-week mark. Can you believe it, honey? We're finally going to have our baby!" screamed Rose, as she jumped into Jonathan's arms. "Now, you're sure. They aren't making a mistake on this, are they? Oh my gosh, I can't believe it. I'm going to be a father. No way. Oh my...holy cow!" gasped Jonathan, while he made his way over to the couch. He felt like he was going to pass out. On the one hand, he had never been this excited in his entire life. On the other, he was scared to death. "Sit down, honey. It's going to be ok," laughed Rose. "You're going to be a great father...simply the best, I'm sure. We just need to find a way to make sure you don't have a heart attack before the baby gets here!"

"You're doing very well, Rose. You've now been pregnant for just over three months and everything is looking good", said Dr. Radtkey, as he continued to examine one of his favorite patients. "Jane indicated that you wanted to have an amniocentesis done today, which is something most of our couples choose to do nowadays. Quite honestly, I'd do the same thing if I were you. Since you're in your early-thirties, the chance of you having any problems is minimal. Obviously, it doesn't mean that there can't be any issues; it just means that the probability of having a complication is quite low. Do you or Jonathan have any questions before we get started with the test?" asked Dr. Radtkey. "No, I think everything is pretty straight forward," said Rose. "Do you have any questions, Jonathan?" asked Rose, as she turned toward Jonathan to see how he was doing. "No, I'm doing fine, honey," responded Jonathan. "I just want to make sure you're feeling ok and that you're comfortable." Deep down inside, Jonathan was afraid, just like every other first-time father. He couldn't stand the thought of anything ever happening to his Rose. She was the love of his life, the one who had changed everything for him. He just wanted this pregnancy, and his new baby, to be perfect. The test results for the amnio would be available soon and then he could relax...maybe. Work had taken a back seat to his family right now, which was exactly the way it needed to be. He had a feeling that it would always be this way. Nothing in Jonathan's life would ever be more important than Rose and his soon-to-be newborn child. This he would be certain of...

William lay in bed, afraid to move, as he could feel his chest tighten and his left shoulder go numb. He began to sweat profusely and could sense something was terribly wrong. He rolled over and fell to the floor, as he began to reach for the telephone that hopefully would get him the help he needed. Slowly, he pulled himself closer and closer toward the dresser. He could see the receiver sitting up near his alarm clock, but it was just out of reach. BJ came running into the room because he could sense something was happening to his best friend. BJ whimpered and tried to help William; however, there was nothing he could do. William needed to get to that phone, but there just wasn't any way he could garner up enough strength to make it. William knew he was in real trouble, as beads of sweat dropped from his forehead to the floor below. He rolled up into the fetal position, while this somehow seemed to make the pain temporarily subside. He didn't want to move…and he didn't want to die. He started to think about all the things he loved so much, how he and Jonathan had somehow mended the fences that were broken years ago. William was grateful for this because it had given him the peace he so desperately needed at this time in his life. He also started to think about all the wonderful times he had experienced with Jesse when he was younger, how she was the rock that kept his family together. He thought about how great it would be to see her again. But…what if she was waiting for him in heaven, and he didn't make it? He knew she was in heaven because she was always rock-solid in her faith. She had always professed herself to be a believer, but William had no interest in what this really meant. "A believer, what in the world does that mean?" he would say. "I'm tired of hearing about your believing. That's just the stupidest thing I've ever heard." The words uttered from years gone by were suddenly brought back to life, and William would give anything to take them back right now. Oh, how he wished he would have asked Jesse how he could have been one of those believers, how he could have been just like her. William felt his entire body start to slow down, and he could tell it was nearly time for him to go. He wanted to say a prayer, but he was way too tired. If only he would have prayed when he had the chance to, he thought, as he cried out to nothing but darkness and silence. He wanted to be with Jesse again, but there was no way. She was in a different place than he was going, and he felt scared and all alone. Peace had left his body, while he began to contemplate his final resting place. Oh, what he would give for a second chance at redemption. But…it was too late. Suddenly, his head hit the floor and he was gone. BJ lay next to him and licked his face, hoping for his eyes to open, but they didn't. William Gunn was dead, and the room went still.

"Mr. Gunn, this is Officer Swenson from the Rocker Police Department. Am I catching you at a bad time? I need to speak with you for a few minutes," said the officer, as he mentally prepared himself to deliver the bad news. This was one of the things he hated the most, a part of the job that he would never get used to. Delivering this kind of news over the phone just didn't seem right, but he needed to let him know. William had nobody else, and Jonathan needed to get the news quickly before the word got to him through some other channel. "Your father was found dead this morning, Mr. Gunn. He had a heart attack in his bed and couldn't make it to the phone to call for help. I'm real sorry to deliver this bad news to you, son, but I wanted you to know as soon as possible. We just got over here about 20 minutes ago and your dad was pronounced dead on the scene. It looks like it happened quickly, so hopefully he didn't suffer. Can I do anything for you right now, son?" asked Officer Swenson, as he sat down in the chair and let out a deep breath. Jonathan was numb. He didn't know what to say. His dad was gone now too, and his children would never meet either of his parents. Jonathan started to cry because the thought of his dad dying at home all alone made the pain cut even deeper. Oh, how he wished he would have been there for him; how he wished he could have done something to help him during his final moments. He and his dad had become very close since Jesse's death, and he knew his life was never going to be the same again. There was a lot of wasted time to make up, but now it was over. Soon, Jonathan would need to head back home because there was nobody else left to go through all of William's belongings. Jonathan had now lost both his mom and dad, and he began to think about all the things he could have done for them before they were gone. Guilt began to suffocate Jonathan with the thought of the potential events that led up to his sudden loss. If only he had one more day with his dad, one more day to hold him tight and tell him just how much he loved him. Unfortunately, the one day he needed most, had disappeared, never to be found again.

Out from behind the plank in the wall they came, one-by-one, as they marched toward William's body lying on the floor. Selera allowed his entourage to lead the way toward the prize he wanted for his own. His inability to take Erika's life back in the garage was still eating at him; however, William's soul would provide him with a brief sense of reprieve. Selera had been assigned to the Gunn family and all of their close friends by Satan himself, and he was focused on making sure that this particular victim was his for the taking. This meant that Selera's assignment was very clear, with no room for error. He was given clear direction to target the soul of any non-believer within this circle and ensure that their final destination was with him. He was also provided with the distinct privilege of delivering these souls after they died. Since William had never accepted Jesus Christ as his Savior and had turned his back on his own personal salvation, he would now be paying the ultimate price. He would belong to Selera, and he would be the one who would ultimately deliver him to his boss as well. Selera's team quickly moved into William's body as he lay still. Out came the soul in a matter of minutes, while Selera anxiously waited for its delivery. They handed it to him and slowly squealed in unison. The sound was deafening, but only to their ears, as this activity could not be picked up by any earthly forms of life that were nearby. This win would help ease the pain of Erika getting away earlier, but Selera would never give up. He would continue to go after Erika and anyone else who fell under his jurisdiction. Selera thought back on Jesse from years gone by and quickly became angry because of her escape. She had been off limits due to her faith; however, with William it would be much different. This would make Selera look good to his boss, which was what he needed most after the Erika debacle. However, he would never give up. Someday, he may even have the opportunity to take Jonathan's soul with him. This would help make up for Jesse's salvation, thought Selera, as he made his way back to his hole. For now, he would focus his attention on what he came for because William's aftermath would definitely score him some much-needed points. He couldn't wait to take William home to his boss. Selera knew this would make him very, very happy...

Jonathan made his way back to Rocker soon after he received the call from Officer Swenson. Jonathan insisted that Rose stay back until he determined what needed to be done in order to get all the funeral plans in place. He didn't want any unnecessary distraction for Rose and was willing to come back and get her if need be. Jonathan pulled up in front of his house, and there were two police cars parked near the old mailbox that read "The Gunn Family". That old box hadn't changed for years, Jonathan thought, as he could still remember his mother saying they should repaint it before the weather sets in. The painting upgrade never happened, and the letters were even more faded now than back when Jesse made her suggestion. He felt sick to his stomach, while he made his way through the front door. "You must be Jonathan," said Officer Swenson, as he met Jonathan just inside the front porch. "Yes, sir, I'm Jonathan Gunn. I assume you're Officer Swenson?" asked Jonathan. "Yes I am, son. I just want you to know that we're all very sorry about your father. We all knew about your dad growing up. Any of us who ever played baseball around here all had heard of William Gunn. I heard your father was really something else." "Thanks, Officer Swenson. I appreciate all you've done here. My dad was a great guy. He was a terrific father, that's for sure, and I'm really going to miss him a lot. Over the years, he had also become my best friend. Where is his body now?" said Jonathan, as he fought hard to choke back the tears that seemed to be pressing on the inside of his eyes. "His body is still back in his room, Jonathan. In fact, the coroner just left a short while ago and will be sending his team in here soon to take the body out. However, we did ask him to give us a little extra time because we were hoping you'd make it here before they took him away. We just thought it was important for you to see where he was when he died. Like I told you on the phone, he went pretty quickly. I don't think he was in any pain when he died, based on the fact that it happened so fast. The coroner, old Doc Mason, said he felt the same way."

Jonathan slowly made his way into his dad's bedroom because he needed to see him one last time. He knew his appearance would change once the embalmers got involved; therefore, it was important for him to see his dad alone before they took him away. As he walked into the room, Jonathan's sadness transformed into one of fear, and he felt like he was going to throw up. There was a presence in his dad's room that was unlike anything he had ever experienced before. In fact, the room felt damp and cold, due to the draft that seemed to be blowing in from the floor vent. Jonathan cupped his fingers and blew into his hands. From a distance, Jonathan looked over at the vent and for whatever reason; this was as close as he wanted to get to the darkness that seemed to be calling out his name. Never before had this room ever felt like this, as Jonathan could still remember the sweet fragrance of his mother and the warmth that was there throughout his days as a child. He slowly made his way over to his father's body and leaned down to take one last look. As he stared into his face, Jonathan could feel his heart begin to race uncontrollably. Fear seemed to paralyze his body, and he began to think about his father's final minutes before he was gone. Jonathan could still remember when his mother died, and her look was much different than what he was staring at right now. There was a sense of peace when she died, and even though it was a very sad time for Jonathan, he knew she was in heaven because of that indescribable look on her face. This was much different today. William's body seemed to be contorted to one side, and his expression was one of total emptiness. His body almost looked like it was being tormented, like something was now residing inside him. Jonathan took one last look and quickly began to head for the door. He wanted to get out of that room because this person lying on the floor was undoubtedly not his father anymore. Jonathan made his way out the front door and fell to his knees and began to sob uncontrollably. As he wiped the sweat from his brow, he realized that his dad may not be with his mother right now in heaven. The thought of them being apart was more than he could bear, as he covered his eyes and began to whimper like a wounded puppy. And even though he wanted to get his father's face out of his mind, he just couldn't shake it free. That look…that empty look of death. It was something he would never forget, no matter how hard he tried.

Jonathan refused to stay at his house that night because he knew it would be far too difficult to be there alone. Not only would the sadness be overwhelming, he just couldn't erase the thought of that look on his dad's face. Instead of staying at home, he found a local hotel that would allow him to bring BJ as well, and they settled in just after 9:00 that evening. Jonathan needed to speak with Rose because he was in dire need of her perspective right now. As much as he wanted to tell her about his dad and what he saw, the last thing he wanted to do was upset her. He just needed to hear her reassuring voice and somehow forget about what had just taken place over at his house. She would bring him peace, he thought, as he made his way over to the phone that lay next to his bed in the room. "Hello," said Rose, as she answered the phone. "Hi, honey. Sorry I didn't call you earlier, but this has been quite a night. I went over to see my dad, and then I needed to answer some questions, just routine stuff, for the officer on charge. They were nice guys and really helped me tonight. BJ and I are here at the hotel, not far from the house. I just couldn't stay there tonight, honey. I hope that's ok. It was just way too tough to be there after what happened to my dad. How are you doing?" Rose took a deep breath and was happy to finally deliver some good news for Jonathan. She knew it would come at a perfect time; however, she hoped he was sitting down when he got it. "Sweetheart, I know it's been a very long day for you, and I wish I was there with you right now to share this news in person. Dr. Radtkey's office called with the results from the amnio, and the news is good. I just hope you're ready for it right now?" Jonathan sat back in his chair, rubbed the back of BJ's neck, and responded, "Please, give me some good news, honey. This has been a very long day." "Dr. Radtkey said everything looked great with the test. Looks like we're going to have two healthy babies, a boy and a girl," said Rose, as she waited patiently for an answer. Silence was all she got. "Jonathan, are you still there?" she asked. "Yes, I'm still here, but I think I heard you say two babies. Is that what you just said or do we have a bad connection?" asked Jonathan. "Yes, that's what I said, dear. Two babies, a boy and a girl. Is that ok, Jonathan? Are you ready for two babies, honey?" Jonathan buried his head in his hands and slowly began to cry. Rose could hear him on the other end of the phone but didn't say anything. "This is the best news you could have ever given me tonight. Thanks, babe. I love you more than you will ever know. I'm going to get things organized here in the morning, and then I'll head back home to get you for the funeral. A hug from you is the best medicine I could ever ask for with all that's happened. I can't wait to feel your arms around me once again. That's what I really need right now." Rose just smiled and closed her eyes. There was no way she could ever love anything more than she loved Jonathan…he always knew exactly what to say to make her feel perfect.

The funeral brought William's friends from near and far. Most of the attendees lived in the Rocker area, but there were a large number of folks who came in from out of state as well. Jonathan was completely blown away at all the support he got from everyone who was there; however, he just couldn't shake the thought of what he saw in his dad's room on the night of his death. He kept going back to the man he saw in his room shortly after he died; this was not the man he knew. That look…Jonathan just couldn't shake that look. It was almost as if someone, or something, had already taken over his body. And the cold, damp feeling that Jonathan felt when he was in the room with his dad...what was that? Jonathan practically grew up in that room, and it never felt like that before. Something had happened to his dad after he died, and it scared Jonathan more than anything he had ever been around in his life. No matter how much he wanted to discuss it with Rose, he said nothing to her. He would keep it to himself for now because it was important that she focus on her upcoming delivery. Whatever that feeling was, Jonathan knew he never wanted it to get close to his children after they were born. If only he knew what it was, he would do something about it right now. He had never been exposed to that kind of emptiness before, and it was unlike anything he had ever felt in his life. Jonathan knew he didn't like it one bit. It was as if he had touched death itself when he was with his dad in that room; the kind of death that represented something he hoped would never set foot in his life ever again. It was the kind of death that one stayed away from, the kind that was never talked about while growing up. Why? Because it represented the darkness that was hidden from the world we all live in. Oh, how it broke Jonathan's heart to think that maybe, just maybe, his dad was part of that frightening world right now. If only he could reach out and take him back, he would. Jonathan knew it was too late for him to do anything, and that was what hurt him the most.

Chapter 12

"The Final Hour"

The twins were born without any complications, and Jonathan and Rose were the proud parents of two beautiful, healthy children. Jonathan had never been happier in his life, as he graciously posed for pictures with his perfect family. The smile never left his face because he was given something far more beautiful than anything he could have ever imagined. His son, Jake, and his daughter, Jesse, quickly became the light of his life. The memories were abundant and every day was an adventure, but the days were here and gone before they knew it. Just like all parents experience firsthand, Jonathan and Rose would look back at their time with the kids with both gratification and regret. Gratification for all the wonderful things they did as a family...but regret for not doing more. Before they knew it, the kids were no longer kids and they were off on their own. And that is when it all happened. Without any advanced warning, their worlds were about to be rocked like never before. Something that began as a relatively harmless pain in the lower back soon became something far more serious. Before they knew it, their lives were completely flipped upside down, and now they were dealing with their greatest challenge imaginable. Life's real purpose was multiplied exponentially on a daily basis, and every breath seemed to contain more relevance than the one before. Each day truly had meaning because there was a realistic, finite endpoint attached to them, and they knew it. Jonathan and Rose had loved each other for the past 30 years, and the thought of going through life alone at this juncture was more than either of them could handle. However, it was a reality, and now the two of them were scrambling for lost time before it was too late. The sequence of events was like a nightmare gone mad. The pain came on a Monday, intensified to the point of an excruciating level by Thursday, a trip to the doctor and specialist by Friday, and results back the following Monday. In one week, their lives were changed, and everything was torn apart. What started out as lower back pain was quickly diagnosed as pancreatic carcinoma, and the prognosis was not good. The problem with this type of cancer is that by the time the symptoms are felt, the tumor is more than likely at an advanced stage. Life had thrown the two of them a curveball that may not get fouled off this time around. This could, in fact, be their last turn at bat.

To go back in time and have the opportunity to relive the lives of his children was exactly what Jonathan needed right now; however, his dream was about to come to an abrupt end. It was time for him to wake up and tackle the day, a day that may, in fact, be his last. Oh, how he wanted to go back in time, back to when Jake and Jesse were born. "Please, let me go back one more time," he begged to himself. "Please, give me another chance to do it all over again. Just one more time is all I ask." Unfortunately, his cry for help was being offset by a deadly tumor that was just starting to pick up steam. The cancer started out in his pancreas and soon made its way into the surrounding organs as well. It moved like a wildfire, and it took everything healthy with it. Good cells were the target, and they soon disappeared like a thief in the night. Jonathan could feel his body try to fight off this deadly rage inside him, but the destruction the tumor caused was something nobody could ever prepare for. He knew he was no match for the aggressive nature of this unsuspected enemy, as it had taken up residency inside him under its own terms. The tumor seemed to be laughing in his face, daring him to take it on. Jonathan was no match for this particular opponent, and deep down inside, he knew this would undoubtedly be his last stand. As difficult as it would be, he would never let it show to his family. He would fight with everything he had, and he would reflect an image of strength and courage in the eyes of his family. But...deep down inside, he was afraid. He was deeply afraid of what was yet to come...

Jonathan could sense he had visitors to check up on him once again, and quickly, the prodding would begin. These were the kinds of visitors a person never wants to wake up to, the ones in the white jackets looking for answers. The only good thing, he thought, was that he was back in Rocker Memorial Hospital where it all began over 50 years ago, almost to the day. This was where Jonathan was born, and he felt a small degree of peace knowing that he was back here at home in familiar surroundings. Jonathan Gunn was a dying man, and oh, how he wanted his life back. Rose looked over at the man she loved with all her heart and soul, as he seemed to be disappearing right in front of her eyes. Fear had wrapped its ugly claws around Rose, and it seemed to be squeezing her with every breath. How would she handle the days that were in front of her? How would their children react to the loss of their father? Numerous questions continued to swirl around in her head, as Rose attempted to play out every scenario that was potentially in front of her right now. And then, for the first time ever, she began to think about where Jonathan would be going when he died. Before today, she thought about this next stop, but it was always just part of a discussion, no different than any other subject. Just like so many of their friends, in one breath they were talking about heaven and hell, and in the next, they were discussing something totally irrelevant like a ballgame that took place over the weekend. However, now the discussion about one's final resting place was real. Rose knew a little bit about heaven and hell, but she really didn't like to think about what happened when a person died. The subject literally scared her half to death so she stayed away from it, just like so many other friends she knew. Today was different though. As she watched Jonathan grimace with the pain that had now overtaken his body, she began to realize that he could be leaving her soon, and that she may never see him again. However, where would he be going? This was the question that was starting to eat at Rose, that almost seemed to tease her in her time of need. Unbeknownst to Rose, there were other forces around her that had now entered into this equation as well. Little did she know that these forces would have a direct influence on his final destination. The battleground for Jonathan's soul was being established, and the key players were about to enter the building. Rose had no idea what was happening around her, which was a good thing. There was no way she could have survived the maneuvering that was now taking place because the ultimate prize was at stake. All players knew that this was not a trophy, plaque, or meaningless form of recognition. This was the soul…the most treasured gift of all. Jonathan's final destination was up for grabs, and the fight between good and evil was officially ready to begin.

They entered the old warehouse in single file, each following the lead of the other in front. For nearly a century, this underground coalition of soul savers had been meeting weekly throughout the country. Their ability to stay out of the public's eye and keep everything under wraps was truly incredible, considering they had been on the firing line of taking on the enemy for such a long time. The concept was relatively simple; however, their ability to implement such a plan was incomprehensible when one looked at the intricacies of the organization that was formed long ago. Their corporate structure was buttoned down with a definitive chain of command, clearly understood by all. They were known internally as the Janitor Brigade, and they had infiltrated nearly ever hospital in the country. Their call to action was quite simple. In every hospital, there were a very high percentage of patients who died every night without any salvation whatsoever. When this happened, Satan would be waiting in the wings with his team, quickly devouring their souls and taking them with him for his own. The Janitor Brigade's mission had one metric of measurement, and that was to get to these patients before they were gone. Their job was to save as many of these dying patients as possible before their final breath was taken. Discussing Jesus before they were gone was their assignment; however, they also needed to make sure the dying patient was willing to accept Him into their hearts with no compromise whatsoever. Although many of the patients called upon passed away before this divine exchange was able to take place, the Brigade's ability to save these souls before they took their final breath was staggering. Even though it was impossible to get to every patient in every hospital before they died, the Brigade's hit rate with those that were visited was extremely high. However, at every juncture, the opposition was extensive as well. In many cases, an entire life hung in the balance until that final breath was taken. At that point, souls were taken to either heaven or hell. There was no in-between, and the Brigade knew it.

Training of the chosen janitors was extensive and included distinct factors before they were brought into the Brigade. First of all, the janitor identified for each hospital needed to have an unwavering heart for God and a true willingness to take on the opposition, no matter what the cost may be. This opposition could impose significant danger to the assigned janitor, as the spiritual war at this last battlefield was indescribable. The janitor sworn into the Brigade needed to have a clear understanding of what this coalition truly meant. Their life would no longer be the same, and their assignment to the targeted hospital meant that saving souls was the primary focus in their life, regardless of when the opportunity presented itself. They would be on call 24/7 while they were in the Brigade, and this was made clear to them before they agreed to the terms. Secondly, the identity of the Brigade needed to remain a secret; therefore, anyone chosen would be sworn into this divine pact with extensive background checks intensely conducted as well. No family member would know about the Brigade, and the janitor chosen would only be known as just that...a janitor...within his circle of friends and family. His employer knew absolutely nothing about the Brigade as well. The janitor simply worked for the hospital and met the requirements of his job. However, this appearance of "only a janitor" provided the individual chosen with the perfect umbrella of protection when it came to the Brigade. These janitors had total access to the floors and were looked upon by hospital staff as a non-threatening extension of the environment they worked in. The Brigade was something that nobody on the outside knew about because their entire organization would be placed in significant jeopardy if there was ever a leak. Through the grace of God Himself, the Brigade had never brought on a member that compromised the identity of the organization. Nearly every single hospital in the country had a member of the Brigade assigned to it, and not one of them had ever been exposed. Finally, the patient targeted needed to be the perfect fit. Accessibility to the patient was critical, and timing needed to be ideal as well. Never could a member of the Brigade subjectively choose one patient over another because every patient was viewed in the eyes of the Lord as being equal. God would lead the janitor down the path that had been presented; therefore, it was imperative that the janitor continually turn to God for direction. Some patients would be targeted in the middle of the night, while others would be targeted during the day; it all depended on their final hour. The timing was left up to the Lord Himself; however, it was critical that the assigned janitor be willing to move quickly when the sign was given. Not every patient targeted was saved because just like during their days when they were healthy, personal salvation would come down to personal choice. In addition, it had to come from the heart and not just the lips. This was when it became very difficult because many patients were totally incoherent during their final hours. Therefore, the patient's understanding of what he or she was doing at the time of this intervention needed to be clearly understood for salvation to take hold. If this was not the case, then their eternal resting place was subsequently put at risk. And finally, one of the greatest challenges experienced was the opposition at this stage of the game. The enemy was manning this battlefield with their highest ranking personnel because this was where most souls were still up for grabs...right up to the very last breath. Janitors on this final battlefield needed to be ready for anything because the enemy would stop at nothing. There were no rules regarding the battle, as the prize was far too valuable for good sportsmanship. Everything, when it came to a man or woman's soul, was considered fair game.

James had been assigned to Rocker Memorial Hospital for a number of years and was considered to be a true warrior in the eyes of the Lord. He was one of the strongest members of the Brigade because he had saved thousands of souls over his illustrious career. James would soon be leaving the Brigade, as the daily challenges he faced had started to take its toll on him. However, since James was still assigned to the hospital, he approached every day on the job like it was his first. He had an incredible memory, which allowed him to keep a very close eye on the patients as they came and left the hospital. James realized that his most recent success rate at Rocker Memorial was being watched very closely by the enemy, and he knew that his personal safety was in even more jeopardy than in year's past. He had no doubt in his mind that he needed to be very careful right now in his position. Rumor had started to circulate throughout the Brigade that the enemy would soon be bringing in additional reinforcements to overtake James within Rocker Memorial. Far too many souls had been saved by him, and the enemy was growing tired of these losses. James knew that his success would be targeted by the enemy's strongest soldiers, and he needed to be more diligent than ever regarding everything he did. And just like James lived to save souls, the enemy's job was to deceive them right up until their final breath. Who would the enemy be bringing into Rocker Memorial, and when would he or she rear its ugly head? The battlefield was about to intensify, and not only were the patients in the hospital at risk, James was as well. The enemy viewed the Brigade as a major threat to his web of deception; therefore, James was one of his primary targets. Every possible temptation would be thrown his way, and it would be imperative that James maintain his absolute focus and spiritual strength. This was the only way James would be able to survive…and he knew it.

In many instances, James was the final person who could speak to the dying patient before they were gone, and his objective was crystal clear. For those patients who had been saved during their lifetime, his job was to reinforce the decision they had made to ultimately accept Jesus Christ into their hearts as their personal Savior. James found that these discussions were the easiest for him to have because he could sense an incredible peace in the heart of the dying patient. Although their passing was always sad, James knew that these patients would be spending their eternity in heaven, and this gave him an incredible sense of joy and serenity. During their final hour, James would keep these patients focused on the decision they had made, which allowed for a peaceful departure from this earth. On the other hand, there were also the discussions that reflected the intensely painful part of his job, as far too many faced the painful stench of death itself. This was the part of the job that truly broke James' heart. Many of these patients didn't want to hear about Jesus because bitterness had taken over their hearts and minds long ago. For these patients, James would continually try to overcome this negativity through God's Word, but some wanted nothing at all to do with it. No matter how hard he tried, James would often find his words to simply fall on deaf ears. Many patients had been duped by the enemy long ago that they were either not worthy of heaven, or that it was too late for their own personal salvation. James knew both of these perceptions were false; however, he also knew that his opponent would stop at nothing to mislead his targets and play out this final act of deception. James' job was to share the Word of God with these patients and do all he could to help save their souls before it was too late. Fortunately, a high percentage of them realized that this was, in fact, their last chance to be saved. For these patients, pride had finally vanished and personal salvation was attained. This was what made James' position, as part of the Brigade, so incredibly valuable. But…in order for this salvation to occur, the timing had to be absolutely perfect. It would have been so much easier, James thought, had these patients been saved before they were in their death bed. He couldn't help but wonder why so many had waited until now. For most, their wait would cost them everything because their souls were gone before James could take the Lord's lead and intercede. He wanted to save every single assignment he received, but this was not possible. This was the part of his job that he would never get used to, the part that he could never accept.

James had become one of the most successful members of the Brigade because he simply wouldn't give up. All James needed was an opening, and he would do everything possible to spread the Word of God. He'd been doing this now for almost 20 years; however, James could sense that the battleground at Rocker Memorial Hospital was ready to intensify to levels he had never seen before. Since James had the highest save rate in the country for the past 10 years running, Satan didn't like his personal accolades one bit. He was about to make a change in his own army, and he believed he had the perfect answer to overcome James and get rid of him once and for all. He needed to bring in someone who knew the playing field well; someone who could make an immediate impact and send James reeling from day one. His choice became an easy one, as he was about to reassign an old nemesis to the area. Rocker Memorial was ready to feel this change of guard, and James would need to be ready. From this point forward, one thing was certain. No patient was safe...

Jonathan was barely into his second week of intense treatment, and Rose was already getting worn out. She and Jonathan both agreed that they would only notify the kids regarding Jonathan's serious condition if it became obvious that he wasn't going to make it. The last thing they needed right now was for the kids to be flying back to Rocker and disrupting their lives for something that may not happen. Whether it was self-denial or the unwillingness to give up, they both felt strongly that they would only burden Jake and Jesse if there was no other option. Deep down inside, Rose was beginning to wonder if they were getting close to this discussion since it had become obvious to her that Jonathan's condition was deteriorating each and every day. Rose had spent every night in the hospital since Jonathan arrived, and she could feel her personal stamina beginning to run out. Both agreed that a couple of night's sleep would be good medicine for her right now because they knew the situation would only get more intense in the coming days. Jonathan's medication was being dispensed at a higher rate every night, as the pain in his back had greatly intensified since the initial diagnosis came their way. Pancreatic cancer was the immediate enemy for Jonathan, but just like every other patient in the hospital, there was a spiritual war going on that represented the most important battle of all...the battle of salvation. James hunkered down and prayed with all the strength he had because he knew God would be his one true answer during his time of need. He had no idea where his enemy would show up next, but he had to be ready for anything. The battle was officially on, and James would be in the crossfire once again...

The clock struck 2:00 a.m., as James slowly made his way out to the west wing of the hospital. This was the telemetry unit, which acted as a sort of step-down repository of patients who had just been upgraded from critical to stable condition. This was one of James' primary targets because he had experienced considerable success in this area over the years. There were a couple of reasons why James spent so much time in this unit. The patients on this floor were coherent and clearly understood the discussions that were taking place. In addition, James had easy access to all the rooms in the unit, due to a lower degree of nursing supervision on the floor. He had developed a predictable routine over the years and had befriended key nurses on each of the floors that he cleaned on a regular basis. This rapport became a critical component regarding the access he enjoyed because James would simply become part of the environment and clean around any activity that was taking place. He waited for the perfect opportunity to get into the patients' rooms, as this was where he would implement his strategy and converse with the individuals who were resting. The night shift was best for James because most family members had gone home and patient access was easiest. James found that patients were far more receptive at night, and this was typically when he had his greatest success. But…this specific playing field was now on the enemy's radar as well. The night shift, as James knew it, was about to change…

James began to make his way on to the floor and methodically moved closer and closer to the targeted rooms. He carried his mop and surveyed the playing field around him. He prayed for God's guidance and made his way into the first room. Inside was Mrs. Gray, who had been admitted seven days earlier with chronic obstructive pulmonary disease. She was still in very bad shape; however, she had somehow survived this past week and was now at least stabilized enough for James to intervene. Previous discussions with her had been very difficult because she just wasn't in the proper state of mind to clearly understand the importance of the subject at hand. James was hoping that tonight would be different. As he made his way over to Mrs. Gray, he could tell that something, or someone, had gotten to her first. James had been around long enough to recognize the deathly smell of his nemesis, and the bitter aroma seemed to reach out and slap him in the face as he moved closer. Somehow, the enemy must have gotten to Mrs. Gray, and James could only hope that he would be able to intercede quickly. He needed to convince her that Jesus was the only true answer to her salvation, and that her eternal peace rested solely with Him. James moved closer to her body, as she began to turn away from him and look toward the wall. Just as James moved in to see if she was awake, Mrs. Gray turned toward him and her eyes met his straight up! The whites of her eyes were fiery red and her breath smelled like death had recently moved in to stay. James began to speak, but Mrs. Gray immediately put her finger up to his lips and whispered, "I know all about you. Now, get out of here before I call the nurse. I don't want you to set foot in this room ever again. Do I make myself clear?" James was speechless and slowly backed up toward the door. He made his way out into the hallway and sat down in the chair. Sweat formed on his brow, while he could feel his heart begin to race. Only once before in his career had James ever had this happen to him, and that was nearly

15 years ago. The enemy was officially here, and he had sent James a strong message. Somehow, the old serpent had gotten to Mrs. Gray by creating a level of trust. There was a strong possibility that this deception reflected a strategy that James hadn't seen before. He put his head down and began to pray for discernment because he knew it was important for him to clearly assess the playing field he was about to enter. Satan's army was in the hospital, and it was critical for James to identify who was in charge. He realized that this would be an extremely important battle for the entire Brigade, and he could sense that his personal battle would have residual impact on many other areas of the country as well. He needed to pray with absolute focus because this was when he was the strongest. He put his head down and closed his eyes. Immediately, he could feel the Holy Spirit grip him, and peace seemed to resonate throughout his body. He could not be afraid, and he could not hide. He had a fight to fight, and its outcome would be felt by many. As difficult as his job had been in the past, he was heading into uncharted waters now…and there was no turning back.

She made her way into the hospital room and, without hesitation, she was talking with the patient. His name was Neil Gustafson, and he had been in the hospital for the past two weeks. He had been diagnosed with liver cancer six months earlier and, subsequently, had spent numerous days in and out of the hospital since that time. His faith was shaky at best, as Mr. Gustafson had never grown up with any clear direction regarding his eternal destination. However, just like so many other patients who fell on James' watch, Mr. Gustafson represented a perfect example of someone who could go either way as he headed into his final hour. "Hello, Mr. Gustafson. I hope you're feeling better today," the woman said, as she reached over to touch him as he lay on his side. Mr. Gustafson tried to respond, but he happened to be very weak on this particular day. "Why don't you just go to sleep, Mr. Gustafson?" the woman whispered. "There really isn't anything to live for here in this sad world anymore. The quicker you go to sleep and rest, the quicker you'll be with your wife once again. Just go to sleep. Nobody is even going to miss you here. Your life is with her now. She deserves it, don't you think?" With that, Mr. Gustafson looked over at the nurse and began to slowly nod his head in agreement. Wouldn't it be much easier for me to just call it quits and leave this world once and for all, he thought, as he found himself becoming more and more tired by the second. The woman continued to encourage him, and she could see that his life was slowly beginning to fade away. Mr. Gustafson could feel his will to live subside, as his body was beginning to shut down. He glanced up one more time and there she was, eyes piercing through his and on into his soul. Her smile seemed to be glued on, and she had him believing every word that came out of her mouth. Her lips slowly mouthed the words one last time, "Your wife is calling for you, Mr. Gustafson. Now, go and show her just how much you really love her. She's waiting, and she needs you right now." And just like that, he was gone. The nurse nodded in passive contentment and reached over and closed his eye lids for good. They would never open again…

Within seconds, they came out from the floorboard and quickly descended upon him. They reached into his chest and dismantled his soul in one fell swoop. Their gnashing teeth created a noise that vibrated the room, and the woman looked on and smiled. Mr. Gustafson lay in bed and would never move again, but this would be the least of his problems. His opportunity for eternal peace and salvation was gone, and he would not be receiving a second chance. His life here on earth was over, and now his family would never see him again. His children would soon find out that he had passed, and they would weep for their loss. However, their weeping would undoubtedly turn to whaling cries if they truly knew where his soul was now. James had met Mr. Gustafson days earlier, and they had started to have productive discussions regarding heaven and hell. He was always encouraged to have these kinds of discussions with the patients of the hospital, as it reflected a perfect segue into his passion for Jesus. James was always quick to point out that there was no "gray area" after death, and that everyone would either be going to heaven or hell. Over the past couple of visits, James felt like he had made significant progress. Mr. Gustafson had decided that it was finally time to look at his life differently, and James was excited about the possibility of bringing him to Jesus for good. What in the world went wrong, James thought, as he heard the news the following day? This man was truly interested in hearing about Jesus, and James knew from past experience that he was close. In just two days, James had experienced two quick setbacks with Mrs. Gray and Mr. Gustafson. This just didn't happen to him at this point in his career. James could sense that he was up for his biggest battle ever, and it was one he just couldn't afford to lose. Rocker Memorial Hospital had always been a stronghold for saving souls because James had diligently fought for the Word of God since he arrived many years earlier. He had formed a partnership with the Lord on the day he was saved, and nothing was more important than sharing his own personal salvation with others as well. Oh, how James wanted everyone to experience this same sense of peace, as the thought of this not happening ripped his heart apart. He wasn't going to let this happen again. He took out the patient roster and went to work. James needed to know every single detail about every single patient in the hospital. The enemy was definitely present now, and James had to be stronger than ever.

Although there were always a number of patients who really didn't want to think about their final resting place, James pulled no punches when it came to the subject. Without any hesitation whatsoever, James would clearly illustrate through Scripture just how easy it was for everyone to get into heaven. This was the part that continued to eat at James the most. If the pathway to heaven was so easy, then why wasn't everyone on earth saved? Accepting Jesus as one's true Savior was clearly the ticket to entry; however, pride and apathy continued to be the obstacles for many here on earth. James had been on the firing line now for a very long time, and he could literally see the human body's impact when a soul was saved. The presence of the Lord Himself was everywhere in the room when personal salvation was experienced, and visible peace was the ultimate result. On the other hand, if the soul wasn't saved, James could sense this as well. Life was literally sucked out of the body, and death gripped hold of the sleeping flesh like a vice. No matter how many times he'd been around this, James would never get used to it. The sound of the soul leaving the body and not going to heaven was awful, but it wasn't near as painful as the shrieking laughs that would accompany its departure. It was something James would never get used to, something he would never forget.

James started to think about his opponent because he knew it was critical for him to completely understand what he was up against. His ability to effectively establish a strategy regarding next steps would be critical, and it needed to be flawless concerning all facets of the plan. From the moment James got home that evening, he took every profile out of his secured cabinet and began to review specific details regarding all hospital personnel and patients. James had developed an uncanny ability to record every single chart when he was on duty, and then every night when he got home, he would review all pertinent details regarding both lists. The list of patients was constantly changing; however, James knew who every patient was at all times. He memorized their room number and the reason they were admitted. He also tried to prioritize these patients during his rounds, based on the severity of their illness. Certain forms of cancer, like pancreatic, always went to the top of the list due to its high mortality rate and rapid spread of infection. Knowing the history and condition of the patients made it much easier for James when he actually entered the room. His ability to reach out and call them by name immediately broke down any wall of apprehension that may have existed. Understanding their illnesses gave him an idea of what he was dealing with as well. This memorization would also be utilized with key hospital personnel. He knew everything about the staff at Rocker Memorial. On this particular evening, James focused on the same routine as he began to review his work…he prayed. James realized that God had blessed him with a photographic memory, and he knew it was important for him to continually sharpen this critical gift. Thanking God for this valuable asset was the first thing he did every night. Once he had completed this prayer, he went to work. Tonight, it would be imperative for him to initially review every single staff member. James had a feeling that this was where the enemy had infiltrated the hospital. Based on the sequence of events regarding Mrs. Gray and Mr. Gustafson, James could sense that someone on the staff was targeting the patients that fell specifically under his span of control. James had heard about this in other parts of the country; however, this kind of occurrence was rare. Reports had come in from other hospitals where Satan had gotten to a member of the staff and, as a result, he had literally taken on the Brigade during the patient's final hour. Was this happening now in Rocker Memorial Hospital as well? Was a nurse, or possibly a doctor, now a pawn for the enemy? James began to focus on the files and went through every line item in the chart one-by-one. Something had changed recently, and he needed to identify what had taken place before more patients were taken away. Not one patient in the hospital was safe, and James knew he needed to identify this conduit to hell before it was too late. Everyone, including himself, was now at risk.

Jonathan was finding it to be nearly impossible to refrain from taking the pain medication that was available to him, as he found himself needing it all the time. His mental state was still in good shape, but how long would this last? He knew the tumor was beginning to take its toll on him simply because he was too tired to do almost anything. He was still a very young man; who could have ever imagined that he would be confronted with something like this before he reached the age of 60? Where in the world did his life go? Just yesterday, he was playing baseball with his dad and hugging his mom. He kissed his beautiful wife on their wedding day and cried when the kids were born. Jonathan looked over and there was Rose, resting on the chair near the window. She had been there all day long once again, and it broke his heart to think about what would happen to her if he were to die. As much as Jonathan didn't want to get the kids involved, he could sense that his time was soon drawing near. He didn't want to alarm them with his condition, but the thought of leaving them without saying good-bye was something he just couldn't let happen. It was time for him to move forward with the plan, the one he dreaded most. "Hey, honey. Do you think you could come over here for a second?" asked Jonathan, as he reached out for Rose's hand. Rose quickly made it to her feet and practically ran over to the bed where Jonathan was lying. "What is it, dear? Are you ok? Please, let me know if I can get you anything," responded Rose, as she grabbed hold of Jonathan's hand. "Honey, I think it may be a good idea to have the kids join us here in the next couple of days. I really want to see them and give them a hug. It's nothing you need to worry about. I just want to tell them that I love them. Do you think you could give them a call and see if we can work this out?" asked Jonathan. He could see the tears begin to form in Rose's tired eyes. She just shook her head in agreement and wrapped her arms around the man she fell in love with many years ago. She held him as tight as she could and never, ever wanted to let him go. Jonathan's request to see the kids meant only one thing for the two of them, and Rose knew it. Jonathan knew in his heart that he would be leaving soon, but he did everything possible to remain as positive as he could. Rose's background told her differently because she knew just how deadly pancreatic cancer was at this stage. If only there was a way to freeze time right now and somehow find a way to stop the pain, Rose would do so in a heartbeat. Jonathan was her everything, and the thought of not waking up next to him every day, was more than she could imagine. She picked up the phone and began to dial Jake's number first. Rose knew that she may need his help when it was time to call Jesse because her entire life had always revolved around her daddy. Jesse was the one she worried about the most...

James had a strong feeling that the enemy had entered into the hospital through a new hire; therefore, he began to go through the hire dates of the staff one-by-one. Over the past 30 days, there had to have been a new addition that was planted by the enemy, so this was where James focused his immediate review. After going through every single employee in the hospital, it turned out that there were only three new hires in the entire hospital over the past month. Since two of them were in administrative positions in Human Resources, it came down to the final new hire he had identified. Her name was Crystal Selera, and she was a nurse who was hired specifically for the telemetry unit. Her experience was excellent, and she had all the credentials necessary for this type of position. She seemed to move around quite a bit from job to job, and this raised a major concern to James as he continued to assess her background even closer. If she was indeed a plant by the enemy, this would be a major problem for James because this was the unit where his greatest work had been done. It would make sense that this unit would be where the plant occurred; however, it was very important that James not just assume she was the one. He needed to keep a level head because any distraction could cause major interruptions to the entire operation right now. This was a critical time for total focus on the job at hand, as James could feel the battlefield heating up quickly. In order for him to effectively do his job, he needed to have absolute concentration on the Word right now. James was confident God would once again lead the way; however, he also realized that he was facing a ruthless opponent without any mercy whatsoever. James' responsibility was enormous, and he knew he could not face the enemy alone because if he did, he would not survive. If his total dependence on God was not razor sharp, this would undoubtedly be his final battle as well.

James made his way toward the nurses' station, as the evening shift had just begun. He had gotten so good at his job that nobody even realized he was in the area. His ability to blend into the environment secured him full access to any of the rooms on the floor. Since James had reviewed the work schedule for the week, he knew this would be the shift that Crystal would be working. He needed to find this woman and assess her for himself. Her recent hiring may mean nothing at all, but he needed to make sure he looked at every option regarding possible enemy infiltration. This woman was now on one of his most strategic floors, and he couldn't take anything for granted. He slowly mopped his way around the station and searched the premises for the new addition. James slowly made his way around the corner and saw a woman standing next to the cabinet, with her back turned his way. He made his way closer to her, as she began to turn toward him. James looked up and there she was, staring directly at him. Her beauty seemed to pierce right through him, and he couldn't help but become focused on her beautiful, brown eyes. As James began to maneuver his way around her, she turned and moved even closer toward him. Her smile seemed to mesmerize James, and he couldn't help but smile her way as well. "Hello, sir. How are you tonight?" asked the nurse, as she set the patient charts down on the counter next to her. "I'm just fine, ma'am," responded James. "And how are you doing tonight? I don't think I've had the opportunity to meet you. My name is James, and I'm in charge of keeping these floors and rooms clean. What's your name, may I ask?" questioned James, as he waited to hear from this newest member of the team. "Well, James, my name is Crystal, and I just came on board this week. I'm so glad to be here because this is such a wonderful place to work. I'm looking forward to working with everyone here and helping in whatever way I can. I'm really looking forward to seeing you here as well, James. You look like you keep yourself in terrific shape, so I may be asking you to help me move some of this heavy stuff around here, if that's ok? Would it be all right if I bothered you at times with these types of requests?" asked the woman, gently placing her hand on James' forearm. "Oh, that would be no problem at all, Crystal," responded James. "I'm happy to help with whatever you need." "Why, thank you, James. It sure is nice to meet you. I'm looking forward to seeing you here often. Now, you make sure you say hi whenever you make your rounds, ok?" said the woman, as she continued to smile his way. "No problem at all, hope you have a great night," said James. Slowly, he made his way back down the hallway. She seems like a very nice woman, James thought, as he proceeded to work his way around the corner toward the new set of rooms. He continued to think back on the interaction he just had with her and was convinced that she was, without a doubt, the most beautiful woman in the entire hospital. I probably don't need to be too worried about her, he thought, as he reflected back on just how friendly and pleasant she was during their discussion. James couldn't help but smile, while he thought about the reaction she would soon be getting from the physicians in the hospital as well. Heads would definitely be turning when she walked into the room...

Crystal watched James disappear around the corner, and quickly, her beautiful smile was gone. The white color that surrounded her brown eyes took on a fiery red tint, and she began to squeeze the pencil between her thumb and index finger. The pencil suddenly snapped, as Crystal began to foam at the corners of her mouth. Her hands began to shake, and her smile seemed like a distant memory from long ago. Her eyes did not blink, and she seemed to be looking right through the wall at James, who continued to mop his way down the corridor. "I'm going to crush you, old man. Just like this pencil, I'm going to break your bones and watch you crumble at my feet," she whispered, as she wiped the corners of her mouth with the napkin that was in front of her. "You'll be no match for me, and every single patient in this hospital will soon come my way. None of them are safe from me. I will rule this hospital and then I will move on to the next, and I will stop for nothing." She took a deep breath and gathered herself once again. Crystal was there to do a job; therefore, it was important for her to maintain her composure and not let anyone know what lay dormant under her skin. Her outward appearance needed to be innocent and sweet, at least for now. She would wait until the time was right, and then she would unleash her fury and wipe out anything in her path.

Jake and Jesse made their way down the hallway and got closer and closer to Room 224, which was where their mom and dad were waiting. How would their father look right now? He was always so healthy and full of life. Jesse could feel the tears begin to roll down the side of her face, as she got closer and closer to the door. Jake reached over and temporarily wiped her tears away, only to be replaced by new ones moving even faster than before. Jake stopped for a second and reached out for her hand, and they both took a deep breath. Jake looked over at Jesse and whispered, "I love you, sis. Everything is going to be ok. Dad's really tough, and he's going to beat this thing. You and I just need to take care of each other and mom right now. She's really going to need us, more than ever." With that, they opened the door and began to make their way over to the bed that held their father. Both of them could feel their stomachs start to turn because his appearance had changed dramatically since the last time they saw him. His skin had taken on a yellowish-tinge, and his face seemed to be tightly squeezed by the skin on his cheeks. Rose looked up and saw both of them and sprinted across the room and into their arms. She did everything she could not to cry, but there was no way for her to hold back the tears anymore. For what seemed like an eternity, Jake and Jesse just held on as tight as they could. Rose was finally able to release the emotion that had been building up since the initial diagnosis came their way. Jonathan didn't move and lay sound asleep through it all. Not a word was spoken, but all three of them knew what they were up against. They realized, more than ever before, that they could not make it alone. They needed to help each other get through the days that were ahead of them, which would be unlike anything they could have ever imagined. Their own personal nightmare was about to begin, and there would be no turning back now...

The night was soon upon them, as the afternoon flew by quickly for both Jake and Jesse. For about an hour, Jonathan had opened his eyes and talked to them about their trip to Rocker. They laughed about all the things they used to do as kids, and the room was finally filled with joy for the first time since Jonathan was admitted. There were moments of sadness, but Jonathan quickly moved into new lighter conversation in order to break the awkward silence. Jonathan was extremely tired on this particular day, but the kids seemed to invigorate him once again. Their presence made him feel better, even though this temporary state of euphoria had a lot to do with the pain meds he was on. Rose needed a lot of help getting things in order at the house; therefore, the three of them agreed to head back a little after 7:00 that evening. Jake really wanted to help his mom get everything together so they could be ready for the days ahead. He knew there would be a ton of work regarding her finances, and he wanted to make sure all the details were finalized. Jonathan woke up just long enough to say good-bye to his family before they went home, and he soon drifted off once again. He was finding it more and more difficult to stay awake, as the medication was designed to literally knock him out before the unbearable pain took hold of his tired body. He felt like he was getting close to the end because the actual thought of dying was beginning to consume his every thought. Just like so many others in the hospital who found themselves at this final stage, the next 24-48 hours would be the most important time in Jonathan's life. His final resting place would be determined one way or the other, and the race for Jonathan Gunn's soul was officially underway.

James made his way toward the telemetry unit, as the patient load on this particular evening was very full. There would be a number of targets for James on this night; however, his primary focus would be on the terminally ill cancer patients who seemed to make up a significant portion of the unit. James' research regarding the patients and their respective medical conditions supported a very strategic approach to the task at hand. Just like every night before, James had prayed and asked God to lead him to those patients who needed him most. The two names that quickly came to the forefront were Jonathan Gunn and Angela LaRue. Angela had been admitted with a rare form of cancer that had attacked her internal organs; however, the pancreas had not been part of this deadly attack just yet. Having said that, Angela's liver, kidneys, and stomach were being devoured by the spread of this ruthless enemy, and everyone on staff knew her days were numbered. These two would be the patients that James would focus on immediately because he had a strong inclination that the enemy would be doing the same thing. Just like every night before, James would wait until the Lord directed him on a path that would not jeopardize his identity. He could sense that the enemy would more than likely be close by, due to the timing of their imminent departure. James began to review the names and profiles once again. Jonathan Gunn…James just shook his head in disbelief, and tears slowly began to form in his eyes. How in the world did he ever end up here?

James slowly made his way past the nurses' station in search of anything out of the ordinary. Three nurses were behind the counter and seemed to be discussing a situation that had happened earlier in the day. James was always careful to pick his spots and tried to consciously keep his head down and work when the staff was busy. He tried to see if Crystal was working tonight as well; however, she was nowhere to be seen. Maybe she was off on this particular night, he thought, as he made his way around the corner toward the rooms on the second floor. Just as James rounded the corner, out came Crystal from behind the door, as she had been watching his every move from the darkness. Crystal made her way down to the corner of the hallway and stopped to look in the direction James had just gone. There he was, 30 feet from where Crystal was standing, pushing his mop closer and closer to where both Jonathan and Angela were sleeping. James had his back to Crystal and had no idea she was there, but he could sense something was different about this particular shift. Whenever the enemy was near, James could feel a draft almost consume his body, and he would pray intently for God to intercede. Immediately, the draft would subside and James would feel at peace once again. Tonight, the draft and the stench of death itself seemed to be everywhere, and James knew his prayers needed to be even more focused than usual. Crystal watched his every move because she needed to see where James would be heading next. It was important for her to follow his path, so she could circumvent any progress he may make. James slowly made his way into Room 228, which was where Angela had been for the past two weeks. He looked up to see if she was alone because he needed to make sure nobody else was present for what he was about to do. Angela's body had vanished from nearly 130 pounds to just over 80, and James could sense that she would be leaving soon. He needed to somehow get to her quickly, before it was too late.

As James made his way into her room, Crystal maneuvered her way past him and on to Room 224, where Jonathan was sleeping. Since Rose, Jake, and Jesse had all gone home for the evening, Crystal would have him all to herself. This was exactly what she wanted because she knew she needed to get her words into his head without any interruptions. Just like James, she had a precise strategy that would involve specific prioritization. Both Angela and Jonathan would be at the top of her list as well due to their conditions, and she knew she needed to move fast. Crystal would have to circle back and go after Angela once she was done with Jonathan, but this was the one she wanted right now. He would be her sole focus, as she had been salivating over this opportunity for a very long time. The taking of his soul would ease the pain of the others that had somehow gotten away.

James walked in and slowly made his way over to Angela. He checked to see if she was awake, but it became apparent very quickly that she was highly sedated and incoherent regarding everything around her. This was when it became very difficult for James since he desperately needed to get her attention and engage her in a discussion with him. He slowly made his way over to where she was lying and purposely bumped into her bed because he could sense that her time was running out. Angela was unresponsive and didn't even flinch, while he proceeded to make numerous noises around her. For the time being, James knew he had to move on and get to Jonathan before it was too late. Hopefully, he could get back to Angela when she came to, as he could sense by her appearance that she would soon be gone. She just had that look, the one that James had unfortunately seen so many times before. The last time he talked with Angela, she seemed like she may be willing to assess her life differently and make a commitment to Christ before it was too late. What really bothered James about this particular case was Angela's innocence and sweetness; he couldn't ever remember meeting a nicer woman. For whatever reason, she just hadn't seen a reason to strengthen her faith. Over the years, she had fallen into the trap of the enemy, as her brackish, lukewarm mindset had taken hold of her actions. She didn't even want to broach the subject with James because she felt like the "heaven and hell discussion" was just too troublesome for her to even think about right now. She felt like she had done all the right things throughout her life, and that this would ultimately be her ticket into heaven. The idea of accepting Jesus as her Savior and confessing her sins to Him just wasn't something she felt was necessary. James had continued to point out that it was very important for her to go down this path in order to get into heaven and experience eternal peace, but she just responded with, "Oh, don't be silly, James. I know God will take care of me. I've always been a good person, so I'm sure I'll get into heaven. I'm really not convinced there even is a hell, so don't talk about this anymore. It's just far too upsetting for me right now." This kind of discussion would take place often, and Angela made it clear to James that she didn't want to think about such a scary place at this point in her life. Like others before her, James needed to be careful not to push too hard and totally alienate patients with this belief. It was a fine line for James to walk because he also realized that he needed to quickly make a move before it was too late. His ability to get back in for additional dialogue was critical. Oh, how he hoped he would have one final shot with Angela when she came to! His prayer would be that he could actually get back in there before it was too late, before she was gone forever.

Angela continued to be non-responsive, and James knew he needed to move on with his next option. He made his way out the door and back into the hallway, and he would now focus all of his energy on Room 224. As he began to move closer and closer toward the room, he could feel a cold draft seem to reach out and almost stop him in his tracks. It was at this point in time when James realized the extent of what he was up against. Without any doubt whatsoever, James knew that he wasn't alone tonight in his attempt to capture the souls that were about to move on to their final destination. As James began to reach for the knob that would open and take him into Room 224, he could feel his hands start to shake. Jonathan Gunn already had a visitor. Hopefully, for both James and Jonathan himself, this would not turn out to be his last.

Crystal slowly made her way down to where Jonathan was lying and quickly went to work on his mind. She leaned down and began to whisper in his ear, "Hello, Mr. Gunn. How are you feeling tonight? It's ok if you just decide to get some rest and go to sleep for good because I know you're getting very tired of all this pain. Soon, you'll be taken to a place far, far away that will be unlike anything here on earth. You will go there and then, when the time is right, your family will join you some day. However, the only way this will happen is if you decide to go when I'm here with you. I want to make sure you get away from this awful pain soon. I've spoken to other patients who also want to go to the place you're going because they know it's safe and quiet. Mr. Gunn, it's very important for you to do what's right for your family right now. I see the pain in their eyes when they leave your room. Your condition will only get worse, and their pain will only get worse as well. The only way to stop the pain for everyone involved is for you to come with me. If you truly love your wife and children, then now is the time for you to finally do the right thing. Please, squeeze my hand if you can hear me."

James had made his way to the doorway of Jonathan's room. He rested his ear next to the crack that was exposed by the opened door, and he knew immediately that this was not the beautiful Crystal he had seen the night before. Without a doubt, the raspy sound was indeed the voice of the enemy. James could feel his heart begin to race because he knew exactly what Crystal was about to do. If Jonathan were to wake up right now, there was a strong possibility that he would quickly fall into her deadly grasp. Her delivery was smooth, and her words cut like a knife. It was obvious to James that she was a seasoned veteran at this game, as he waited by the door to see what Crystal's next move would entail. His mind began to race because he needed to do something before Crystal took Jonathan's soul back to her boss. James closed his eyes and asked for the Lord to quickly intercede...he knew he needed His strength in order to move on. And then it hit him! James had a plan that he needed to quickly employ if he wanted to save Jonathan from the darkness that was gathering steam. He had hoped that he didn't have to resort to the events that were about to unfold; however, he realized that he truly had no other choice. The plan had dangerous consequences if it failed because everything James had done up to this point was about to be put at risk. He knew that if he were to implement this plan and it didn't work, then his position in the Brigade would more than likely be terminated. The unit's purpose that had become his sole focus in life would undoubtedly be exposed for all to see. Despite the fact that everything was about to rest on the events that were quickly unfolding, James knew in his heart that this was a risk he needed to take. He quickly made his way back out to the hallway and down the staircase to the lobby of the hospital. He had to get home because there was something he just had to do! Leaving Jonathan with Crystal was a dangerous option for him to take, but right now, he simply had no other choice. Hopefully, Jonathan would still be there when he made his way back...

Crystal tried everything in her power to capture Jonathan's attention; however, his response level continued to be nonexistent. Maybe it would be better right now, she thought, to pay Angela another visit? She had no other choice but to move on to option B, as her appetite for someone's soul at this juncture was reaching fever pitch. After she was done with Angela, she would come back to Jonathan, hoping for better results the next time around. If only she could just get him to wake up, she felt strongly that he would be quickly woven into her deadly web of thorns. For the time being, she would have to wait for this to happen, which went against her nature. When it came to the final hour, her lust for the ultimate prize was like that of a blood-thirsty predator. Crystal made her way back down the hallway and moved quickly into Angela's room, while she continued to rest alone. She intentionally bumped up against Angela's bed, and with that, Angela's eyes began to open. Crystal quickly moved in for the kill and could sense that her timing was perfect. Within minutes, their discussion revolved around where Angela would be going once she passed. "So, sweet Angela, aren't you getting tired of being sick? You know there's a much better place than here that awaits you. You won't be sick anymore if you're able to just rest and go to sleep once and for all. The same peace you feel when you're asleep right now will be experienced around the clock. Just close your eyes and try to get some rest, ok?" encouraged Crystal, as she could feel Angela start to slip away. Angela's eyes began to close, and her heart slowly started to wind down. As every breath became more and more faint, Crystal became more and more excited about what was in store for her team. Within minutes, Angela took one final breath, and then she was gone. Suddenly, as if on cue, out came Crystal's followers as they moved in quickly for their prize. They giggled in unison, as they dismantled her soul and began to carry it away. Crystal just sat back and smiled, as her thirst was slowly being temporarily quenched. Angela's body was whole, but her soul now belonged to the enemy. The smile that was on Angela's face, just minutes before, would never be seen again. Crystal nodded at her team, and they quickly departed through the floorboard. Angela now belonged to them, and this made Crystal very happy. She was hungry for more, which meant it was time for her to move on to Jonathan. Unfortunately for Crystal and her hungry followers, Jonathan already had a visitor...

James made his way into Jonathan's room and quickly moved over to where he was sleeping. James needed to wake him up because he could not risk Jonathan's exposure to Crystal once again. James began to move Jonathan's head upward and could sense that he was finally coming to. "Mr. Gunn, please wake up," whispered James. "My name is James, and I work here at the hospital. I want to speak with you about something, something very important." Jonathan looked into James' eyes and began to squint as tightly as possible. Where had he seen these eyes before? Even though Jonathan was losing his faculties very quickly, there was something about this man that triggered his thoughts from years gone by. "Who are you, sir? You look very familiar. Do I know you?" asked Jonathan. "Mr. Gunn, I need to speak with you about something very important, ok? Please, listen to me. I really need you to focus on what I'm about to say. If you're unsure as to whether you're going to heaven or hell when you die, then I'd ask that you do something very important for me right now." Jonathan looked over at James and became agitated with the discussion that was about to take place. "Look, if you're going to try and lecture me about God right now, I want nothing to do with it, ok? If I had anything to say to him right now, I'd ask him why I'm dying at such a young age? Why am I going to be leaving my kids without ever experiencing the joy of being a grandparent? I have a lot of "whys" on my mind right now, so the last thing I need from you is a lecture on eternity. I've had others try to tell me about this heaven and hell thing before, and quite frankly, I'm just plain tired of it. Now, why don't you just leave me alone so I can get some sleep?" James could tell that Jonathan was beginning to slip away, and he knew he only had one more shot to connect with him. However, if he were to fail with this final attempt, then his entire cover could be blown and the Brigade's presence in this hospital, and others as well, would be highly compromised. James prayed about the options that were in front of him and decided he had no other choice other than to move forward with his plan. He simply had to take the risk. He closed his eyes and continued to pray for God's strength. James knew Crystal was near, and Jonathan Gunn's final hour would soon be upon them. He moved closer toward Jonathan, and once again, memories from long ago slowly started to seep into the back of his mind and capture his thoughts. James reached down and put his hand on Jonathan's shoulder, and at the same time, he reached into his coat pocket and took out the envelope. Jonathan opened his eyes and watched as James began to open the seal.

"Many years ago, there was a young man who had a profound impact on my life," said James, as he sat down in the chair next to where Jonathan was lying. "This young man always treated me with the utmost respect, even though I had been shunned by my parents at the age of 12. When I arrived at the juvenile detention center, I didn't want to live anymore. In fact, I strongly considered taking my life shortly after my arrival. For whatever reason, there was a young man there who believed in me and made me feel good about myself when others preferred that I leave this earth. My parents never visited me after dropping me off, but this young man was always there to take care of me. Whenever I started thinking about taking my own life, he was like a guardian angel looking over me. He became the most important person in my life, and the thought of not having him there with me every day was more than I could handle. One day, he sat me down and told me he'd be leaving for college and that he'd no longer be working at the center. Next to the day that my father dropped me off at that place, this particular day was the worst day of my life. I felt like he was leaving me because I had done something wrong, and I was scared to death that he would never come back again. The day he left, he stopped by my room and he knocked and knocked on my door…but I wouldn't come out. Instead of yelling at me, he simply slid an envelope under my door, and he told me he loved me and that he was going to miss me. I didn't get up until he had left, but after I knew he was gone, I went over to the door and picked up the envelope. The words he wrote to me on that awful day turned out to be the words that ultimately saved my life. They were the words that got me through the scary nights and gave me the confidence I needed to never give up. No matter what I was up against in life, I knew there was at least one person out there in this world who cared about me. Although they took a while to sink in, these words have been with me ever since that day, the day that changed my life forever." James took a deep breath and began to read the letter to Jonathan, hoping and praying that he would somehow make it through the words that took hold of his life years ago…

Dear Jimmy,

I write this letter to you today with a very heavy heart. I want you to know that leaving you and the Timber Lake Detention Center is one of the most difficult things I've ever done. You've made me a better person, and you've made such an incredible impact on my life. I will be forever grateful for your friendship and love over the years. I want you to know that you can do anything you put your mind to, and I'm certain you will make a huge difference in this world. You are going to have a significant impact on everyone around you, and I want you to know that you will always have a special purpose in your life. You are a real difference maker, and this entire world will benefit from what you are about to do. Your positive contribution will be felt by all. I would do anything for you…no matter what that may be. Please, Jimmy, know that it will always be this way. Anything you ever need…consider it done. I'm going to miss you with all my heart and soul, and I will always love you.

Your Friend Always,

Jonathan

Jonathan looked over at James, and with tears streaming down his face, he cried out, "Jimmy Hidalgo, is that you? Is that really you?" And with that, James put his hands on Jonathan's face and said, "I never forgot you, Jonathan. I never forgot what you did for me. You were the most important person in my life, and now I'm here to pay back my debt. When my father dropped me off at Timber Lake, I had nobody. I was all alone, and all I wanted to do was die. My parents didn't want me, and I had no reason for living. However, you recognized deep inside my heart that I was going to make a difference in this world. You gave me something that nobody else could give me, and that was a belief that I could do anything I put my mind to. Your words have been in my heart and in my mind ever since. I only have one request from you right now." "I'll do anything for you, Jimmy, anything at all," cried Jonathan. James leaned down and said, "Will you let me tell you about Jesus and how He can bring you peace? How He is the only way to true salvation, and how He can make the darkness go away?" Jonathan wiped his tears away and said, "Please, Jimmy, tell me about Jesus. I want to know everything." James began to tell Jonathan about how Jesus died on the cross for our sins and that anyone who believes in Him shall not perish but will have eternal life. As Jonathan listened to his old friend from years gone by, a profound change began to take place in his heart. The physical pain he was going through was soon replaced by a divine stillness in his heart that he had never felt before. For the first time ever, Jonathan truly felt like he had attained the peace that he was so desperately searching for…something that had somehow avoided him over the course of his lifetime. When James finished his message, Jonathan put his arms around James' shoulders and tried to hug him with what little strength he had left. Jonathan looked into James' eyes and, fighting back his tears, he spoke with a conviction in his heart that he had never felt before, "I accept Jesus Christ as my Savior, Jimmy, and I believe that He is the way, the truth, and the life. I believe that He died on the cross for my sins, that He was raised from the dead, and I want more than anything to spend eternity with Him." James put his arms around Jonathan and gave him a nod that said it all. "Jesus loves you, Jonathan, and so do I," James whispered, as he closed his eyes and thanked God for the miracle that had just taken place.

Jonathan could feel his body begin to slow down, but he did have one more request from his old friend. "Jimmy, what will happen to Rose, Jake, and Jesse if they don't know about Jesus and don't accept Him into their hearts like I just did?" asked Jonathan, as he began to shake at the answer that he thought may be coming his way. "Well, Jonathan, if they don't know Jesus like you do, then you will not be together again in eternity. I have to tell you the truth because you've meant more to me than anyone here on earth. Your family needs to accept Jesus as their Savior just like you just did, acknowledge that He died on the cross for their sins, and they need to ask Him for forgiveness. If they don't, then you'll never see them again." Jonathan began to shake and cried out, "Will you get in touch with them and tell them that I want to see them right now, before it's too late? Their number is over there on the table. Please, get them here as quickly as possible." James made his way over to the telephone and placed the call. Jesse answered and could tell in James' voice that they were needed at the hospital immediately. She could feel it in her heart that the time was near. Quickly, the three of them got changed and made their way out to the car. Within minutes, they arrived at the hospital and ran as fast as they could up to Jonathan's room. James was sitting in the chair as they entered through the doorway. Jonathan gestured their way, and they walked toward his bed. Jonathan put out his hand, and Rose squeezed it with everything she had. He began to whisper to the family that meant everything to him, the one that he would be leaving soon.

"Thanks for getting over here so quickly. I want you to meet my good friend, James. Someday, he'll tell you all about our lives together because he was my best friend when I was younger. In fact, I just found out how special James truly is, and he has given me the greatest gift one could ever imagine. James has opened up my eyes regarding something that I need to tell you about, but I need you to promise me something, ok?" asked Jonathan, as his voice started to lose momentum due to the condition he was in. "Sure, Dad, we'll do anything for you. Anything you want us to do, we'll do it right now," responded Jake, while his voice began to crack with built-up emotion. "I'm going to be leaving the three of you soon because God has determined that it's now my time for me to go and be with Him. I had no idea what this meant before today, but James has made it very clear to me. He's also made it very clear to me that I still have one more wish before I go. This is where I'll need your help. I want you to be with me after I leave here as well, and the only way this will happen is if you accept Jesus Christ as your Savior, just like I did here today. Please, give me your hands and pray with me right now because I cannot bear the thought of leaving you and never seeing you again." Rose, Jake, and Jesse all huddled around Jonathan and began to pray, with Jonathan leading the way. James watched on with tears in his eyes because he knew in his heart that Jonathan and his family would be together again when they left this world. He knew, without a doubt, that they would all be in heaven one day, just like Jonathan had wished. Tears fell on Jonathan, as his family could sense that he was about to go. Even though Jonathan couldn't bear the thought of leaving his beautiful family, the peace he felt in his heart was unlike anything he'd ever experienced before. Jonathan looked up at Rose, Jake, and Jesse and knew this was it. "I love all of you so very much, and I promise I'll be waiting in heaven for you. Don't be sad because God is taking me to a better place. We'll all be together again, and for that, I am forever grateful," whispered Jonathan. And with that, he closed his eyes and took one final breath. Rose held on to his hands with everything she had, and the kids buried their heads into their daddy's shoulder. All three of them could feel his chest exhale one last time, as their tears fell on his motionless body. Despite the fact that he was gone now, all three of them could see on Jonathan's face that he had truly found the peace he was searching for…and all were grateful that they, too, were blessed with this gift as well. Peace had somehow burrowed its way into their hearts in the midst of all their pain, and they knew that it was only because of their newfound friend, Jesus. Without Him, their sorrow would have been insurmountable, but with Him, they knew their father would be in good hands. And someday, they knew they would be safe in His hands as well.

Chapter 13

"Conclusion"

Revelation 20:11-15

"Then I saw a great white throne and him who was seated on it. Earth and sky fled from his presence, and there was no place for them. And I saw the dead, great and small, standing before the throne, and books were opened. Another book was opened, which is the book of life. The dead were judged according to what they had done as recorded in the books. The sea gave up the dead that were in it, and death and Hades gave up the dead that were in them, and each person was judged according to what he had done. Then death and Hades were thrown into the lake of fire. The lake of fire is the second death. If anyone's name was not found written in the book of life, he was thrown into the lake of fire."

What Next?

Whether we are just starting out in life or we are approaching our final stages, *we must never forget that eternal life is available to all who seek it*. We need to live for the moment, which means that today is the day we must act on our faith. Our sense of urgency must be high, and our commitment must be strong. We should never look back but instead we must live for the Lord, for He will never leave us nor forsake us. He, and only He, is the way, the truth, and the life. We must fight the fight and finish the race strong. We must stay focused on the prize and realize that this stop on earth is only temporary, and that our final resting place will be determined by our actions while we are here. There are no limitations regarding entrance into heaven, as everyone is eligible for eternal salvation. However, we cannot wait and we must take action today because we do not know what tomorrow may bring. And for some…tomorrow may be too late.

CPSIA information can be obtained at www.ICGtesting.com
Printed in the USA
LVOW092212130512

281508LV00008B/1/P